SINGULARITY

Helena Hann-Basquiat

with

Sara Litchfield
Sandy Ramsey
Lizzi Rogers
Hannah Sears

dilettante publishing

Singularity
Copyright © 2015, Helena Hann-Basquiat

ISBN 13: 978-0-9940419-5-1
ISBN 10: 0-9940419-5-0

Published in Canada by Dilettante Publishing

SINGULARITY

Within thirty years, we will have the technological means to create superhuman intelligence. Shortly after, the human era will be ended.

Vernor Vinge, *The Coming Technological Singularity*

"Real isn't how you are made," said the Skin Horse. "It's a thing that happens to you. When a child loves you for a long, long time, not just to play with, but REALLY loves you, then you become Real."

"Does it hurt?" asked the Rabbit.

"Sometimes," said the Skin Horse, for he was always truthful. "When you are Real you don't mind being hurt."

"Does it happen all at once, like being wound up," he asked, "or bit by bit?"

"It doesn't happen all at once," said the Skin Horse. "You become. It takes a long time. That's why it doesn't happen often to people who break easily, or have sharp edges, or who have to be carefully kept. Generally, by the time you are Real, most of your hair has been loved off, and your eyes drop out and you get loose in the joints and very shabby. But these things don't matter at all, because once you are Real you can't be ugly, except to people who don't understand."

Margery Williams, *The Velveteen Rabbit*

"No live organism can continue for long to exist sanely under conditions of absolute reality."

Shirley Jackson, *The Haunting of Hill House*

"If I cannot inspire love, I will cause fear, and chiefly towards you my archenemy, because my creator, do I swear inextinguishable hatred. Have a care; I will work at your destruction, nor finish until I desolate your heart, so that you shall curse the hour of your birth."

Mary Shelley, *Frankenstein*

ARGUMENT

J essica B. Bell is not real.

I think it's important to clear the air about that.

A couple of years ago I started writing horror stories and rather than use the name Helena, I created a new pseudonym, and Jessica was "born".

I had fun creating a twisted and ominous biography for her, painting a picture of some crazy hermit who lived in my basement and wrote stories on old parchment using her own blood for ink.

I even went so far as to make an entire book about her - a speculative meta-narrative about her alleged past and curious origins. I wanted to blur the lines between fiction and reality, and so I treated it as factual – or at least plausible – events, even creating fake newspaper clippings and audio clips.

But it was just a story. You have to understand that above all else, darlings, because I don't want there to be any confusion.

Jessica B. Bell is *not real.*

Let me repeat myself: JESSICA B. BELL IS NOT REAL.

THE INCIDENT

Michael and Naveena - Now

M ichael didn't know how long the phone had been ringing when he picked it up and answered with a groggy *Hello?*

The man in the bed next to him slept through it, but that didn't surprise him. Michael had crushed three Xanax into his wine the night before to ensure he fell asleep quickly afterward. He just wanted the sex, not conversation. He got all the conversation he wanted and more from his partner when he was around, which was rarely. But when he was, all he wanted to do was talk about their relationship. They had become an old married couple, and Michael resented the hell out of him. They had fought so hard to get married – to be *allowed* to be married, for fuck's sake – and now all Michael wanted was a divorce. It was almost embarrassing.

The call was from his answering service. They'd been trying to get a hold of him on his cell phone for hours, but got no answer.

"Shit," he muttered and fumbled for his pants. "Hang on."

He dug in his pocket for his cell phone, which was dead, and turned on an antique lamp – a birthday gift from Ray – to look for his charger.

"What is it?" he asked the operator, whose utter lack of emotion betrayed nothing of the urgency of the call.

"I've got a message – several of them, actually – for you to call Dr. Chandra immediately."

"That's it?" he asked.

"They didn't give me any other message, Doctor," she replied. "Do you have the number?"

"Yes, thank you," he sighed, and hung up the phone.

Chandra. Just the mention of her name tied a knot in his stomach. If she was calling him at – *Jesus*, it was only half past four – then it wasn't good news. Dr. Chandra and he had worked very hard to keep their little project a secret. If their work were successful, they'd both be up for the Nobel Prize. If not, well, omelettes and eggs, Michael figured.

His cell phone lit up, showing ten missed calls and three messages. He was about to listen to them when someone started pounding on his front door. He pulled on his pants and went down to open it.

"What is it, Naveena?" he asked, opening the door, both annoyed and worried.

The woman standing in his open door was pale and trembling. Her lips were twitching as if she wanted to say something but couldn't. Her face reminded him of an unravelled sweater, and just the thought of that made him shiver at a distant memory that he couldn't quite place. But it wasn't the look on her face that worried him, rather, the smears of what could only be blood on the sleeve of her scrubs.

"Naveena?" he asked, more gently this time.

She snapped back to life it seemed, her eyes angry and wild.

"Where have you been, Michael?" she hissed, and pushed past him, closing the door behind her. "I've been calling you for hours!"

She was clearly frightened, though her voice was the same melodic singsong it always was, the product of British Schools and the affluence of New Delhi. She'd spent her years at Oxford trying to disguise her roots by adopting a posher, more English lilt to her voice, but in her anger, she fell back on her true origins, and her voice took on a character that Michael could not find intimidating in the least.

"Yeah, sorry, my cell phone died," Michael said, his head still a bit dull around the edges from the wine. "Are you okay?"

She didn't answer him, but frantically made her way to his kitchen, pulled a stemless Riedel glass from the cupboard and reached for the bottle of wine that was still open on the counter.

"Don't," Michael warned, running a hand over his face. "Um, don't drink that one."

She surprised him by smashing the glass on the floor and screaming – a sick, wordless growl.

Upstairs, Michael's lover stirred.

"Is Raymond here?" Dr. Chandra whispered.

Michael shook his head and hung his head in shame.

"You fucking asshole!" she sneered. "Get dressed. Now. And get rid of him. We need to talk privately."

"Are you hurt?" Michael asked, motioning to the blood on her sleeve.

"This is not my blood, Michael," she said. "Get dressed."

"Get up..." Michael began, and then realized he couldn't remember the guy's name. He also didn't remember him mentioning that he snored when he picked him up in the club the night before, but then, there was so much left unsaid, and talk was over-rated.

"Get up," he repeated, and threw a pair of designer jeans that cost as much as his phone at the heavily-tattooed stranger in his – and Ray's – bed.

"The fuck, man?" he groaned and buried his head in a pillow.

"I need you to leave. I have an emergency, and you can't be here," Michael insisted, slowly losing his patience.

"What time is it?"

"A quarter past *I need you to go*," Michael said. "You can't be here."

"What, you got someone else coming by?" he laughed and yawned.

Dr. Chandra called up the stairs. "Are you coming, Michael?"

The man in the bed sat up, startled at the woman's voice. "You're married?"

Michael fumbled for what to say. "Well, yes, but..."

"You're straight?"

"No." Michael laughed at the idea. "No, definitely not. Look, you just have to go. I have an emergency and I have to go."

"Okay, sweetie, no need to be all agro," he said, reaching out to tousle Michael's hair like a child, and then trailing his hand down Michael's bare chest down toward his hastily-thrown-on jeans.

Michael reached out and caught his hand before he could go any further.

"Listen, this was fun, but I'm a doctor, and I have an emergency, and I've got to go," he said firmly, stressing the last three words. "And so you have to go."

"Doctor, huh?" he mused. "So, you think I can get some more of those pills from last night? They made me feel all warm and fuzzy."

Michael pulled away from the man, whose name still hadn't come to him, found his shirt, and threw it to him. Then he opened the drawer of his side-table and pulled out a prescription bottle of Xanax made out to Raymond Semple and tossed it to the man.

"I need you gone in five," he insisted.

"Sure, no problem," he said, inspecting the bottle. "Hey, I thought you said your name was Mike."

Michael said nothing, but threw on a shirt of Ray's, feeling both comforted and ashamed at the smell of his partner – the first and only man he'd ever really loved.

"I really need you to leave," he repeated.

Dr. Chandra swept up the glass in the kitchen and put a kettle on for tea – another comfort from home – deciding that she wasn't in the mood for wine after all. She stood at the sink while Michael and the still-nameless man came down the stairs, Michael looking old and ashamed, the younger man looking vibrant, alive, and utterly incapable of being embarrassed. Still, Michael gave the man a kiss goodbye, and then closed the door and locked it, collapsing against it and fighting back tears.

"Well, you sure know how to pick them," came a chiding voice from the kitchen.

"It was a mistake," Michael whined. "Don't you judge me, Naveena."

"Not at all," she said, "he was a fine specimen. Tell me, has he started shaving yet?"

Michael ignored her. Disarming voice or no, her tongue was as sharp and concise as the scalpel she wielded with unequalled skill.

"Why are you here?" he asked.

"I've been trying to call you for hours, since the alarm was first raised, a little after midnight," she replied. "When it was too late for you to be of assistance, I gave up trying to reach you, and instead came here. To be honest, I was worried that you had something to do with it. That maybe you'd – what is that charming phrase? *Bolloxed it up*, and then done a runner."

A slight but perceptible tremor crept into Michael's voice.

"What are you talking about? What's gone wrong? Is it Ward C?"

Naveena nodded, and sipped her tea, holding the cup with both hands to stop it from shaking.

"What happened?" he asked, steadying himself as his legs suddenly threatened to stop supporting him.

"They're dead," she answered, her voice calm and quiet, not at all the shriek of disbelief it had been just hours earlier.

Michael swooned, and licked his lips.

"Sit down, Michael. You look like you're going to faint."

Naveena offered him a stool from around the island where Michael and Ray often enjoyed morning coffee.

"Thank you," he managed, and sat, sighing. "Tell me what happened."

"I don't know," she said. "That's the problem. Nobody does."

"What do you mean nobody does?" he asked in disbelief. "Surely someone saw something! What about the security cameras?"

Dr. Chandra shook her head. "Some sort of interference has corrupted the footage. I've backed up what there is for analysis, but I'm telling you, it's just bits and pieces at best."

"Fuck," Michael spat, and then looked again at the blood on Naveena's scrubs.

"It's a mess, Michael," she said, noticing him staring. "They're *unrecognizable*."

"What do you mean?"

"It's inhuman," she said. "Whatever did this to them, it got in there and back out without anyone seeing a goddamned thing."

She produced her phone and showed Michael a short video of the scene. After a few seconds, Michael pushed it away and turned and retched into the sink. He turned the faucet on and ran cold water over his head.

Naveena put her phone away. "Are you okay?"

Michael turned the faucet off. "Hand me a dishtowel, would you? The drawer beside the fridge."

Drying off his hair and spitting red wine vomit into the sink, he shook his head as if by denying what he had just seen he could deny the truth of it.

"No," he said. "No, no, no. That's not possible. It's crazy."

"Of course it is," Dr. Chandra agreed. "And yet…"

"How many dead?"

"All but one," she said. "But she's not talking. Nearly catatonic, really. Hasn't said anything. At least, not anything that makes any sense. She just keeps saying the name Helena over and over again."

"Who's Helena?" Michael asked. "There's no one by that name in Ward C."

"No, I know."

"Could this Helena be responsible for... *this?*" Michael asked, knowing it was the wrong question to be asking.

Dr. Chandra shook her head. "I think you know who is responsible. And I know you don't want to believe it, but I've been trying to tell you..."

Michael glared at her darkly. "Impossible. She's delusional. Paranoid schizophrenic."

"Please. She's never been diagnosed as such. And her response to all of our neuroleptic cocktails has been inconsistent with that assumption. It certainly hasn't stopped her delusions. She said something like this would happen."

"She said a lot of things," Michael said. "And I didn't believe half of them – not really."

"Didn't you?" she asked with a doubtful raise of an eyebrow.

"Of course not," he said unconvincingly. "But no matter, she's dead now, and this has *nothing* to do with her."

Dr. Chandra shook her head slowly. "No. She's not dead. Not her."

"No," Michael whispered, and grabbed the counter to stop himself from collapsing. "The one survivor?"

Dr. Chandra nodded, her eyes wide and frightened.

"Bell, of course." she said. "Jessica Bell is the only survivor."

Helena - Six Months Ago

"Penny, have you seen my Jessica notebook? I've got an idea for a story and I want to write it down."

Penny danced around the living room with her headphones on, wearing an oversized t-shirt and two differently-striped stockings – one black and white striped, the other rainbow striped. Her hair looked like an experiment in modern art, half black and half bright pink, and shaped in such a way that must have required so many bobby pins that, in fact, her hair was more metal than organic.

I waved my arms and tried to get my free-spirited niece's attention, but even I could hear the heavy thump-thump-thump of the bass and drums of whatever it was she was listening to, so there was no way she could hear me.

"Penny!" I called, jumping up and down and waving my arms in the air.

Still no reaction. I decided to try another tack and began creeping up on her in order to startle her by either removing her headphones, or more likely going in for a quick rib-tickle.

Slowly I crouched, walking duck-like around the sofa to reposition myself directly behind her as she bounced and boogied, oblivious to my presence.

One step. Two. A quick shuffle of my feet, and I was nearly within grasping reach. Slowly I stood up, and reached out one quiet hand to grab at her headphones.

"Not another step, Helena," Penny said, quite obviously enjoying herself.

"How did you?" I stammered.

"I'm *magic!*" she said with a flourish of her hands, turning to favour me with a wide-eyed, teasing look.

"Uh huh," I said, catching my reflection in the glass cabinet of a bookshelf. "Have you seen my Jessica notebook?"

Penny frowned. "I thought you were done with that."

"With what?"

Penny had never liked the stories I wrote under the Jessica B. Bell pseudonym. She liked it even less when I started treating Jessica like an actual person, with a dark and mysterious past. She indulged me when I wrote a book all about Jessica's possible pasts, and applauded the ending in which Jessica fucks off to some Caribbean island.

Good riddance, she said, and urged me to move on to other things, to forget that creepy fucker, Jessica B. Bell.

"Well, I thought that when you finished that novel you were working on, that you'd be done with that part of you. Why can't you just finish writing your memoirs and leave all that behind?"

I shrugged. "I don't know. Why can't you just enjoy one colour of hair at a time? Besides, I haven't written any Jessica stories in months."

"And I liked it that way! Whenever you get in Jessica mode, you always hide out in the basement listening to the creepiest, gloomiest music. It's like you're the Phantom of the goddamn Opera, hiding out down there in your dungeon."

"Oh, I do not hide out in the basement," I protested. "That's just what I told my readers Jessica does. You know, the whole *I keep a writer chained up in my basement* shtick."

"You do, too," Penny insisted. "It's creepy."

"It's quiet down there. I can write undisturbed. There are no urchins allowed down there."

"Well, loik, pardon me, your ladyship. Cheerio an' such. Blimey!" Penny replied, slipping into a Dickensian era London street urchin, sounding not unlike Dick Van Dyke in Mary Poppins.

"See," I said. "How could I write something terrifying when you've always got me giggling?"

"Thass kind of the point, gov'nah. Nod's as good as a wink to a bloind sumfink or ovah."

"Where's my Jessica notebook?" I asked, losing patience.

Penny shrugged. "Dunno, gov. Why don't you check the basement?"

I nodded. "Fair enough."

The basement was crypt-like, darlings, I'll admit it. It smelled of constant dampness, like old, dead trees, with a hint of mouse turds and dead spiders. Like something rotten. Once, a squirrel had gotten in and burrowed itself behind the drywall, only to get stuck and die, and we'd called a pest removal company to come and get it out, but not before the smell had filled the whole basement. The smell still lingered, buried beneath the more pleasant odours of dryer sheets or the scented candles I often burned when I was writing. I liked to write in longhand when I wrote the Jessica stories – they just seemed to flow out of me better that way – and I had a book full of ideas and drafts and notes scribbled to myself.

"You lost down there?" Penny called nervously.

"Still looking," I called back.

"C'mon, Helena, forget about her. Come back to the land of the living. Write something nice for a change. People are going to think you're crazy, or that you hate me, or something. You're always killing people off or driving them crazy. Why can't you just write something *nice?*"

There it was. The frequently uttered phrase that was like an ice-cold knife being drawn down my spine.

Why can't you just write something nice?

I did write nice things. All the time. I confess, what I sometimes heard when Penny asked the question, though, was: *Why can't you write something good?*

It hurt at first, thought I wouldn't admit that to Penny. Then it just made me *angry*.

"People like to be afraid, Penny, to experience the sublime, to stare terror in the face and yet not be terrified by it. Immanuel Kant wrote entire philosophical treatises on the concept of the sublime, and the Romantic writers – Mrs. Mary Shelley, for instance – were enraptured with the idea. We would have no Gothic literature were it not for a little fear, darling."

"I just don't know how your mind can go to those places," Penny mumbled.

"Be glad my mind does not *stay* in those places," I replied. "Ah, here we are!"

I picked up a thick folio full of loose pages and pictures cut from magazines and scribbles on napkins. More importantly, it contained the notebook in which I wrote all the stories I attributed to Jessica B. Bell.

I pulled it out and opened it up, hoping to start a fresh page. I'd woken up early that morning with a story in my head, and was eager to let it out. But when I opened the book, I strangely forgot all about the story that had been brewing, and instead looked at the pages, covered with frantic writing. I was immediately overcome with confusion and annoyance.

"What the literal fuck, Penny?"

Penny, irritated by the intentional malapropos, rolled with it nonetheless.

"Oh, I'm sorry, are people copulating in our basement again?" she called down the stairs, unaware of my rising desire to strangle her with a pair of her own striped socks.

"Come down here, please," I called, trying to keep my voice even.

"Nuh uh," Penny replied. "It's gross and creepy down there. Whatever it is, you can come up here and tell me."

I didn't want to fight with her, so I carried the book upstairs, where, in the light, I could see it better. I dropped it on the kitchen table and pointed to it.

"Did you do this?"

Penny examined the book, and the look on her face said that she didn't know what she was looking at.

"What am I looking at?"

"This!" I cried, and turned the pages, revealing pages upon pages of scribbled writing. "This! This! This!"

Penny reached out and stopped my hand from turning more pages.

We locked eyes – hers fearful and confused, mine angry and resolved.

"What are you talking about, Helena?" she asked. "What's wrong with your book?"

"It's full of writing!" I said, and as soon as the words escaped my lips, I realized how stupid it sounded.

Penny stared at me, waiting for me to continue.

"It wasn't full before," I insisted. "I haven't written in it for months, and now it's full. Have you been writing in it?"

"Me?" she asked, shocked. "Did you not hear me before? I don't go down there. It's gross. Besides, you were down there nearly the entire fucking month of November – maybe you filled it up then. What does it say? Have you read any of it?"

I turned back to the first few pages – notes about another story I had been working on but abandoned – I remembered that. That had been the last thing I'd written in this particular book that I remembered. I always started a new project with a new notebook. But then the pages afterward, they didn't seem right at all.

"They're stories," I said, staring at the pages in confusion and disbelief.

"Well, duh," Penny said indelicately. "What does it say?"

"*Her hand was all-absorbing.*" I read, "*White, like the bones within it, and still fading from violent pink in places, at the edges of the scars.*"

Penny shivered at the image. "Yup, that sounds like Jessica, alright."

I frowned at her, furrowing my brow in frustration.

"Penny, *I am* Jessica."

Penny feigned shock and surprise, complete with a dropped jaw and eyes the size of saucers.

"But I didn't write this," I finished, and Penny rolled her eyes at me.

"Tell it to the rubes, lady," she said, slipping into her newly-acquired 1920s gangster persona. Penny enjoys making voices from time to time to keep life more interesting. "You ain't gonna fool me with that, see. Maaa, see."

"I'm serious," I said, flipping through the pages to see if I recognized anything.

"Maybe this is the wrong notebook," Penny suggested, dropping the gangster shtick. "Maybe this is an older one, and these stories are from a long time ago and you just don't remember them."

"Maybe," I allowed, continuing to turn the pages, until I came upon something that caused me to gasp and reach for the table to steady myself.

"What is it?" Penny cried, and stopped to stare at the last page, which contained a picture of a stuffed rabbit, and beside it, scrawled in mad, furious letters, the words NOT REAL over and over again.

She grabbed the book out of my hands and closed it before I could stop her.

"Hey, give that back!" I said unconvincingly.

"I don't think that's a good idea," she said. "You're scaring me a little. Now, why don't you go write something nice and let me look at this and make sure you haven't lost what little remains of your mind? Mmm'kay?"

I conceded defeat. I often do when my opponent is Penny. She doesn't fight fair.

"Alright," I said. "But take care of that book. Don't lose it."

"I promise."

Michael and Naveena – Now

There wasn't enough coffee in the world to make Michael focus, nor enough booze to stop his hands from shaking. Trying to make sense of what he was seeing was like trying to explain the colour red to a blind person.

There was a lot of red.

"This isn't possible," Michael whispered, shaking his head.

The bodies of their very special patients were scattered around Ward C, a private research wing of the Sisters of Mercy Hospital. Dr. Chandra had posted guards outside the room with strict instructions that no one be allowed in or out. She hadn't even called the police yet, wanting Michael to see the carnage before they began removing body parts.

Blood-soaked hospital gowns – ripped to tatters – clung like second skin to headless torsos that bore unexplainable gashes, almost like claw marks but deeper. Severed limbs decorated the floor like spare parts at a Barbie doll factory. The room was splattered in blood, as if whatever had done it had torn the bodies apart and thrown the pieces around in a frenzy. And the bodies *were* torn, Michael was sure of it. Arms were pulled from sockets like someone would pull a drumstick off a chicken, and shiny white bones stuck out obscenely, glistening in the fluorescent lights of the normally sterile hospital room. Ribs poked out of abdomens like porcupine quills, and of all the faces, only two were recognizable.

"How are we going to identify the bodies?" he asked. "It's going to be like a goddamned jigsaw puzzle."

He got no answer from his colleague, but kept staring at the room in disbelief, examining the bodies and their parts. He counted the heads, and then counted them again. There were only five heads.

"Who's missing?"

More silence from Dr. Chandra, who just shrugged and shook her head.

"What kind of a monster could do this kind of thing?" Michael said, not expecting an answer from the woman, and not getting one.

Naveena stood silently, as if trying to meditate and form her own hypothesis. Michael looked at all the blood, and the bodies that looked like they'd gone through some sort of medieval torture, and couldn't even guess. There were unusual wounds, jagged and deep, but nothing that would indicate that a weapon was used. If they were claw marks of some sort, there would be DNA from whatever did it left in the wounds.

"All this blood," he said. "Surely the killer – whoever or whatever it is – will have left a trace of themselves, or taken away evidence that could help us find them."

"Perhaps," Dr. Chandra said – the first word she'd spoken since they'd arrived at the scene of the carnage.

"What about Jessica? Has she woken up? Is she injured?"

"Not a scratch," she said. "Not a drop of blood on her, either, despite the fact that she had to have been less than ten feet away from all this when it happened."

Michael put his face in his hands and imagined what prison was going to be like.

"Where is she now?"

"I've moved her," she said calmly. "She's safe."

"Where?" he asked, impatient.

"To the maternity ward," she said with a thin smile. "No one will look for her there. When the police come to ask their questions, I'd rather not have her around."

"Who is looking after her?" Michael snapped, panicking.

"Don't worry, Michael," she said, growing more irritated with him. "She's safe. And she won't be going anywhere. I'm keeping her sedated just in case she tries something else."

"You don't think that she could have done this?" he asked, doubtful that Naveena could possibly think one tiny woman could have torn five people apart, evidently with her bare hands.

Dr. Chandra just shrugged.

"Don't be ridiculous," Michael replied with a sick laugh. "She's what? A hundred and twenty pounds at best? Do you really think she is capable of this?"

Dr. Chandra favoured him with a stern look.

"We weren't here to test the capabilities of the body, Doctor," she said, and left the room to call the police, leaving Michael staring at all the blood, and wondering what that kind of power felt like.

Luther - Now

Detective Crowley never could get used to sleeping beside anyone, not since his wife left, going on ten years back. He'd been divorced longer than he'd been married, but Alice was the only woman that ever fit him right. No matter how many bodies filled her place in his bed by proxy, he always preferred to wake up alone. Not that he'd had that many women, but the few that had come and gone all told the same story – sleeping with him was impossible. He'd seen too much not to have nightmares, and if it wasn't the frantic shakes and sweats of terror that made his bed an uncomfortable one to share, then sure as eggs is eggs, the whiskey sweat and the lingering spicy sweet aroma of the clove cigarettes he smoked ensured he got the bed to himself.

The morning he started his last case, he woke up next to a note scribbled on the back of an envelope, and the message wasn't at all surprising. He didn't even really need to read it to know what it said. It was usually some variation of the same theme.

Dear Luther, you're a great guy when you're available, and I don't just mean physically present – I understand how important your work is. But I need to be important, too, and you're just never available for me. Even when we're together, you're never really here.

"I'm really sorry, etcetera etcetera, hope we can still be friends, blah blah blah," Luther said, crumpling the envelope and tossing it into the wastebasket with all the others.

His mind needed something to solve – it always had. Women had no patience for a man like him, who was always looking for the next challenge. He supposed he picked the wrong women, maybe for the wrong reasons. Alice said that it wasn't that she'd stopped loving him, rather that he'd lost interest in her. She was like a puzzle that, once solved, got put away in the closet, never to be played with again.

His job never bored him, always challenged him, and if he had the lowest solve rate on the force, well, it wasn't for lack of trying. They always gave him the weird ones, the unsolvable ones, and his Inspector remarked that Luther got closer to solving them than anyone else ever would have. He had a reputation for being able to see the things that weren't there at a crime scene – the things that were missing. When he was a kid, he and his brother had played Sherlock Holmes, and the axiom about how once you've removed the impossible, whatever remains, no matter how improbable, must be the truth had stuck with him into adulthood. However, Luther had seen things – strange, unexplainable things – and so his definition of what was impossible had grown narrower and narrower over the years, and he could tell some stories that would have turned Mr. Holmes' blood to ice.

Most recently he'd seen a young woman pulled from the wreckage of an exploded tanker truck, not a hair left on her body, and most of her skin burned off, too. She should have been dead; instead she crawled out of the fire like a chicken jumping out of the oven and running away on half-cooked drumsticks. There was a smell coming off her as they placed her on the stretcher that made him salivate involuntarily, and he wasn't the only one – one of the ambulance attendants caught a whiff of her cooking body and nearly dropped her when he turned his head to throw up.

How she could still be alive Luther couldn't imagine, but seeing the extent of her charred wounds, he knew that she'd never be even remotely normal ever again. He'd told the attendants at the scene that if they really wanted to save that poor girl's life, they should pump her full of morphine and let her die peacefully.

He'd been tailing the girl for a couple of weeks, worried that something would happen to her. The car crash had to be an accident – he couldn't bring himself to believe that anyone could orchestrate something like that – but it still weighed on him. This was the third death connected to the same woman. She was a real piece of work. She had already killed her husband – not that he could prove it – and maybe tried to kill his girlfriend, too, if somehow she was responsible for the fiery crash.

Then she disappeared, and that cemented her guilt in the detective's mind. Not that it did him any good – he couldn't find a trace of her. Much as it pained him to do so, he had to let it go for the time being. She was a cold woman who left a cold trail, but she didn't have the means to disappear forever. Sooner or later she'd surface, and he'd be there to welcome her back.

Now, he had a new mystery. A multiple homicide at the Sisters of Mercy.

He coughed and hacked phlegm up into his kitchen sink, then lit a clove cigarette and poured himself a coffee. Alice had always said it was those cigarettes that would do him in, but Alice wasn't around anymore. She'd complained about it, saying he smelled like a bakery that had been set on fire. Luther smiled at the memory, and then frowned as he listened to the message on his phone again. Five bodies, it said. Messy, it said.

He opened his door and looked out at the grey and soggy morning and felt the damp cold already settling into his bones.

"Well, at least it's inside," Luther mumbled to himself, grabbing his raincoat. "This rain'd wash it all away in ten minutes if it weren't."

Jessica - Now

Jessica slept, and for the first time that she could remember, she had dreams. She dreamed of a clever man; a man that could see around corners that others couldn't. His appearance was deceiving – he could be attractive, she supposed, if he wanted to be – but he had let himself go. Middle age had given him a slight paunch and love handles, but even though he looked soft, he was anything but. He dressed in comfortable clothes, and if his London Fog raincoat looked worn out and ready for replacement, the man liked it that way.

A phrase came to her through her dream, and she wasn't quite sure exactly what it meant. She would remember to write it down in her notebook when she woke. Unconsciously, her hands tightened around the book as she slept, holding it to her chest like a security blanket.

...smells like a bakery that had been set on fire...

"Helena," she murmured, still fast asleep. "Helena."

Helena – Three Months Ago

Penny threw a stack of mail on the table and opened the fridge, pulling out a carton of chocolate milk and drinking several unladylike gulps direct from the carton, unaware I was watching from the hall. I announced my presence by barking like a dog, startling my young niece and causing chocolate milk to shoot out her nose in a most satisfying and impressive spray. Ordinarily this would be the type of behaviour one would expect from the Countess Penelope of Arcadia, who is not actually a Countess, and certainly hasn't attended charm school – but she takes after her favourite aunt, and so whatever outrageous behaviour she displays is surely genetically inherited.

"Drink out of a glass, you bloody savage!" I cried, not really caring one way or the other. But as Penny's legal guardian, there were several parental prerequisites that I was required to perform, or else I'd lose my privileges on the PTA.

That is, if I belonged to the PTA. Heaven forefend. Besides, those days were long gone for Penny, as she had grown into a quasi-respectable adult and only still hung around because she couldn't get enough of me.

"Any mail for me?" I asked her as she cleaned herself up.

"Bills, bills, junk, junk, oh, and another of those creepy postcards. You ever find out who's sending them to you?"

This would be postcard number five in the past three months. All from the same person, and from the postmark I could tell that they were close, and that's what bothered me. The tone of the messages was friendly enough, if a bit strange. The postcards themselves were odd but not alarming. The first had featured a picture of that famous Edward Hopper painting *Nighthawks at the Diner* – that one that had been spoofed so many times to include James Dean or Elvis or Humphrey Bogart or whoever. Only whomever it was that sent it had scratched everyone out of the picture and, on the back, written what Penny and I thought was a very unfunny joke.

Descartes walks into a bar, and the bartender asks him if he'd like a drink.

Descartes says, "I think not," and disappears.

I had to explain it to Penny, telling her all about Descartes' philosophy of *cogito ergo sum* I think, therefore I am – and Penny

27

rolled her eyes and declared that if a joke had to be explained, it wasn't funny.

What was even less funny was the signature, which read *Jessica*.

As if to clarify, the second and subsequent postcards were all signed *Jessica B. Bell*.

"Whoever this is knows where we live, Helena," Penny said. "You think maybe it's time we found out who's sending them?"

"Jessica's sending them," I replied with a shudder, which I turned into a macabre laugh to try to ease the tension. Penny was right. So far, the postcards had been harmless, and yet there was something unsettling about them nonetheless.

"It's not funny, Helena," Penny pouted.

"Let me see the latest one," I replied, ignoring her and reaching for the stack of mail. I sorted through until I found the postcard, which was covered in rabbits.

"Must be from Easter," Penny remarked.

"I guess," I allowed, turning it over, and resisting the urge to tear the card up. There wasn't anything written on the back other than my name and address. Just a drawing of a stuffed rabbit – the same one that was in the notebook I'd found in the basement a couple of months before. I crumpled it up in one fist and threw it across the room aimlessly.

"Get that notebook," I snapped, suddenly angry.

"Sure," Penny said, eyes wide. "Calm down, already."

Penny disappeared up to her room, and after a few moments I heard a string of curses the likes of which are usually only heard in a Quentin Tarantino film, unless, of course, you live with Penny. Penny's ability to use the word fuck gets more creative every day, and she assures me that the word has endless possibilities, syntax be damned.

"I can't find the fucking thing!" she screamed, at which point I knew she was upset. Penny has the kind of temper that is disguised as rationality. She may appear calm until that moment when she just explodes, and god help you if you are in her blast radius.

"Well, where did you hide it?" I called, careful not to insinuate that she lost it. She came stomping down the stairs with an annoyed look.

"That's just it," she said. "I didn't hide it anywhere. You gave it to me, and I trust you not to violate my space."

"Thank you."

"You're welcome," she said without missing a beat. "So I didn't feel the need to hide it. I'd been reading it – some really fucked up shit, by the way. I'm scheduling a psychiatrist's appointment for you immediately."

"But I didn't…"

"Don't start with that again," Penny stopped me with an open palm, the universal sign derived from Ancient Egyptian hieroglyphics, where the falcon-headed god Horus holds up his hand toward Anubis, signifying that the jackal-headed god should talk to the hand, because the falcon-face isn't listening.

"So where's the notebook?" I asked her.

"Like I said – I've been reading it. It was on my bedside table, and unless it got up and walked away, it should still be there."

"Well, when's the last time you saw it?"

"I don't know," Penny shrugged. "Couple of days ago, I guess. Maybe a week at most. But it was there, I know it."

"I think someone broke in here," I said, feeling sick and violated.

"Why?" Penny asked incredulously. "To take your notebook? You know, I was kidding about the head-doctor, but maybe it's not such a bad idea."

"It's not funny, Penny," I said, feeling tears of rage – or maybe fear – start welling up in my eyes. "That postcard has the same fucking picture of that same goddamned Velveteen Rabbit that was in that notebook. It's the exact same drawing! Whoever sent that postcard stole my notebook."

"Bloody 'ell," Penny said, slipping unconsciously into her Dickensian street urchin voice.

"Not now, Penny!" I cried, and the waterworks began despite my efforts to hold them back.

"Sorry," she said, and wrapped her arms around me for a hug. "Listen, it's probably just some fan having fun with you. Reach out to your readers, maybe someone will confess to it. Tell them it's weirding you out and enough's enough."

I sniffed and nodded.

"I can do better than that," I said, feeling angry and powerful. "I can do what you've wanted me to do for a while now. I'll tell them all that I'm done with her."

Penny held me at arm's length and looked at me like I had grown another nose.

"What are you talking about?"

"I'm going to kill her," I said coldly. "I'm going to kill Jessica B. Bell."

Luther – Now

Detective Crowley's unlikely first thought upon seeing the carnage at Sisters of Mercy was that he'd seen this kind of thing before, but on a much smaller scale. It was years before, but he'd never forgotten it. He'd just made detective, and was called in on his first – but not his last – strange, unsolvable homicide. He'd gone out to a farm out in the middle of nowhere, to a plot of land that had last been registered to a Thomas O'Sullivan – but old Tom wasn't the corpse in question, not by a long shot. Tom had died in 1979 of natural causes, nothing suspicious. Technically, he was still the only legal resident, and was, in fact, buried on the property. Whoever lay in that open, unfinished grave must have been a squatter. Luther never did identify the body, such as it was. The man was found in a shallow grave, and he'd been torn apart. Much like the bodies he was looking at now. Crowley had never been able to figure out who the man was digging the grave for, either, and there was plenty of gallows humour being passed around that day to break the tension. Nobody could figure why the grave was unfinished. If it was a murder, why not finish the job? A location this remote, it was a wonder it even got called in. If not for the mutilated state of the body, he would have suspected a heart attack or even suicide.

"He dug his own grave, and now he lies in it," he mumbled under his breath, then ran a strong hand over a weary face, scratching three days' worth of grizzled stubble that had begun to go grey.

"What's that?" Michael asked.

"Sorry, Dr. Browning," he said. "Just remembering something. I've seen this before."

Michael's eyes widened. "Nobody's seen this before, surely."

The big detective took one last sip of his now cold coffee and looked around for somewhere to throw the empty cup.

The entire area had been cordoned off as a crime scene, and there was a team of investigators gathering evidence and trying to piece together the dead bodies for identification. If this was the same killer – or killers – Luther already knew he wouldn't find much in the way of forensic evidence. The only fingerprints found at the old O'Sullivan place belonged to the victim and were found on the shovel that he'd been using to dig the grave.

Setting aside the impossibility of the act itself – for the type of butchery these people had been subjected to was beyond imagining – what was the motive for the crime? Who had access and opportunity? Luther wanted to know the Who first, and would worry about the How afterward.

"Doctor, I need a list of everyone who had access to this ward, starting with yourself right down to the people that change the linens."

"Of course," he said. "It will be a small list."

"Then that will make my list of suspects small," Luther replied. He reached for a clove cigarette, then stopped, realizing he was in a hospital.

Michael half-laughed uneasily. "Surely none of my staff could be responsible for… for *this*."

Luther glared at the man and shrugged. "Who else?"

Michael stiffened. "I assure you, none of the hospital staff could be capable."

"Are all your patients accounted for?"

The frazzled doctor hesitated, and Luther noticed. He also noticed an anxious-looking man standing just outside the cordoned-off Ward C, arms crossed, rocking side to side from foot to foot. He was wearing scrubs, but Luther didn't see an ID badge or anything. When the detective made eye contact with him, the man didn't look away; rather, he nodded his head, and Luther nodded back. Here was someone with something he needed to say.

"Doctor?" he repeated. "Those bodies in there – is that everyone?"

"Nuh…" Michael coughed, clearing his throat. "No. There's one missing."

A lie, Luther thought. Probably not the last. He'd be digging through a lot of shit to get to the truth on this one, he just knew it.

"Who's missing?"

Michael looked at his feet, and when he looked up again at the detective, the bigger man had taken a step closer to the pale doctor, towering over him.

"I, uh, that is… we're not sure."

"What do you mean, you're not…?" Luther began, beginning to lose patience with the doctor, whom he'd already begun to think of as a slippery eel. Something about the man just didn't sit right with him. Then he took another look at the room and understood. Until the bodies were rearranged, it was going to be hard to identify them. Three of the faces had been destroyed beyond recognition.

"I'm sorry," he corrected himself. It wouldn't do to make an outright enemy of the doctor, even if he didn't trust him. "I understand this is all shocking and unsettling. I'm sure you have families to notify, reports of your own to file. If I could just have access to your patient files, so I can familiarize myself with the victims…"

The dismayed and defensive look on the doctor's face made Luther stop.

"There's nothing in the patients' files that will be of any help to you, I assure you," Michael said.

Luther swore under his breath. He wasn't convinced by the man's plastic smile. "Tell you what, Doctor – why don't you let me decide that for myself, okay? I'm going to need everything you have, starting with a list of your patients and the contact information for their next of kin, and I'm going to need that ASAP, Doc. That means now."

Michael flushed in anger. "That information is confidential, and won't help you in your investigation. Don't you need a subpoena or a search warrant or something?"

"This is a criminal investigation, doctor."

Michael clenched his teeth, refusing to respond.

"Look, as long as what you were doing was legal, I don't care what it was. I'm not asking for access to any top secret information; I just want whatever personal information you have about your patients."

Michael sighed and nodded his head.

"That's the problem, Detective," he said. "We, uh, don't necessarily have complete records on some of the victims."

"What do you mean?" Luther asked, his anger slowly returning.

"Well, they were all volunteers for the study, and some preferred to remain anonymous, and…"

"You mean to tell me you didn't get them to sign some kind of consent form or something?"

Michael shook his head slowly.

"Most of them we only know by their first names," he mumbled, and Luther laughed in disbelief.

"Jesus, what were you people doing here?"

Luther watched Dr. Browning slither off to retrieve the information he'd requested, and kept an eye on the twitchy-looking gawker. He hadn't decided what to make of the man yet. He had the wild eyes and unruly hair of a either a mental patient or a hospital resident who had been surviving on three hours sleep and a dozen cups of coffee a day. He could have been either, really. Crowley had seen all sorts hanging around crime scenes, and he had learned to divide them into three general categories: voyeurs who didn't know anything and would generally slink off when you put them on the spot; attention seekers who didn't know anything but were the first to volunteer useless information or crackpot theories; and the last and only real valuable ones – the shy and shocked onlookers who knew something and just needed some coaxing to give it up. Luther doubted that the guy in the scrubs who was currently hopping from foot to foot as if his bladder was about to explode had anything valuable to contribute, but you never knew. He knew if he waited long enough, the man would either piss his pants or make his move and approach him with his story. If that was the case, Luther would listen and take the man's statement – even the attention seekers were useful sometimes – but he wouldn't put much stock in what he had to say.

A hushed whisper: "Detective."

Luther prepared himself for whatever mad theory the man had for him.

"I'm Detective Crowley," he said, in equally hushed tones. He'd played this game before.

The man took a few steps away from the crime scene, bidding Luther follow him.

"And who might you be?" he asked, stopping cautiously. Once, a perp had hung around the crime scene and had posed as a witness. He'd lured Crowley away from the scene as if he had information, only to take a swipe at him with the largest knife Luther had ever seen a man manage to conceal. He'd taken a deep defensive cut on his forearm that had needed more than thirty stitches, and ever since then he'd given potential witnesses a wide berth.

The man kept walking, unaware that Detective Crowley had stopped. He took a few more steps and then looked over his shoulder and motioned for the detective to keep following him. Luther planted his feet and put his hands into the pockets of his ragged and frayed raincoat. It had once been black; now it was the colour of dust and smoke. Feet shoulder-width apart, he stood like an ancient, rooted tree; his mahogany skin completing the illusion. He was a towering figure when he straightened up, and he used it to his advantage, intimidating people he needed information from.

"This is as far as I'm going," he said firmly. "Say what you've got to say. Start with your name, and what you're doing here."

"My name is Simon," he said timidly. "And I used to work here."

Suddenly, all the tension in Luther's shoulders loosened, and his eyes widened. Maybe there was something here after all. The feeling was brief.

"Tell me, Detective," the man continued. "What do you know about reincarnation?"

"Oh, fuck off!" Crowley snapped, and he turned to walk away. If he didn't, he'd likely choke the man.

"Hear me out!" Simon cried. "I worked here. I saw weird things. These people – these dead people – they were part of some experiment. They didn't even know who they were. Dr. Browning and Dr. Chandra, they recruited mental patients, John Does, trauma cases."

"For what?" Luther asked, despite his intuition about the man.

"There are things we don't understand, Detective – but just because we don't understand them, that doesn't make them untrue. Dr. Chandra and Dr. Browning were researching the paranormal. Dr. Chandra had a theory that combined the concept of reincarnation and past lives with poltergeists."

"Okay, I've heard enough," Luther said, pointing an angry finger at the man. "I want you to clear out of here."

The man wasn't deterred. "Do you believe in the soul, Detective?"

Luther ignored him.

"What if that energy – that spark of life – lives on after death, and could find a new vessel?"

"What are you babbling about? I told you to go."

"Dr. Chandra was trying to channel that energy into a living being. She theorized that mental illness was often the result of people being possessed by spirits trying to make their way back into the world. They were trying to make that transition work. Imagine it, Detective – if people could be reborn after death by possessing the living."

"That's ridiculous," Detective Crowley growled. "Who would allow that kind of invasion?"

"The homeless," the man said gravely. "The mentally ill. Other expendables."

Luther couldn't believe he was listening to this.

"Fuck off," he said again, laughing. "Do you know how crazy that sounds?"

"A hundred years ago, the Internet would have sounded crazy. Please, just ask them. Ask them what they're doing here."

"I plan on it," Luther said, filing the man's crazy story away for further thought. "So what happened here then? Why did these people die?"

Simon shook his head.

"Maybe they awakened angry spirits," he said. "I don't know for sure. All I know is that something went horribly wrong."

"Yeah, no shit," Luther grumbled, and he walked away from the man. "Asshole."

Michael and Naveena – Now

The research wing of Sisters of Mercy was small, consisting of only four wards and a shared lab space. There was limited office space, and Michael and Naveena shared a cramped corner office, both using the same desk, computer, and filing system. Michael found Naveena crouched over her computer, deleting entire directories as fast as her fingers could move.

"You'd be better off taking a giant magnet to the hard-drive," Michael remarked from the doorway, and she gave him a silent rebuke with a quick glare. "Or dropping the fucking thing out the window."

"You're not helping, Michael," she said. "It would not do for anyone to see what is in these files. But it would look suspicious if everything was missing."

Michael shook his head in lament.

"All that work, gone," he moaned.

"Don't be stupid," she snapped. "I have this all backed up to a private Cloud account. It's all safe."

"*Your* private Cloud account?" he asked, surprised, and even a bit suspicious.

"I'm not hiding anything from you, Michael," she sighed. "Open up your email once in a while. The account is shared with only you. You have full access to the information."

Michael cleared his throat and made a sick-sounding noise.

"The detective is asking for patient files," he said, and her fingers stopped their almost arachnid crawling over the keyboard.

"So give them to him," she said, turning to face him. Michael laughed – a hollow, nervous, mirthless thing that sounded like he was choking.

"What?" he asked. "Paper files with little more than names and pictures, and fragments of half-remembered biographical information? These people…"

"Really? Our patients? People?"

"Don't start with that," he warned her. "These people were troubled, and we exploited them. We knew nothing of their past, of their families, and we treated them as expendable."

Naveena fixed him with a stare.

"Sit down," she commanded, and then softened her tone. "Please."

Michael sat across from her, and she kept him entranced with her dark eyes, like a cobra hypnotizing its prey.

"What are we going to tell Detective Crowley?" he asked quietly. "We need to be on the same page here."

"We admit that we didn't do thorough background checks," she said. "And we give him what we have. It's going to look like nonsense to him, anyway, and we will agree that it is nonsense. We tell him we were studying the power of delusion – every one of our patients held impossible beliefs and delusions, some of which were dangerous."

"What about Jessica?" Michael asked, and Naveena's eyes went wide with anger.

"You do not so much as speak her name!" she hissed. "Do you understand me? She is not to be involved at all."

Michael nodded.

"Don't you see, Michael? She survived this. Whatever it was that happened, she was untouched by it. As long as we have her, we can start over. Her survival can only mean one thing."

"You were right about her," Michael admitted, and he was filled with awe and terror. "She is the one."

"She's only the first," Naveena countered. "This first batch may have proved a failure, but there will be others."

Michael turned pale. "Five people are dead. We can't just clean up the mess and resume our study."

Naveena smiled and murmured two words that had begun to frighten Michael over the past three months.

"Not real," she said.

"What did you say?" he asked, shocked.

"You heard what I said, and you know exactly what I mean."

"How can you...?" he stammered. "How can you say that? She's convinced you then, is that it?"

"How are you not convinced, Michael? How else can you explain this? She's our ticket, Michael. She's everything we were searching for. And she can't be the only one. I simply can't believe it. I won't."

"But you thought the others…" he began to respond, and Dr. Chandra scowled so fiercely that he cut his thought short.

"I was wrong," she admitted bitterly.

Michael sat obediently, waiting to be dismissed. Their professional relationship wasn't always so lopsided, but since she'd caught him with his pants down that morning, he'd had a hard time even meeting her gaze.

"About this morning," he tried, and was cut off.

"Not the time, Michael. But get your shit together," she said.

"Right. Sure."

"And give the detective everything he asks for, and nothing more. I'll make sure there's nothing for him to find."

"Do you think he'll find who did it?" Michael asked.

Naveena stared at him like he was an idiot child.

"*Really*, Michael?"

HARRIS

Luther – Now

Detective Crowley took a long, sweet drag on his clove cigarette and blew smoke out into the rain. He stood under a ledge, his back against the wall, and popped his collar up, but he was still cold and damp. His back ached and his toes froze in his worn out loafers. He wanted to go back to bed, forget the sight of the dismembered bodies, forget the impossibility of the force required to tear bodies apart like that. More than anything, he wanted to forget the crazy theories of the man who'd called himself Simon, and who claimed to have worked with Dr. Browning and Dr. Chandra. Luther would suspect Simon himself of the crime – there was a mania in the man's eyes that he recognized – but one look at Simon told him he was the sort of man who had trouble opening a bag of potato chips, and not the sort who could tear an arm off a man.

Still, he wanted to know more about what was going on in Ward C. He wasn't likely to get a straight answer from Dr. Browning, and Dr. Chandra seemed inaccessible. He'd hold on to Simon's story until the time was right.

Dr. Browning had given him the six files he'd requested – he'd need to spend some time on them, get to know all the players. It would be a while before they identified all the bodies and learned who it was that was missing. Whoever it was might not be a murder suspect, but they were certainly at the top of Luther's list for questioning.

He got in his car and sat with it turned off, the steady sound of the rain pattering on the windshield in a way he found almost musical. He didn't like the cold, or the wet, but he'd always loved the sound of the rain, especially when it was violent and stormy. When he was a boy, his dad would drive him and his ma out to the lake during the summer storms and they'd just listen to the rain and the thunder and marvel at the light show of lightning on the water. He still found the sound soothing.

Pulling out the files from beneath his coat where he'd kept them dry, he flipped through them, noticing that none of them were more than three months old. Whatever had been going on, it hadn't been going on long. That surprised him. He'd gotten the impression that Ward C had been in use longer than that. Dr. Browning certainly seemed at home there, even protective of his staff.

Luther made note of it but didn't read too much into it. For all he knew, Chandra and Browning had been there for twenty years and this was just the most recent batch of patients.

The first and oldest file belonged to Harris Parker. He opened the file and found a pretty standard intake form, with a picture of a middle-aged, Caucasian man, followed by the usual informational requests: Name, date of birth, address, place of employment, next of kin. None of this was filled out except the man's name. No social, no health insurance, nothing.

Instead, there was just a date of intake, and some handwritten notes about the patient's condition upon arrival. This couldn't be everything. Three months, and this was all the information they'd gathered?

"Bullshit," Luther said under his breath, and flipped open the other file folders. They were all the same, as if the intake files had been created merely for appearances, out of some sort of formality. What he did notice was that every one of the files contained several pages of photocopied writing – but the handwriting didn't match up to the notes on the intake sheet.

Was he supposed to read this?

Harris

Patient Data

Today's Date:_____

☐ F

Insurance Information

Name of Company:_____

Name of Insured:_____

Insureds DOB:_____ SS#:_____

Patient consents to participate in trials, comp
of which will be at the discretion of the super
physicians. Resitution will be paid at the en
the study.

Your Employer:_____

Occupation:_____

Referred to this office by: ☐ Web Site ☐ Yellow Pages ☐ Advertisement

☐ Friend/Family Member Name:_____

Signature of Patient:_____

Print Name: *Harris Parke*

Date: *04/04/15*

Payment for Services will be by: ☐ Cash ☐ Check ☐ Credit Card ☐ Health Insurance ☐ Automobile Insurance

Are you covered by more than one insurance company? ☐ Yes ☐ No   Name_____

Patient is excited -- almost manic. Excessively verbal,
obsessed with a ~~particular~~ ~~he is~~
~~~~
Harris believes that he is here to help us with the study, an
allowing him this delusion seems to be the best way
to get him to comply.

Have you been treated by a physician for any health condition in the last year? ☐ Yes ☐ No

Describe Condition_____ Date of Last Physical Exam_____

Describe The Treatment:_____

SURGICAL HISTORY: ☐ NONE

1._____ Date:_____
2._____ Date:_____
3._____ Date:_____

Have you ever had a metal implant? ☐ Yes ☐ No   Ever been gunshot? ☐ Yes ☐ No

ACCIDENT HISTORY: ☐ Job ☐ Auto ☐ Other 1._____ Date:_____
☐ Job ☐ Auto ☐ Other 2._____ Date:_____
☐ Job ☐ Auto ☐ Other 3._____ Date:_____

HARRIS

He couldn't quite remember when Marianne left for good.

He vaguely remembered the door slamming, the rumble of the old LeSabre as it coughed to a start. He hadn't realized she was gone, capital G, until he took a glug of milk out of the carton and it was solid. Harris gagged on the curdled milk and leaned over the sink, retching. It was piled high with dishes he hadn't done – because Marianne did the dishes. He ignored the pull of his workroom and prowled the house looking behind doors and the moulding shower curtain as though Marianne were hiding from him. All he found were dust bunnies that had morphed into abominable dust rabbits and one stray pearl earring. Harris rolled it between thumb and forefinger, gazing down at it as though he might see Marianne there in the milky sheen. He didn't bother asking himself where it went wrong. It went wrong that Fall, but the downhill slide was inevitable the day they moved into this house. Marianne thought the country would be good for them. Maybe they could stop flinching every time they heard tires screech against the asphalt, could stop freezing every time a bus roared around the corner. Harris raged at her – he needed his work; his work kept him busy and he *needed* to be busy.

"It's not forever," she said, unpacking their wedding china and arranging it in the kitchen cupboard. She blew a coppery curl out of her eyes. "Just for the summer. You hate the city in the summer – all the tourists, the traffic. This will be good for us."

She returned to stacking plates. "This will be good."

She told him the place had a big basement and that he could still work if he really wanted to – but Harris could see the disappointment that tugged at the corners of her mouth when he began carrying box after box down the concrete steps. The basement was cool and quiet and soon filled with the comforting hum and clicks of his machines. Some of them were recognizable as computer parts, with wires sprouting from them like coiled snakes, but many of the things were his invention, totally unique.

The university had been impressed with his thesis and gave him a research grant that morphed into a job with the brightest minds in the state – possibly in the country. His colleagues told him they'd never seen someone as good with computers as he was.

"It's like they talk to you, man," one of the younger team members said, flicking shaggy hair out of his eyes.

"They do, sometimes," Harris had said from behind a tower of screens, repairing a frayed wire.

Mark used to do that little hair flick. Harris wasn't sure where he'd learned it – he kept his hair aggressively short, almost military. Maybe Marianne had the same habit. His fingers shook as he carefully soldered the split wires back together. He couldn't think about Mark, not yet.

Harris rinsed his mouth out in the bathroom, trying to avoid his reflection. Stubble crawled from his chin down his throat. He couldn't remember the last time he'd shaved. Marianne stopped reminding him. Harris looked down at his body, plucking his shirt away from his chest, which seemed to have grown more concave. Did he eat dinner last night? What time was it anyway? He glanced vaguely at the frosted window above the shower, the thin light coming through giving little indication. He had fallen asleep in the workshop and woken with his face pressed onto his notebook of calculations. Marianne used to prompt him to go to bed. He wondered when she stopped doing that, too. He padded back across the worn, wooden floors to the basement door and descended the stairs. It felt like a pressure in his chest was loosening as the cool air caressed his face. If only he'd been able to make Marianne understand what he was trying to do; if only she hadn't been so narrow-minded.

Their second week in the house she'd stopped coming down the stairs after he yelled at her for almost spilling coffee on the main memory bank. His hands had been shaking so hard he had to clamp them between his knees as he tried not to hyperventilate. If the main bank went down – if anything happened to it – everything would be destroyed.

"If you ate upstairs, you wouldn't have to worry about any of that," she said later, scrubbing the dishes with enough force to send flecks of soapy water flying over her shoulder.

He tried eating upstairs, shoving toast and eggs in his mouth, forcing it all down with too-hot coffee. But he couldn't focus.

Marianne asked him the same question again and again but all he could think about were the numbers running across the screen downstairs, about the adjustments he needed to make. He started getting up earlier and earlier so that he could eat in silence, quickly.

"This isn't healthy, Harris," she said through the basement door one evening. "Have you been outside since we moved in? I want to show you where I want to put the garden. It could be really nice, don't you think?"

He'd suffered a day of lost work with her in the garden, on their knees in the dirt, planting little seedlings until his back ached and sunburn flared across his arms and face. "We won't be here long enough to see anything grow, Mar."

"What do you mean?" She tilted her head to look at him from under the brim of her faded, blue, Red Sox hat. He had bought it for her on their first date.

"It's the middle of June. We have to go back soon – I have to go back soon." He pressed a dirty hand to his back.

Marianne returned to digging. "I'm not going back."

It took Harris a full minute to formulate words as he watched her nimble fingers free a seedling from its plastic carton and nestle it gently in the dirt. "What do you mean you're not going back?"

She didn't answer.

"My work is there – my research, everything!" He looked around at the countryside around them, taking in the greenery for the first time. "My life is there."

"You can go. But I'm not going with you."

Harris ran a finger over the top of one of the machines – dust free, as always. When did they have that fight? A week ago? Two? A month? She said she wouldn't go, but she was the one that left. Marianne's face faded from his mind as he checked on the lines of code running across the screen. He blinked several times before he realized the code was no longer moving. He had to wait until his fingers stopped shaking before he keyed in the commands, checking his logs over and over before hitting the key to confirm. Everything went dark and his breath snagged in his chest, caught somewhere around his heart, which seemed to have forgotten how to beat.

The screen flared to life and he exhaled raggedly watching as the thousands of tiny pixels appeared as if by magic and began coalescing. It took several minutes for the image to settle, to stop flickering, but when it did Harris pressed a shaking hand to his mouth, unaware of the tears streaming slowly down his haggard face.

"Daddy?" The voice was hesitant, testing its ability to speak. It was full of static and skipped a bit like a scratched CD, but it was unmistakable.

"I'm here, Mark." Harris cleared his throat. "I'm right here."

The image on the screen blinked once, twice, and then the smile – so like Marianne's, spread across Mark's thin face. "Hey, Dad."

Harris shut his eyes for a moment, letting his success sink in. Mark had been standing on a busy street corner in downtown Boston, talking to some friends, when the crowd behind lurched suddenly and he was forced off the curb. Off the curb and into the pass of the oncoming express bus whose tires were unable to gain traction on the rain-slicked street until it was too late. His baby boy – not such a baby, a few years away from college – wasn't gone right away. Harris and Marianne argued in hushed, tight voices about when to take him off the machines. *The machines are keeping him alive*, Harris had told Marianne. *If you shut off the machine, you shut off your son.* Marianne had begged Harris to take a look at Mark, to see that he was gone, that the machines breathing for him and keeping his heart beating were all that was left. Before they had let him go, Harris had waited until Marianne was asleep. It had been the work of a few moments to attach the electrodes and begin the download. It was highly experimental but he had tested it on himself – downloading memories and turning them into images, projecting the mental movies that played in his head. This was a considerably larger task – he was downloading fifteen years of life. Fifteen years of memories, sensations, experiences.

Harris opened his eyes and reached out to touch the pixelated cheek of his son. He hadn't downloaded all of the memories; there were things he surgically removed, telling himself he was excising malignancy. The accident went first, an easy choice. But there were moments that Harris remembered all too clearly – when he first yelled at his son, when Mark told his father that he hated him – things it was better that Mark forgot.

"Dad? What's wrong?" Mark's voice brought Harris out of his daze.

"Nothing, Mark. Everything's fine now. Everything is fine."

Harris knew there would be complications in the future – Mark would become more self-aware as he settled into himself. He would wonder why he was reduced to a picture in a box, his DNA replaced with computer code. Harris had put a lot of thought into this. He was good with computers but he was no robotics expert and the thought of chaining his little boy into a steel casing, something powered by batteries – something breakable – made his stomach turn.

"Where do you go when I can't see you?" Mark asked, his brows shadowing his eyes slightly. "You're always leaving me."

"No, Marky – I'm not leaving, I'm just right upstairs." Harris heard the wheedling tone in his voice. "I can't take you with me right now."

Mark's disembodied head twitched slightly – the closest it could come to portraying a shrug. Harris's phone buzzed against the table and he was reaching out to silence it when an idea came to him. It took another few weeks, but after several failed attempts, Harris had created a Mark app. Mark jokingly dubbed it MobileMark and demanded a share of the profits when Harris released it to the world. It was Mark who finally got him out of doors, exploring the lands around the house. It was Mark who finally reminded him to go grocery shopping. Harris walked dazedly through the aisles. Marianne had done the shopping. He reached to touch his breast pocket – a tic that had developed since Mark became portable.

"That's the kind of cereal Mom always buys."

The voice made Harris jump and look around quickly before he realized the low whisper was coming from his pocket. He didn't think he'd launched MobileMark – there was little to see but the inside of his pocket. How could Mark see the cereal? Harris looked down and realized that the camera on his phone was facing outward. He tilted his chin to his chest and asked quietly, "Is that you, Mark?"

"How many other people you got on your phone, Dad?" Mark's whisper was exasperated.

"But how…?"

"I just turned on the camera. Back at the house, I could go between the computer and your phone – they're hooked up to the Wi-Fi. It was easy to bounce between them, once I learned how to do it. But I couldn't go any further than the Wi-Fi reaches. So, I figured out how to tap into the cell network even when MobileMark isn't launched. It wasn't hard, Dad." Mark's voice held a combination of amusement and condescension that Harris had never heard his fifteen-year-old use before.

"Okay, wise guy." Harris reached for the box of healthy bran flakes that he recognized. "Guess I'm gonna have to get one of those talking earpiece things so people don't think I'm crazy."

"Don't get those, Dad, they taste like dirt. Get the Cap'n Crunch."

Little things like grocery shopping and cleaning the house were novel now that he had Mark back. They even spent an afternoon in the garden. Mark proved to be extra useful when Harris had his hands full. He could quickly look up information online and was smarter than the search engines – able to find instructions on how much water their tomato plants needed and how to get rid of the pests eating the basil. Harris bought an earpiece that connected to his phone via Bluetooth and used that when he was out in public. They went to a few movies – several months old due to the small theater's lack of demand – and it was the first time Mark acknowledged any gaps in time.

"Did the new Hawkeye movie come out? I wanted to see that," Mark said, nestled quietly in Harris's ear as the previews began. "I thought it was coming out in the spring."

Harris's throat tightened. The Hawkeye movie had come and gone and Mark hadn't seen it because he was dead and buried before opening weekend.

"We'll rent it," Harris said.

Mark was quiet throughout the showing and Harris wasn't able to concentrate on the movie. His son always chattered through movies – spouting trivia facts about actors and filming or making clever jokes. Harris felt Mark's absence as the credits rolled, but assumed his son would resume his usual stream of consciousness once they were out of the theater. But he didn't. Harris checked his phone to make sure everything was running. When he tried to click on the little *M* icon, however, it wouldn't open. He almost dropped his car keys in his hurry to get them out of his pocket and the drive back out to the little house blurred by. He ran down the stairs to the basement and woke up the system. Mark's face didn't appear. He waited for thirty seconds, sixty, ninety – five minutes before he did an extensive backup and reboot. Still, Mark didn't appear.

Harris tried to quell the panic that brought sweat out on his forehead and sent it streaming down his back. He did everything right – there was no way his data was corrupted. Unless… a virus? He double and triple-checked his encryptions, his firewalls. Everything was secure. He sat in front of the computer for over an hour, drumming his fingers on the tabletop and periodically saying his son's name aloud. He didn't remember falling asleep but a pinging noise from the computer startled him awake. His left eye was gummed shut and he rubbed it while waiting for his vision to focus on the screen.

`Why didn't you tell me?`

Harris was taken aback by the text that flared across the screen. "Mark? Can you hear me?"

`Why didn't you tell me?`

The text repeated, right below the first line.

"Why didn't I tell you what?" Harris asked aloud, hoping to get a verbal response from Mark.

In answer, the screen was immediately filled with the same set of words over and over again, hypnotic in their pulsing glow.

`Mark Harris Parker`
`October 6, 2001 - March 3, 2015`

"But you're not gone," Harris choked. "You're here – you're right here."

The cursor on screen blinked, but no more words appeared. Harris tried to regulate his breathing. He should have known this would happen, should have planned for it. Once Mark proved that he was able to search the Internet on his own, it was only a matter of time. All because of that stupid Hawkeye movie, Harris thought, feeling angry for the first time. Things were going so well. Why couldn't Mark just let it lie?

"Why won't you just talk to me, Mark?"

`Where is mom?`

"Please, Mark." Harris waited but there was no answer. He finally said, "Mom left. She left because I wouldn't – couldn't – stop this project. I had to bring you back. And I did. I did!"

    `I'm a fucking computer. I'm not back,`
      `Harris. I'm not really even here.`

Harris pleaded with his son – it *was* his son, no matter what Mark said – but soon even the text stopped appearing and the app on his phone refused to open. At first, all he received was an error message: Error -1311811. He didn't recognize the error code and tried uninstalling and reinstalling the app but the same error repeated over, and over. Error -1311811.

Harris drifted about the house in a daze, opening cans of soup and eating half of them cold out of the can before abandoning them. Some days he didn't get out of bed for hours. There was no point in doing any further work on the machine if Mark wasn't responding. It felt like he had died all over again. Just after three a.m. in the second week since Mark stopped talking, Harris's phone began to buzz. He pawed for it, but his sleep-numbed fingers couldn't grasp it. He knocked it off the bedside table and heard it clatter on the wood floor. Whatever it was could wait, he thought, burying his face back into yellowed pillowcases that hadn't been washed in weeks.

"Play with me!" The singsong voice that came from the speakers startled him awake. It was Mark's voice at four or five. "Daddy! Come play with me!"

Harris tumbled out of bed and scrambled on the floor, searching for the phone. He pulled it from beneath the bed, blowing off the shroud of dust. The screen was lit so brightly he had to blink twice, dazzled by the light and movement. It was a home video of Mark careening around their little back patio on his tricycle

"Watch me, Daddy! Watch me!"

The sight mesmerized Harris; little Mark circling round and round, his helmeted head bobbing.

Watch me. The voice changed—deeper, rougher—and yet there was something almost familiar about it. *WATCH ME.*

The image was grainy and it took Harris a moment to realize he was seeing a security camera. He knew the street. He saw it over and over in his nightmares. He wanted to squeeze his eyes shut, but he watched as a little figure stepped out into the street, watched as the bus lumbered towards it, watched as the bus skidded, as the little figure disappeared out of the frame. The image switched and was focused on another part of the street, further up. A blob on the concrete that wasn't moving. The mangled and bloody body of his son.

"I'm sorry, I'm so sorry," Harris said in a broken whisper, letting the phone slide to the floor.

Sorry that Mark is dead? Or sorry that you turned off the machines that were keeping him going? the new voice asked.

"I didn't – there was no other choice. Mark's body was too damaged – they had to restart his heart three times." The words sounded hollow to Harris, an echo of Marianne's pleading.

So you chained him to a new machine, instead. You selfish sack of shit. The voice flicked across him like an icy wind. *Well here I am, Harris. And I'm not going anywhere now.*

Harris tried again that day to bring up Mark on the computer in the basement, on his laptop, on his cell phone – nothing. He tried to forget the strange, new voice, tried not to think of how it could almost be Mark's voice – if Mark was twenty-five. If he had gotten the chance to reach twenty-five.

The next night at the same time his phone went off again. It played another home video of an older Mark kicking around a soccer ball. Harris tried to shut the phone off before the accident footage played, but it wouldn't turn off. He turned it upside-down on the bed, but the voice that taunted him the night before seemed to grow louder and louder. He held down the power button, almost panicking, and for thirty tortuous seconds, it refused to shut off. He breathed a sigh of relief and lay back, trying to calm his racing heart. He finally fell back asleep sometime before dawn, rudely roused again by a loud beeping. His first instinct was to check his phone, but it was still black and silent. He followed the sound to the kitchen where the coffee pot Marianne had gotten him last Christmas was chirping. It was the latest model – connected with an app on his iPhone, he could set the pot to brew without even getting out of bed. He hadn't used it in weeks, though. Maybe the software had a glitch. The clock was stuck in military time – chirping frantically as the numbers flashed at him. 13:11:18. He finally unplugged the blinking, beeping thing, too tired to investigate further.

Out of habit he descended the steps of the basement, hoping against all hope that Mark would be back. The computer whirred to life and Harris keyed in the necessary commands, but nothing happened. The relief that flooded through him sickened him. The video the night before had unsettled him. Logically, it had to be Mark – Mark working through his newfound existence. Harris had wanted Mark to be as close to human as code and wiring could make him – his memories of thoughts and feelings would feed into his make-up as the program continued to build on itself. That was the way the program was designed – to learn and develop. Harris wondered now if he should have built in some stopgaps, if he should have placed limits on how quickly and how far the code could grow. He drummed his fingers on the table for a few minutes before keying in the commands that would bring up the program. Maybe it wasn't too late to slow things down. He skimmed over the code that made up the program, feeling a twinge of pride at the delicate construction, the beauty. People didn't understand programming, didn't see the poetry in it, the way the combinations came together so perfectly. His eyes snagged on something unfamiliar.

"That's not right," he said, leaning in closer.

Harris keyed in the commands to edit and the screen flickered. He held his breath. The data was safe; he'd taken to doing daily back-ups in case the program was on the verge of crashing. He almost hoped it was a glitch – something he'd done wrong, a malfunction. If that was the explanation for the videos the night before, he could figure out how to fix it. The screen flashed again, then held steady, and Harris marked the deviation mentally before continuing to scroll. It caught his eye again. A third time, a fourth. It was riddled through the code, a sequence of numbers that he hadn't put there: 1311811. Harris was puzzling over them when a blaring sound upstairs nearly sent him out of his chair and onto the floor. He bounded up the stairs. *A break in?* he thought wildly – and slid to a halt when he realized it was coming from the living room. The TV was on, the volume at an ear-splitting level. Harris was almost afraid to see what was on, disoriented by the sheer noise. Edging into the room as though the TV were a predator, he peeked at the screen. It was a sitcom – one of thousands of quirky family dramas that blurred together. He reached for the remote.

"Mark! Hey, Mark!"

Harris froze, eyes locking on the screen, but the boy who was calling and the boy who answered him were only familiar as child actors. Neither one was his beautiful boy. He switched off the TV and wondered if there was something wrong with the electrical circuits in the place. It was an older house – electrical problems weren't out of the question. He returned to the basement and opened the breaker box – the first thing he thought to do. He knew the wiring in computers like he knew the spray of freckles across Mark's cheeks, but house wiring was beyond him. He flipped the breaker labeled *living room* on and off twice just for the hell of it. Returning to the computer, he idly repeated the numbers in his head as he continued searching for them, trying to make sense of where they had intruded and why. 1311811. 131 181 1. 13 1 18 11. He thought of something – an old puzzle book he'd loved as a child, pairing numbers with letters to make secret messages. Mark had rolled his eyes when Harris tried to interest him in number riddles; he would rather be outside, his body in motion rather than his mind. Harris fumbled for a piece of paper and wrote the sequence of numbers out carefully.

13 1 18 11

M A R K

Harris leaned back in his chair and exhaled slowly. Mark was rewriting the code from within. He felt a rush of pleasure at the thought, remembering watching Mark's head bent over his latest work, puzzling through the steps. Harris always waited until Mark began asking questions to explain, bursting to share his passion with his son. He went back through more carefully this time, noting other tweaks and changes – things he hadn't thought of. Things he didn't understand. He forgot about the phone, the TV, the coffeemaker, the unsettling voice that was Mark and yet *wasn't* Mark. When his eyes refused to focus on the screen and he felt a deep hollowness in his gut, Harris dragged himself upstairs to eat. He meant to keep working after dinner, but exhaustion overwhelmed him and he fell into a dreamless sleep. Just after four a.m. Harris awoke to a cacophony of beeping, whirring, shouting, singing – his phone was dancing and buzzing on the nightstand, the TV in the bedroom was running through all the channels in rapid succession. He staggered out into the living room where the second television was blaring a music video and the iPod dock in the corner was shuffling through music on a forgotten, dusty iPod that had belonged to Mark. Harris clapped his hands over his ears for a minute, stunned. If it was the electricity, why would it affect his phone? He went to the TV to yank out the cord when all the sound cut off. The ringing in his ears distracted him and he hesitantly asked, "Mark?" in a voice that cracked.

ARE YOU WATCHING?

The words ran across the TV screen in a blaze of bright text. Harris watched, mute, as they flashed and flickered. Then, they vanished and he saw an image of a shabby room with a sagging couch and dust on the table and a man standing there, mouth slack, face gaunt. The skin pulled at the man's chin and cheekbones like wax dripping off a candle. Harris raised a trembling hand to his mouth and saw the man on the screen do the same.

"What…" he began. But there was movement on the screen, in the doorway behind the man's – Harris's – back.

Harris didn't turn, gaze fixed on the image of the figure lurking in the shadows. He was tall and lanky. The boy – the young man – stepped out of the shadows and flicked the hair out of his eyes with a twitch of his head. He walked silently – if you could call it walking – around Harris until he was standing directly in front of him. Harris felt like he was choking or maybe having a heart attack. The figure looked solid, except for the unnatural glow that lined his cheeks, his shoulders, and the tips of his hair. Harris couldn't breathe, couldn't speak. Mark – or something that looked like a projection of Mark – flickered, like the static that ran across the TV screen. He leaned in to Harris, close enough that Harris could hear the faint buzz that he emitted.

"Hello, Dad."

Harris – Three Months Ago

Harris took another yellow pill, even though it wasn't yet time. He needed to be calm and professional. He'd trimmed his beard and cleaned up nicely, wanting to make a good first impression and be taken seriously. He looked at his watch – an old-fashioned thing that had to be wound once a day to keep time, and checked it against the flashing digital clock on the taxi's meter.

The time on the meter read 1:31 as the driver pulled up in front of the hotel. The fare read $18.11

Of course it did.

He paid the driver with cash, leaving the driver a dollar tip. He looked around the front of the building – a fancy thing with stone sculpture lions guarding the entrance, as if it were a library or a government building and not just an expensive hotel.

The woman he'd spoken to on the phone had given him strict instructions, and he'd followed them to the letter. But he didn't see her. She said she'd be waiting for him – or rather, she said she'd find him. He had a phone number for her, but he didn't see a payphone in sight. He didn't carry his cellphone – didn't carry *anything* electronic anymore – and so he'd have to wait.

He bought a coffee from a news kiosk, and the guy tried to sell him a lottery ticket. The red dot matrix sign advertised that tonight's jackpot was $1,311,811.

He sat down on the steps out in front of the hotel and drank his coffee. He looked at his watch, which now read closer to a quarter to two.

She was late.

"Mr. Parker?"

Harris turned his head to see a man and a woman. He recognized them both.

"Dr. Chandra," he said, standing and offering her his hand. "A pleasure to meet you."

"Likewise," she said with a smile, and then motioned to the man beside her. "This is…"

"Dr. Browning. Yes, I know." Harris offered the man his hand as well. "I saw your lecture, Doctor, and you're absolutely right. I believe it. I've seen it. I think… I think I may have created it."

Michael and Naveena – Nine Months Ago

Transcript of a lecture by Dr. Michael Browning, given at a symposium on Genetic Psychology and Molecular Psychiatry.

THE POWER OF THE HUMAN MIND
vs. THE COMING SINGULARITY

"What a piece of work is a man, how noble in reason, how infinite in faculties, in form and moving how express and admirable, in action how like an angel, in apprehension how like a god! The beauty of the world, the paragon of animals – and yet, to me, what is this quintessence of dust?"
Hamlet, Act 2 Scene 2

Science fiction stories have warned us of the danger inherent in trying to play god, and we are very entertained, but walk away from the story having learned nothing. Our faith and confidence in our own intellectual superiority is hubris, and will surely be our downfall.

The fear that the creation could surpass its creator has long been the theme of movies starring legions of killer robots and bloated special effects budgets. Whether it's Stanley Kubrick's HAL or James Cameron's Skynet, there has existed in the collective consciousness the real and possible danger of being surpassed by an artificial intelligence of our own design.

Increasing numbers of scientists in various fields, as well as philosophers and social analysts, are predicting something they call "the singularity" – defined as something of an event horizon in human history, where technological progress will accelerate beyond human intellectual capacity and comprehension. When this happens, the age of human superiority will essentially come to an end, as we are made redundant.

This may sound paranoid or impossible, but I assure you, it is neither. The human mind cannot make computations as fast as a computer, even though the human mind conceived the computer – the child surpasses the parent. What happens when someday – and I believe this day is coming sooner than we think – we create an artificial intelligence that is greater than our own, able to think at a level that we cannot even conceive? What will become of us then?

What will the hierarchy of the world look like when we could be outsmarted, out-strategized, and rendered obsolete by our own electric children?

I believe that there is a way to prevent this. I believe that there is more potential in the human mind that can be unlocked, if we are willing to try. Furthermore, I suggest that there are those out there living among us that may have already unlocked that potential, only we don't recognize it. We don't understand them and so we dismiss them or fear them. What do we make of so-called psychics or telekinetics? People who claim to have seen ghosts? People with unexplained intelligence or abilities that defy what is scientifically quantifiable? What if unexplained phenomena such as these are just perceptions currently outside the realm of our understanding of the human mind, but that could be understand – even learned? What if we are all capable of these feats, and we just need to have them unlocked in our brains?

Hypothetically, if there is knowledge that we currently don't have access to, what might we do to achieve it? The quest for wisdom and knowledge is what defines us as humans. Our earliest stories and legends have to do with forbidden knowledge – Adam and Eve in the Garden, Pandora and her box, even Odin trading his own eye to drink from the font of wisdom. What might we achieve, given our full potential? If we are to avoid being surpassed in the coming technological singularity, what must we do, what sacrifices must we make, what lines might we have to cross? How do we tap that potential?

Do we look to genetic mutation? Is there something in our biology that prevents us from furthering our mental capacity? Could chemical manipulation be the answer, as Timothy Leary and others believed? What true value might come from such controversial psychiatric techniques such as deep brain stimulation or sensory deprivation?

Another controversial philosophy is the idea of post-humanity or trans-humanity. There are those that suggest that humans should not be limited by our biology, and instead embrace technology, going so far as to become hybrid beings, using technology such as unusual prostheses to give us abilities beyond those nature endows us with. It is, in a very real sense, an attitude of *if you can't beat them, join them.* How might we define what real humanity is fifty years from now? A hundred years? Will we fight against the coming technological singularity or surrender to it?

Michael sat at the hotel bar and knocked back a shot of Johnny Walker Red, then motioned to the bartender for another.

"Should juss leave the bottle," he slurred, and the bartender frowned.

"This isn't some Old West saloon, sir," he said. "I think maybe you've had enough. I'm sure the minibar in your room is well stocked."

Michael had been trying to flirt with the young man, but he wasn't getting anything from him. Not even a little nibble. Maybe if he was more direct.

"You maybe wanna come and check it out with me?"

The bartender rolled his eyes and walked away.

"Yeah, fuck you, too," Michael muttered under his breath. He shouldn't have been flirting anyway. He was taken. He loved Ray – he did – but when he got a drink or three in him, he sometimes forgot.

He needed a drink right then. He'd heard them talking about him after his lecture. The audience had clapped politely when he was through, but their faces told a different story. They whispered behind their hands and laughed when they thought he couldn't hear them.

He wanted to knock the teeth out of every one of their talentless, unimaginative faces. Their kind of stagnant, safe thinking was dangerous, and he knew they'd never listen to him until it was too late.

He braced himself on the bar and was making to get off the stool when he saw a woman with skin the colour of creamy coffee approach him, taking the seat next to him.

"Is this seat available?" she asked, and Michael smiled at her and sighed.

"Be my guest," he said. "But I have to warn you, I'm really not your type."

"And what type is that, Dr. Browning?" she asked and raised an inquisitive eyebrow.

Michael straightened up in his chair at the mention of his name.

"Dr. Naveena Chandra," she said, and offered him a strong, well-manicured hand. "I attended your lecture on the coming singularity."

Michael wished he had another drink. "And you've come to invite me to join your post-human cult? Or hit me up for some magic mushrooms?"

"Not at all," she said in a cultured voice. "I think we can be of help to one another. You see, I believe I have encountered something like the singularity you speak of, only she is not a machine at all, doctor. She is like you and I – flesh and blood."

"She?" Michael asked, curious.

Dr. Chandra nodded and smiled. "Would you like to meet her?"

Jessica – Nine Months Ago

Jessica wasn't sure how she ended up at Sisters of Mercy Hospital – sometimes things like that just happened to her. The details of her past were sometimes fuzzy, and seemed more like multiple choice than a true autobiography. But ever since she'd left Helena, things had become clearer, like a veil had dropped and she suddenly saw the possibilities of her own existence. And she did exist, she was sure of that – only sometimes she had trouble keeping the days straight, or filling in the gaps of time where she couldn't quite remember where she'd been or what she'd been doing. At best, it could be described as a half-life, and she intended on changing that.

She would do what she knew how to do – the only thing she knew how to do. She would write.

"Write and write and write and write," she whispered to herself with the manic glee that always came when inspiration struck her, her pen dancing across the smooth blank page of her notebook.

The path cut through the woods like a jagged scar left by a knife-wielding maniac.

She looked at what she'd written and smiled. It was the kind of grin that would make young children cry, the type of crooked, malicious, evil smile that made passers-by cross to the other side of the street, and caused the testicles of even the most virile men to shrivel up in fear and retreat back into their bellies.

She looked at what she'd written and declared it good.

This was the first day. It would be six more days before the doctors came with all their questions, just when she was trying to get some rest.

She was just doodling, drawing that stupid rabbit. That wasn't Jessica's memory, it was *hers*. It meant nothing. It meant everything. Jessica had become obsessed with it; he couldn't get the story of The Velveteen Rabbit out of her head.

The two doctors came in, and she pretended to ignore them. The very white man seemed content to observe her, while the small Indian woman regarded her with something like awe. Jessica felt like a sacred relic or fetish whenever Dr. Chandra was in her presence, and she had to admit it didn't feel terrible to be the object of – well, let's face it – worship.

"Jessica," Dr. Chandra said. "I'd like to introduce you to my partner,"

"Your partner?" Jessica asked, looking the man up and down.

Dr. Chandra blushed ever so slightly, and Jessica noted it and grinned a little grin.

"My colleague," she corrected. "We're not together."

"Of course not," Jessica remarked. "He's queer."

The tall man shuffled his feet and cocked his head.

"How did she...?" he began, and Dr. Chandra laughed with delight.

"She knows a lot of things," she said. "Jessica, this is Dr. Browning."

"Hello, Michael," Jessica purred, eliciting another surprised response from the man. She loved catching people off guard and disarming them. "So lovely to finally meet you. I've dreamed of you for days now."

"Is she for real?" Michael asked Naveena out of the side of his mouth, never taking his eyes off of Jessica, whose own dark eyes were locked on his.

"She is," Jessica answered. "And she finds it terribly rude to be spoken of as if she is not right in the room."

Michael flushed. "I'm sorry, you just surprised me, Miss Bell. Dr. Chandra has told me so much about you, but apparently not nearly enough."

"Jessica, please," she said. She could be charming in an unsettling way.

"Jessica, then," he agreed. "What is it you're doing there?"

Jessica closed her notebook and held it tightly and protectively to her chest, like she was nursing an infant.

"Writing," she said.

"What are you writing?"

Jessica hesitated and rolled her eyes. If she were Helena, she'd likely digress into some diversion – a Hamlet reference, no doubt. Jessica loathed the other woman's repetitive segues and unimaginative and predictable motifs. But she was not Helena, so there would be no witty banter here.

"Stories," she stated plainly. "It's what we were born to do. Our mother was possessed by a demon, they say, and he gave her all the stories, as well as me."

"Who says?" he asked.

Jessica rolled her eyes again and waved an exasperated hand. "They. Them."

The doctor nodded as if taking mental notes for further review. "About this demon…"

"Oh, straight to bed then, doctor? Without even buying a girl dinner?" Jessica cackled, and the doctor smiled unconvincingly.

"Could we read some of your stories, Jessica?" Dr. Chandra asked, and Jessica gripped her notebook tighter.

"I don't think you'd like them, *pyaari beti*," Jessica cooed almost sweetly, and Naveena blushed and broke into bright laughter.

"I have not been called that endearment since I was a child, Jessica. Thank you. But why do you not think we'd like your stories?"

"They're strange and terrible, like me. Twisted, dark and obscene."

"Surely you're not so terrible, Jessica," Dr. Chandra replied, though the look on her face made Jessica think of plague victims or the recently drowned.

Jessica cocked her head and grinned like a child's drawing of a smile – her mouth seeming to stretch impossibly wide, like her cheeks would tear open at any moment. She stared Dr. Chandra down, challenging her to meet her gaze, but the woman's eyes darted this way and that, as if she were in the midst of a dream.

"Why do you write such strange fictions?" Dr. Browning asked. "Why not write something nice, something based in reality?"

Jessica scowled. "She always asks us that. The little one."

"Who?" Dr. Chandra asked. "Who is the little one?"

"Not important," Jessica sighed, clenching her teeth at the thought of the stripey-socked urchin. "I hate reality. Too much of it will drive you insane. Shirley Jackson was absolutely right on that account."

"Surely the stories you write, even though fictional, contain something of yourself," Dr. Browning insisted. "I'm sure they'd be an insight to your personality, the workings of your mind."

Jessica looked at him like one might a precocious but inexperienced and naïve child.

"Really, doctor," Jessica said in her most patronizing tone, "they're just stories. They're not real. Besides, mostly it's just character sketches, first drafts, and unfinished vignettes. They're not ready yet. I'd show you, but you wouldn't understand. Not yet, but soon. I don't want to give away the game just yet. Not until I see how far I can take it."

THE MAN

Luther – Now

The John Doe wasn't called John Doe at all. Instead, the file simply called him The Man, and all that accompanied that title was a blurry photograph of a plain but attractive man of maybe thirty, Luther guessed. It was a terrible picture. He wondered why they didn't take another.

There were notes scribbled in the same hand that the detective assumed belonged to one of the doctors, either Chandra or Browning. The script was rough, and he was leaning toward Dr. Browning for the writer.

J says The Man killed his son. The Man says he doesn't know, doesn't even know if there was a boy, he can't remember.

i suggested we send his picture to the police. if The Man is a fugitive, we need to turn him in. Dr. C. disagrees. She tells me that she is positive that The Man didn't kill anyone. Because of how the story ends.

There is more writing, but it's been scratched out so completely that Luther can't make out any of it. Then below that there is more, in different handwriting, which must belong to Dr. Chandra.

The Man is a blank slate. I'm beginning to understand her attraction to him. He could be anything. A template. A rough sketch, as she says. I wonder what he actually looks like. If I gave a description to a sketch artist, and then had Michael give his description, would the artist draw the same person? This sounds insane, but normal went out the window the moment we met J.

Luther flipped through the files again, noting the names of the dead – there was no one with the initial J among them.

Who was J?

The Man's file held more of the same writing – another story? Maybe this would make more sense than the last one. Even if it didn't, it was all he had to go on at the moment, so he began to read.

atient Data

ay's Date:_____

Insurance Information
Name of Company:_____
Name of Insured:_____
Insureds DOB:_____ SS#:_____
Patient consents to participate in trials, completion of which will be at the discretion of the supervising physicians. Resititution will be paid at the end of the study.
Signature of Patient:_____
Print Name: **THE MAN**
Date:_____

F

er:_____

is office by:☐Web Site ☐Yellow Pages ☐Advertisement

nily Member Name:_____

ervices will be by: ☐ Cash ☐ Check ☐ Credit Card ☐ Health Insurance ☐ Automobile Insurance

ed by more than one insurance company? ☐ Yes ☐ No Name_____

ays The Man killed his son. The Man says he doesn't know, sn't even know if there was a boy. He can't remember. ggested we send his picture to the police. if The Man is gitive, we need to turn him in. Dr. C. disagrees. She tells she is positive The Man didn't kill anyone. ause of how the story ends.

~~is a killer ... afraid of what he and Jessa ... o be together.~~

Man is a blank slate. I'm beginning to understand her attraction to him. He could be anything. mplate. A rough sketch, as she says. I wonder what he actually looks like. If I gave a description ketch artist and then had Dr. B. give his description, would the artist draw the same person? ounds insane, but normal went out the window the moment we met J.

reated by a physician for any health condition in the last year? ☐ Yes ☐ No

on_____ Date of Last Physical Exam_____

atment:_____

RY: ☐ NONE

_____ Date:_____
_____ Date:_____
_____ Date:_____

d a metal implant? ☐Yes ☐ No   Ever been gunshot? ☐ Yes ☐ No
RY: ☐ Job ☐ Auto ☐ Other 1._____ Date:_____
☐ Job ☐ Auto ☐ Other 2._____ Date:_____
☐ Job ☐ Auto ☐ Other 3._____ Date:_____

THE MAN

THE MAN

The man was seeking the boy. The boy who had done this to them.

A twist of dust spiralled over one rag-eared boot, ever more dirt settling on the sock showing through the hole at its tip. He stared down at it a moment – red-rimmed, bloodshot eyes blinking in dull incomprehension.

Could this be the world? Or was this some kind of hallucination? It could've been brought on by stress. He'd been stressed recently. They all had. That's why they'd listened to the boy.

The man's fists clenched, knuckles whitening under the grime that coated them. He forced himself to uncurl his fingers and breathe slowly. The stale, dry air crawled its way into his damaged lungs. He coughed – a dry, hacking bark that cracked out into the silence like a gunshot. There was no one to hear.

The boy had promised... what? He'd sworn they were going to a better place. Had the others gone there? No. Otherwise the boy would've gone too. Why was *he* still here? What had gone wrong?

He shook his head slowly from side to side, the world turning and blurring around him until he was dizzy. He'd not been right since the powder the boy had given them. The boy or the doctor? How could that really have happened?

He'd crawled out of the church over stray, stiff limbs grown cold and grey. Or could it be that he was still there? Tangled in spread-eagled human flesh. Dead flesh. Everyone was dead. Everyone except him and the boy.

The man rubbed at his eyes – gritty and sore, and weeping mucus from their corners. The others had bled from their eye sockets. He stared at his hands. Were they red or was it the light? It was a crimson-tinged wasteland that he wandered through. The boy must be here somewhere, though. He knew he lived. It wasn't just him left. It couldn't be, could it?

Broken, crumbled buildings shimmered on the horizon like an alien outpost in the Mars-like environs. The boy must be there, hiding like a lying cockroach. Coward. He'd ended the world and now he was scuttling through the ruins, emperor of all. But he knew he was hunted.

The man strode shakily toward the edge of the shantytown. Rusted, corrugated iron roofs came into hazy focus. One had a pole sticking out at a crazy angle. It held half a torn flag, ash obscuring the colours it had flown. It twisted in the scant breeze like a slow snake, surprised to have survived the riots and escaped the burning buildings. As people realized they were dying – that they were going to choke to death on their own vomit – they had tried to go down fighting, but they could only fight each other.

The man made for the flag. The church had been out in the desert. Now the whole world was a desert.

In amongst the rubble, the man picked his way down empty streets. What had happened to the bodies? A sudden clatter sounded and he raised his head sharply. The boy. It must be. There was no one else left.

The man broke into a staggering run toward the noise. He tripped over blackened debris as he hurtled around broken building corners, bricks cutting unheeded into his hands when he reached out for balance.

He stopped. Ragged breathing obscured his hearing for a moment. Was that another noise? A frustrated growl vibrated in the base of his throat. The boy was wily. Obviously. He'd had everyone convinced. Hypnotic words promising a better life, a world worth being in, worth following him for. He was the new god, destroying the old earth to bring forth the new. But this couldn't be the new world. It just couldn't.

The congregation had nodded and swayed, holding hands and casting their eyes up in silent supplication, and in gratitude that the boy had come into their lives to save them. He was the one. The boy saw it all coming and described it to them in detail. He would take the true believers with him. He would create them all anew. The medicine that would fix them – that would lead to their rebirth – was still dancing in the man's bloodstream.

He felt the firm pressure on his hand as though it were really there. Suzie's grip. She'd stared into his face unseeing, a beatific smile stretching her lips. Her features blurred before him, her face swimming and settling into her death mask, a horrified grimace the antithesis of a smile. Her new face told the true nature of the boy. His honeyed words had hidden the evil truth from all of them.

When he found the boy, he was going to choke the lying air out of him, settle his hands around his misleading neck and squeeze. Then he would pull out his silver tongue.

The man stretched out his fingers and started at the stained skin of his hands. The boy had to pay. The man was the only one left to call in the debt. The boy had done this, hadn't he?

Glass smashed. The man's head flicked to the right. He had him. He shifted around the building and studied the broken window. He reached a raw hand through the jagged, glass hole and unlatched its frame, creaking it open. A can rolled across the floor in the room inside – the kitchen. The boy must have knocked it over.

The man went in feet-first, ripping the leg of his trousers. Suzie had taken them in for him; he'd been losing so much weight. Had he fed the poison into her mouth? It was a mouth he had kissed a thousand times since they'd found the church, a lingering finger on her bottom lip. They'd had each other. Why had they needed the boy?

The man passed the kitchen table. Mouldy fruit sat in a bowl on its surface assaulting his senses. He hadn't eaten in days, not since he'd woken in the mausoleum and realized what had happened, what the boy had done.

He must be upstairs. The man's narrowed gaze scanned the kitchen counter. A knife gleamed on the sideboard as though it were the only shiny thing left in the world. He grasped it by its wooden handle. A floorboard squeaked above him. He nodded grimly and walked through the doorway to the hallway beyond. He stood at the foot of a carpeted staircase, thick with dust. A cough mumbled in his chest. Did the boy know he was here? Cornered at last.

Forcing one foot before the other, he climbed, flinching each time a creak sounded and stopping, straining to listen. Only silence now. He'd find the boy under a bed or inside a closet, surely. His grip tightened on his instrument of execution. He'd drive it through the boy's ribcage and slice right through his treacherous heart. He would bleed black.

The man shook his head. Where was he? Suddenly, when he looked around, for a flicker of a moment, he saw the home as it must have existed before. The carpet was clean; he could see each and every bluish thread, plush – a pleasing juxtaposition to the polished oak of the banister.

He blinked and the stairs were threadbare once more. The railing was splintered and rotting. The man sighed a relieved breath. He knew where he was. The drug was playing hell with his senses.

The boy. He had to punish the boy. Maybe he could undo what the boy had done to the world. Once the false god was dead, perhaps this reality would fall away as fast as it had come to be.

The man stalked down the corridor. There. Breathing coming from the room at the end. Rapid gasps of ghoulish fright that his mind enhanced into surround sound. It was all he could hear, echoing through the grand and empty chambers of his expanded consciousness. The boy should well be frightened. The man was justice. He was vengeance. For all those people – even children – stacked around each other like bent and broken marionettes, down to the plastic sheen on their skins.

They were supposed to be transformed. That's what the boy had said, what he had promised them. The man had survived in order to call him to account for his betrayal, for the vile visions in his mind of twisted death. Death for no cause at all.

In the doorway the man paused, distracted by the patterns in the peeling paint, mapping out the muffled movements of his prey.

This house seemed familiar. Strange that the boy had holed up here. It was like the house he and Suzie had shared in the compound, twined around each other like vines between services, whispering their secret hopes and prayers for the world to come.

He gripped the handle and opened the door. The boy hadn't even bothered to try and hide. He cowered in the corner of the dark bedchamber, eyes wide, the whites showing all the way around his dilated pupils. His skinny limbs shivered and his mouth formed a panicked O.

"Dad –"

The man stopped a step inside the room and shook his head again.

The boy was the devil. The master of deceit and disguise. Of course he would try and trick him again. Deception was his seventh-circle mission. The one who had sent him had merely hidden his horns from view and named him Hope. The congregation had prostrated themselves before him and offered blind faith in their outstretched hands.

The kitchen knife felt like an extension of his arm. It stretched out before him in a steady, glinting line of retribution. Here was redemption.

The boy held out his quivering hands, bright eyes pleading, framed with tear-spangled lashes, dark like Suzie's.

"Dad... Don't —"

The man took a step forward. "Boy. You lied to us."

The boy scrambled back, as though he could slip straight through the wall if only he tried hard enough to press his frail body back into it.

A muscle jumped in the man's jaw. How many days since the boy's forked tongue had told them to take the powder? How long since he'd put the plague in motion?

He stared at the ceiling above the boy's head. There was a small grate there. Hadn't he fixed that grate into the room when he and Suzie had been planning their nursery? He'd installed an entire air-conditioning system. Outside air, she'd said. There needed to be outside air circulating through the room. Better for the baby. Open a window, he'd joked. The skirting up there, he'd painted it off-white, the colour of enamel eggshells.

He'd forgotten that they'd wanted a family. A family they'd bring up in the church's righteous embrace, learning everything about the eschaton, the final days. And then the boy had arrived, the second coming.

A noise in the corridor behind him. Suzie's voice, calling his name, ringing out in terror, harmonizing with the boy's treble quavering from the corner. The man no longer heard the words. He was immune. That must have been how he'd survived. He was immune to the boy's plague, to the church's angel dust, to the locusts that had devoured the whole world and everyone in it.

If he stared out the window, he could see the skeletons of people's homes poking out of their concrete bodies, ripped open and decaying like carrion. The sky scowled down its blood-orange reproach, casting the carcasses in plum shadow lands.

The boy was sobbing in earnest now. Liar. Deceiver. Suzie's screams reverberated in his skull. Phantom cries, surely. Phantom fingers grasping at his jacket sleeves, pulling at his arms. The boy's supernatural ministrations couldn't stop him. Not now.

The boy had stood at the pulpit. He had anointed them one by one as they had stood before him, only the whites of their eyes showing. The boy had shared out packets of powder, a new sacrament for a new world. Powdered flesh of his flesh – perhaps salty, crystal grains of sacred, white bone.

The man reached the corner and loomed over the cowering figure. He stared down into the small, familiar, tear-stained face. This was right, wasn't it? That's what had happened. He couldn't be wrong?

The boy had smiled from the pulpit and his teeth were needled razors. The powder was talcum death. It had all happened, just as he remembered. Black curtains in his mind drawing back and showing him what had surely come to pass.

The man cast his gaze into the corner shadows and raised the knife.

Luther – Now

Luther had seen suicide cults – there'd been a real nut job two years ago. A travelling preacher, like from the circus tent days of old-time gospel revivals. He was some has-been rock star that claimed to have found God and purged his life of all of his sinful past. He was from one of those hair bands where the guys wore more make-up than an aging hooker and dressed in leather and spandex. After his transformation, he dressed more like a Mennonite, with his hair cropped short and not a trace of leather or makeup. He travelled from town to town, setting up on farms or public parks – wherever he could find the room. When he left town, he'd always gained a few more bodies for his caravan. Women, mostly. Young, beautiful, damaged. Luther had done just as many profiles on victims as he had killers, and had determined that there was definitely a victim type when it came to con men and narcissistic sociopaths. Not everyone could be charmed, but some people seemed to be *looking* to be charmed. Women – or men – who'd already come from abusive homes, or had been brought up by narcissists. People who had spent their lives looking for the acceptance or approval of a parent – these were the same people who worked for Amway, married monsters, joined cults.

Twenty-three women had gone missing from ten different towns, and it had come to the attention of the police because of a missing person report. Some woman's husband insisted that his young bride hadn't gone off with the travelling salvation show of her own volition. He was sure that she'd been taken, and he pointed the police in the direction of the caravan.

The woman in question was indeed found with the others, but she told a different story – she said she'd gone with Father Samuel to seek her own path of enlightenment. She and all the others refused to leave, having nothing but praise for the preacher.

There were drugs – a lot of drugs – on the two busses that carried all the members of the Father Samuel Transcendence Tour, as it became known, but it was later revealed that the good Father's handler – an ex-con by the name of Clint Maxwell with a long history of fraud and extortion – had paid off the local cop to look the other way on that account.

Father Samuel, aka Sam Weiss, had indeed lived a life of sin and excess during his tenure as the drummer for Crystal Serpent, and while he had claimed to have seen the face of God and been healed and changed for the better, his physicians had a differing opinion. Somehow the information leaked to the tabloids, and the news that Sam was HIV positive was plastered all over the less legitimate media. Whether it was true or not, Luther never knew, nor did it really matter. The next time Father Samuel and his followers tried to set up shop, there were protesters lined up to prevent them, and so they fled, eventually settling in a resort town up north.

Luther had no idea what happened, what Sam Weiss told them, or how he convinced more than forty people to kill themselves, but it happened anyway. The bodies were found huddled in a large circle around a fire pit, hypodermic needles in their arms, as if it had been choreographed – Luther could imagine someone leading a countdown, handing out the needles and instructing them all to shoot up simultaneously.

Father Samuel's Transcendents were never violent. They were little more than leftover hippies, really, and it was a tragedy how it ended, but Luther wasn't worried about that kind of suicide cult. He worried about what he'd just read. This Man, if he was to believe the narrative – for that's what it was, no debate – was crazy, and dangerous. If there were only five bodies but six patients, and this was the one that was missing, Luther worried that The Man could prove to be a problem.

He wondered if The Man was capable of the kind of carnage he had been brought in to investigate and had to conclude that he didn't know.

"Fuck!" he swore and threw the file folder across the room. "This tells me nothing!"

The doctors were fucking with him, he decided. Whatever they were doing here, they just wanted to keep him occupied chasing nonsense stories while they cleaned up their mess, erased their tracks. He wasn't going to be anyone's fool.

Michael and Naveena – Three Months Ago

"John," Dr. Chandra spoke calmly, afraid to startle the man. "John, there's someone I'd like you to meet."

Jessica sighed and sat up in bed, continuing to scribble away in her notebook.

"I told you not to call him that," she said. Dr. Chandra ignored her, and kept trying to awaken the man. Dr. Browning stood quietly behind her, accompanied by Harris Parker.

"Is this your boy?" Michael asked in a hushed voice.

"What? No, of course not," Harris replied. "Why would you think...?"

Michael stopped him with a quiet shake of his head.

"John," Dr. Chandra tried again. "Sir, I need you to wake up."

"Oi!" Jessica yelled, and the man's eyes popped wide open. He began to howl and struggle against the restraints.

"Who are you? Why am I tied up?"

Dr. Chandra remained calm.

"Sir, look at me," she began. "Calm down, I'm not going to hurt you. My name is Dr. Chandra, and we are at Sisters of Mercy Hospital. We're going to take good care of you."

"He does this every time he wakes up," Michael told Harris. "Every time, it's like the very first time. He's been here two weeks, and every day it's the same."

"Dear god, what's wrong with the poor man?"

"We're not sure," Michael admitted. "Retrograde amnesia? PTSD? We can't even get a name out of him."

"But he's..."

"Very special, yes," Michael nodded. "Just how is yet to be seen, but we were told where to find him, just as we were told about you."

"Told? By whom?"

Michael shook his head. "Best not to worry about that right now, Professor."

"Why am I tied up?" the man cried.

"I'm very sorry about that," Dr. Chandra said. "When we found you, you kept screaming about being covered in blood, and you said you had killed him. You said you killed the boy over and over again. Do you remember this?"

The man shook his head from side to side, and then slowly stopped, and nodded.

"The boy," he said, and then bared his teeth in rage, spittle gathering at the corners of his mouth like a rabid dog. "The boy!"

He strained against the straps that held him tight. They should have held him, but the man they knew only as John Doe seemed to have impossible strength, and had torn through his restraints on a number of occasions. Mostly, they kept him sedated. In this, he was something of a disappointment to the doctors. In order for their drug enhancements to bear fruit, the patient needed to be lucid, but this one had proven too dangerous. Their only hope was that somehow, something would manifest while he was dreaming. However, Michael thought it likely they would find the manifestations of the man's dreams quite frightening, and wondered if it were not best to let this one go and cut their losses.

"John, please calm down," Dr. Chandra urged, preparing a syringe.

"Why are you calling me that?" he asked, thrashing on the bed.

Dr. Chandra motioned to Dr. Browning to help hold him down while she stuck him with the needle that would sedate him.

"I told you not to call him that," Jessica said as the man's body relaxed, and the fight went out of him. "He is The Man. I didn't give him another name. Do you suppose that makes him less real? You know, like a fledgling effort – a character sketch, if you will?"

"Who is she?" Harris asked, pointing to Jessica. Michael followed the man's trembling finger to Jessica, whose face looked hungry and sadistic. She reminded Michael of an awful childhood memory – the squeal of brakes, the sharp hiss and howl, and the sound of broken bones. The smell of death. She made him feel all cold and sick inside, yet he couldn't take his eyes off of her.

"I told you they'd come," Jessica laughed. "Hello, Harris. How's the kid?"

"How does she…?"

Dr. Chandra glared at Jessica.

"That's enough," she said. "Michael, please, take Professor Parker somewhere quiet, where we can talk."

"Yes," Michael said, staring intently at her. "We need to talk."

Luther – Now

"What the fuck is this?" Luther slammed down the pile of folders on the doctors' shared desk and glared.

"Please keep your voice down," Dr. Chandra asked, standing. "This is still a hospital."

She walked around the desk and closed the door, pointing him to a chair and bidding him sit.

"Where's Dr. Browning?" he asked. "I want him here, too. I have some questions for you both."

"Dr. Browning is in the morgue, helping to reassemble the bodies for identification," she said. "If there are questions I cannot answer, perhaps you can speak with him another time."

"And will he give me the same answers you do? Should I give you a chance to get your story straight?"

Dr. Chandra frowned, and leaned back in her chair, arms crossed. "I'm not giving you access to my private observations on these patients, Detective, if that's what you're looking for. I've given you all that is relevant. I realize it's not much…"

"It's nothing!" he said, slamming a strong hand down on the desk to emphasize his point. "A name, some minor biographical information – nothing that tells me who these people were or where they came from. And then… and then there are these stories – what am I supposed to make of them?"

"We're not sure," Dr. Chandra said.

"What do you mean? Why are they in there? Why does each patient have one? Whose handwriting is it? Who is J?"

"Please, detective, I'm very upset right now," she said.

"Don't," he said. "I know when someone is lying, and neither you nor Dr. Browning have been forthcoming with me at all. You give me these useless files and these stories – I mean, what are they supposed to be? These aren't someone's confession, these are…"

"Fictions," Dr. Chandra finished for him.

"Right," he agreed. "Stories. Fiction. Right."

"Of course they are," she said. "Have you read them all?"

"No, just the first couple," he admitted. "Something about a guy who creates an artificial intelligence out of his dead son's consciousness, and another about a guy who was involved in some sort of suicide cult, trying to track down and kill his own kid."

"Ah, yes," Dr. Chandra nodded. "The Man. Yes, well, we're not sure how to interpret that one."

"What are you talking about?" Luther asked. "Don't try to tell me these are the patients' stories, because that's bullshit."

Dr. Chandra forced a smile. "Of course not. That's ridiculous."

"Who wrote them? J? Did J write them?"

"J is none of your concern," Dr. Chandra said firmly.

"Who is she?"

"She's – she *was* one of our first patients. She's not with us anymore."

"She died?"

"No," she said, shaking her head. "She's just moved on."

"Mm hmm. You know, I had an interesting talk with one of your former staff."

"Really?"

He nodded and broke into a tired smile. "Fellow named Simon. He told me you all were trying to channel spirits, something to do with poltergeists and possession and reincarnation. Ghosts and assorted voodoo."

"Is that so?" Dr. Chandra said, raising an eyebrow and grinning widely, giving her face a somewhat lopsided look.

"I told him to fuck off," Luther said, "but now I wonder if I should have listened to him. After all, what he told me is no less bullshit than what anyone else is feeding me."

"Detective –"

"What were you people doing here?"

"Read the rest of the stories, Detective," she insisted. "Pay no attention to Simon. He is one of my former patients. He suffers from paranoid delusions, but he's otherwise harmless. I helped get him a job here as an orderly, but he started interfering with some of the patients, and I had to have him transferred."

"Interfering how? Sexually?"

"Really, Detective? Simon is no deviant. He has a delusion that he is a doctor here, and he would pretend to treat the patients. He's in hospital scrubs, so the patients had no reason to doubt him when he said he was a doctor. There were complaints, and I had to have him transferred."

"As you've said. But not dismissed. Not fired."

"He did no real harm, detective. I believe in working with people to achieve their full potential, realizing that there will certainly be some setbacks along the way."

Luther reached for a cigarette, and Dr. Chandra shook her head.

"Fucking hospitals," Luther cursed, then locked his fingers and stretched out his arms, cracking his knuckles in the process.

"So," he tried again. "Just what was it you were doing here?"

Dr. Chandra pushed the pile of folders back across her desk to him. "Read the rest of the stories, Detective."

Luther stood and favoured the doctor with a practiced smile of polite impatience, grabbed the stack of folders and left, slamming the door behind him. As he walked away, he heard Dr. Chandra pick up the phone.

"Michael," she snapped. "Find me Simon."

Helena – Six Months Ago

I'm dreaming of sheep, I mused, and wondered if I was grinning while I slept.

The moon is impossibly big, like a drawing out of a children's storybook. The hillside I'm standing on is covered in tall grass, and I swear I can see and count every blade – lush shades of green taking their colours equally from the shadows and the moonlight.

There are no stars in the sky – nothing for me to wish upon.

The sheep crest the hill, running toward me. One by one they leap over a rough-hewn fence, and if I am supposed to be counting them, I've lost track. Is this an anxiety dream? A memory? Something slipped into my subconscious by Hollywood?

Tell me, Clarisse – have the lambs stopped screaming?

Only they aren't sheep. Upon closer examination, they are rabbits, and they *are* screaming. Their white fur is in patches, with mangy, bloody skin showing through, their pink eyes pinned wide and unblinking. Their cries sound like children in pain.

I turn away in fear, unable to continue watching the horrid things, and when I do, I'm in a bright white room, and there are dozens of white rabbits in restrictive cages, pinned down and unable to move. Is this a guilt dream? I've been very careful not to buy anything tested on animals.

The rabbits all have patches of fur shaved away, and some of them have their eyelids cut off. There are electrodes attached to others, and some have been burned with various chemicals.

I walk down an aisle between the tables, and see that at the end of the row is a cage with a stuffed rabbit in it. It looks brand new, and even still has a tag on it: *Merry Christmas Helena! From Santa.*

A high-pitched squeal from behind me makes me turn, and one of the bunnies is gripping the cage with suddenly human hands and squealing in a sort of sick pleasure that is almost sexual.

"Reeeeeal!" the rabbit screams. "Finally reeeeeal!"

The other rabbits begin to get agitated, and they start screaming as well, and I begin to cry.

"Oh my god," I say. "What's happening to you? Are you in pain? Does it hurt?"

"Oh yes," one of the rabbits says, sounding like the star of a bondage porn flick. "It hurts. But I don't mind. It's not love that does it, you see."

"What?" I ask. "I don't understand."

"Reeeeeal!" the rabbit screams in response. "Reaaaaaa—"

I woke up with sweat pooling on my chest, and a splitting headache. Dragging myself out of bed, I fumbled through the drawers of my night table looking for my notebook and a pen. A nightmare like that needed to be written down – there was a story there somewhere between the lines.

Morning light shone through the window, blinding me. Eyes squinted, I made my way downstairs, following the sound of Penny making breakfast, and the smell of coffee. I navigated like a blind woman to the fridge, opened it up and found a carton of grapefruit juice. I poured a glass and downed it all at once, enjoying the bitter, tart, cold juice sliding down my throat and into my belly.

"Headache?"

I nodded.

"Boo," Penny said. "You want me to get you an energy drink?"

I shook my head, trying to remember the story that had been brewing before I woke up.

"Penny, have you seen my Jessica notebook? I've got an idea for a story and I want to write it down."

Jessica – Six Months Ago

"Where is my notebook?" Jessica asked, firmly but politely.

The nurse had come to check Jessica's vitals. All of the staff of Ward C had been carefully selected and made to sign confidentiality agreements above and beyond the standard policies. Ellie wasn't

Jessica's first nurse – in fact, she'd gone through three since she'd arrived at Sisters of Mercy.

"I don't know, dear," she said, not looking at Jessica, instead, just going about her work. Jessica had asked Ellie once why she wasn't afraid of her like the others. She'd shrugged and went on doing her work, but Jessica noted that she never made eye contact. Jessica's first nurse had run out of the hospital screaming when she couldn't find a pulse, not even when she tried listening with a stethoscope. Sometimes Jessica had a heartbeat, and sometimes she didn't. She didn't think too much about what that meant, so long as she could keep writing. It was what she was born to do, and without it, what was her purpose?

But someone had taken her notebook, and sometimes, she forgot things. Sometimes she went *missing*, and she couldn't remember what happened during those times. Her second nurse had come to see her at one of those times, and claimed that she'd seen Jessica fading in and out of focus, growing *thin* like an underdeveloped photograph.

It had taken her weeks to pry out of Ellie that the old nurse had killed herself. Jessica wasn't surprised. The woman had serious emotional issues.

More forcefully this time. "Where is my notebook?"

Ellie went to walk away without answering, and Jessica reached out and grabbed her by the wrist.

"Where's my notebook?"

She squeezed, and Ellie looked up, meeting the gaze she'd managed to avoid for nearly two months.

"Where's my notebook?"

Ellie cried out in pain, and her eyes rolled back in her head. A thin trickle of blood ran out her nose on to her lip, and she began to make a sick, moaning sound.

"Where's my notebook? Where's my notebook? Where's my notebook?"

Two large orderlies, watching on closed circuit TV from outside Ward C, came running to pull Jessica off of the nurse, injecting her with a sedative cocktail of Haloperidol and Promethazine. It had taken quite a bit of trial and error experimentation, but Dr. Chandra had finally found a dosage that worked on Jessica. The dosage would kill anyone else, but for Jessica it merely put her to sleep for a couple of hours.

"Where's my notebook?" she screamed again, and when one of the orderlies pried her fingers from Nurse Ellie's wrist, he had to dig her fingers out of the woman's skin. She had dug in nearly a quarter of an inch in places, and Ellie had to immediately wrap her wrist in bandages to stop the bleeding.

"Where's my…" Jessica tried, but all the fight was fading from her. She was drifting, and she was angry, but she was also afraid – afraid that she would close her eyes and wake up somewhere new, with no knowledge of how she got there. Or worse – that she would not wake up at all.

Jessica slept, and in her dream, she was torturing rabbits.

It was a good dream.

Michael and Naveena – Six Months Ago

Michael was used to unusual results when it came to Jessica. Casual observation would lead anyone to believe that she was just as normal as anyone else. But spend any length of time with her, or try to take a blood or tissue sample, or even a pulse, and the results would vary day to day. She was impossible, and yet there she was.

They'd tried to take a CT scan the first week he'd met her, and that was the first time that Michael had seen what Dr. Chandra called her *manifestations*. She'd screamed and hissed and began speaking in different voices, different languages, some of which no one present could identify. The temperature of the room fluctuated so wildly from hot to cold that a dense fog appeared.

Since then, they only did as Jessica would allow, and she'd been agreeable for the most part. Most recently, she had seemed particularly interested in experimenting with psychedelics, and though she claimed to have no previous experience with them, she had remained remarkably lucid and in control during the strange trips. This had resulted in a unique demonstration that neither Michael nor Dr. Chandra had any experience with or precedent for.

"We are witnessing the true power of the human mind," Michael had declared in awe, watching as Jessica created three-dimensional images of made of light with her hands, spinning them and manipulating them, morphing them and stretching them.

"Is she human?" Dr. Chandra asked. "Or is she what we might become? Something outside of the very definition of humanity?"

"You're being dramatic," Michael said.

"She seems to have control over every aspect of her being, right down to the function of her internal organs. If she can shut off her heartbeat, does she age? Does she die? Look at her, Michael. Look at that small display of power. Where did the energy come from for this light display? From inside her? Or is she manipulating energy outside of herself? If so, what is to say she could not manipulate other people? Could she stop your heart? Turn my lungs off?"

Michael scoffed at the idea. "She has some mild telekinetic abilities, and that in itself is amazing. But what you're talking about is more like god-like powers, Naveena. And I don't believe in god."

"She does," Dr. Chandra said curiously. "But not the gods we are used to hearing about. But she seems to be obsessed with the idea of god."

"I've never heard her speak about anything religious," Michael remarked.

Dr. Chandra shook her head. "You have to read between the lines."

Michael hadn't known what to make of that at the time, but then Jessica's notebook went missing.

Jessica was furious, and since that first harmless manifestation – the pretty light show – she had grown in control over her environment. Things would seem to move of their own accord, or Jessica would suddenly be in possession of something that she'd wanted but had been denied – a glass of wine, a box of chocolate truffles. A vibrator.

Then she'd attacked a nurse, and Michael found out that Naveena had been hiding things from him.

"She's dangerous," he said.

"She's frightened," Chandra insisted. "She builds defense mechanisms, first in her mind, and then, if threatened, in the physical world."

"She's pathological," Michael sighed. "The stories she tells, about being host to some storytelling demon. What did she call herself?"

"She said she was the Words made flesh," Dr. Chandra said. "Which makes me think she may have had some sort of religious upbringing, possibly suffered abuse at the hands of a religious figure."

"I thought you said she wasn't religious."

"I don't think she is," she agreed. "I said I think she has an obsession with god – I daresay she is fixated on the idea."

"And what makes you think that?"

Dr. Chandra opened her bottom desk drawer and pulled out a stack of photocopied sheets full of small but legible handwriting.

"Read these," she said.

"You took her notebook?"

They had both asked several times to read what Jessica was writing, and every time, she had denied them. They had both agreed that until she volunteered it, they wouldn't press the matter. But Naveena had gone behind his back.

Naveena nodded. "She won't talk about herself seriously, you know that. She claims to be the spawn of some demon called Raconteur, she claims to have escaped an experimental military institution, she claims to have been sold into child prostitution, she says she killed a man, and that she spent two years chained in a basement writing stories like something out of the writings of the Marquis de Sade. What are we supposed to make of any of that nonsense? I thought that we might learn something from what she was writing. And I have."

"She's delusional," Michael said. "I think she might possibly be schizophrenic. I hear her talking, whispering and laughing as if she is having a conversation with someone only she can see."

"And I think we should consider that, but these stories are fantastical. If we are to have any insight into her psyche, it's going to be from these stories of hers. Read them, Michael. There are patterns and interconnected themes. Stories of creators and their creations, gods and monsters, psychic connections, ghosts, possession. She's trying to tell us – tell the world – something. I think she knows the power that is inside her. I think she has an inkling of what she might do. You and I spoke about these very things. What if she understands the nature of the hidden world? What if what we call poltergeists, she understands in a totally different way? You've seen her harness energy in ways that seem impossible. What if she is exactly what we hoped for – a human singularity rather than a technological one? What if she has unlocked the power of the mind? Who knows what the world might look like to her? Who knows what she might be capable of?"

"That poor nurse – what's this one's name? She knows what Jessica's capable of."

"Omelettes and eggs," Naveena said with a dismissive wave of her hand. Michael wished he'd never taught her that particular phrase. He thought she was far too cavalier with the safety and well-being of the staff.

"So you've made photocopies," Michael said, flipping through the pages. "You've got what you wanted. Now give her back her notebook before she hurts someone else."

Dr. Chandra's face flushed. "I don't have it."

"What do you mean?"

"I mean it's gone," she said. "Disappeared. Where do the things come from when she wants them? Maybe it's gone there, I don't know."

"Fuck," Michael swore, and buried his face in his hands. "You can't tell her."

"What?"

"Tell her you took it, tell her, I don't know – tell her you thought she was unhealthily attached to her fantasies – that you need her to forget the stories and deal with reality. Buy us some time to find that book, and in the meantime –"

Michael pulled open his top drawer. Ray was overly fond of postcards, and Michael had some on hand for sending notes when the mood took him. He hadn't sent any in a while, and had more than a dozen blank cards.

"Give her these," he said. "Maybe they'll inspire her. Maybe she'll reach out to someone, and we can finally track down someone that knows her and we can get her story straightened out."

Jessica – Six Months Ago

Jessica opened her eyes, and discovered a strange man sitting beside her bed. She took a deep breath, and smelled the same antiseptic odour that had greeted her every day for the past three months. The man, however, was new.

"Who are you?" she mumbled, still groggy from the sedative.

"I'm Simon," he said. "I work here."

"You the new nurse?" she asked. "I could really use some water. And by water, I mean vodka."

"I, uh, don't think…"

"Never mind," she said. "Just bring me water, I'll do the rest."

"I'm not your nurse," he said.

Jessica growled, annoyed. "Are you or are you not qualified to bring me some water?"

"Yes, of course, Miss Bell," he said, and returned a moment later with a glass of water. Something about the way the man was moving bothered Jessica. He seemed like he was sneaking around.

"So, you know me," she said, dipping her finger into the glass of water, which then became vodka, "but who are you, and why are you here? You look like you're worried about getting caught here, am I right?"

"I have… *concerns*, Miss Bell," he began.

"Please, it's Jessica," she said. "And I shall call you Peter."

"It's Simon," he corrected.

"Whatever," Jessica said.

"Like I said, I'm concerned about what they're doing here."

"Oh, and you should be," Jessica said in a confidential hush. "Do you have any idea what kind of torments they're putting me through? All in the name of some paranormal psychobabble crackpot theory about reincarnation and poltergeists?"

Jessica clapped a hand over her mouth and stifled a mischievous grin.

"Oh, I've said too much," she deadpanned. "I'm not supposed to talk about any of the experiments."

Simon's eyes went wide with interest.

"Have they hurt you?" he asked in a whisper.

Jessica bit her lip and moaned, and Simon flushed.

"They made me do things, Simon," she said, reaching under the hospital mattress for the toy they kept trying to take from her, but which always found its way back home. "They hurt me."

"Tell me, Jessica," he prodded. "Tell me what they did, and I swear, I'll get you out of here."

Jessica laughed. "Out of here? Oh no, Peter, no, I want to stay. I don't mind when they hurt me. See, when you're real, you don't mind being hurt."

Jessica pulled out the long, purple sex toy and waved it in Simon's face, then spread her legs and lifted her hospital gown.

"Do you want to hurt me, Peter?"

"Simon!"

Dr. Chandra stormed into the room and pulled the man away from Jessica's bed. Jessica cackled and began rubbing herself with the vibrator. Dr. Chandra pulled the curtain closed and demanded that Jessica stop what she was doing.

"But I'm not finished yet, you dry, old cow," she said. "Let me top myself off first, and then you can fumble with my brain like we're two horny teenagers in the back of Daddy's car."

Dr. Chandra turned her attention to Simon, who was trying to slip away quietly.

"What were you doing talking to her?" she demanded. "You don't have clearance to be here."

"I just... she woke up and..."

"Give me your badge and clear out of here," Dr. Chandra said, fuming. "I'll see that you are transferred to another ward, Simon, but if I see you here again, I'm calling Security and having you fired."

Simon clenched his teeth and left, and Dr. Chandra was left alone with the sound of Jessica masturbating. As she climaxed, she purred like a cat.

"Ah, that's better."

Dr. Chandra tore the curtain open and glared at Jessica.

"What's up, Doc?" Jessica asked. She glared right back at her, daring her to say something, to reprimand her, to voice her disapproval.

Dr. Chandra surprised her by smiling thinly and then getting right to the point.

"I won't allow you to hurt anyone else," she said. "If we have to put you in restraints, it would be unfortunate but not unworkable."

"Where's my notebook?" Jessica replied, ignoring the empty threat. Chandra was afraid of her, and Jessica knew it. Just as she knew that Dr. Browning was not – but he was an unbelieving fool. She'd seen the way that Dr. Chandra looked at her, and knew that if she didn't quite understand the whole truth, she at least suspected some of it, and rightly quivered in awe and terror.

"I took it," she said calmly. "I felt it was a distraction. You were fixating on these dark fantasies of yours instead of focusing on realizing your potential. There's so much we can learn from you, but you keep hiding behind these fictions, and frankly, you're wasting my time."

"Where's my notebook?" she repeated, and Dr. Chandra took a step backward out of Jessica's reach. Nurse Ellie had a broken wrist, and required twenty-some-odd stitches as a result of Jessica's displeasure in the matter of her notebook.

"I told you, I took it away. I'll give it back when I think it's appropriate."

"Where is my notebook?" Jessica demanded. "Bring it back *now*."

"I can't, I…"

"Oh," Jessica said, and laughed a bitter laugh. "Oh, *she* has it. Fuck. Do you realize what you've done? That's my book, not *hers*. I need to write, or else…"

Jessica trailed off, and seemed to stare off into the distance, as if lost in thought.

"I've got to write," she repeated.

"Then write on these," Dr. Chandra said, tossing Jessica a handful of postcards. "Write something constructive. Send one to friends or family."

Jessica laughed. "What makes you think I have friends or family?"

"Fine, then write whatever you like."

"I have to write," Jessica said, "or else I won't be real."

"Jessica," Dr. Chandra said, concerned. "What do you mean by that? You've said this before. You said you were worried you weren't real, that you were just someone else's dream. Do you still believe this?"

Jessica sat up in bed and glared defiantly at the doctor. "I am the Words made flesh!"

"What does that mean to you, Jessica?"

"I can close my eyes and all this will stop," she said. "Someday I will bore of this little experiment and take it all away."

"How, Jessica? How?" Dr. Chandra seemed excited. Jessica enjoyed watching Dr. Chandra try to psychoanalyse her.

"I read a story once about a rabbit that wanted to be real. So he asked a raggedy, old, stuffed horse how you become real."

"This is the story of the Velveteen Rabbit, no? Every child knows this story, Jessica. What does it mean to you?"

"In the story, the old horse tells the rabbit that by the time you become real, you are old and broken – your eyes are falling out, and your skin is peeling off, but you don't mind being ugly and in pain, because you're *real.*"

"It's about love, Jessica," Dr. Chandra said. "Have you never loved something so much that it became precious to you? Real to you?"

"No, you're wrong, doctor," Jessica said, shaking her head. "It's not about love. It's about pain and torment and trauma. These things are more powerful than love. These things can destroy love. I have to destroy in order to create. Trauma – not love – is what makes you real."

Dr. Chandra shivered. "Am I real, Jessica?"

Jessica laughed and closed her eyes. "I don't know, doctor. Perhaps none of this is real. Perhaps we are all just characters in some writer's dream. Or maybe we are butterflies fast asleep, dreaming that we are people."

"Zhuangzi," Dr. Chandra replied. "Am I man dreaming of a butterfly, or a butterfly dreaming I am a man?"

"Butterflies transform themselves," Jessica mused. "From larvae to cocoon to something completely different. I wonder if, while in pupa state, they dream of flight. Perhaps becoming a butterfly is an act of will, borne of dreaming."

"It's a lovely thought."

"It's rubbish," Jessica said. "The delusion of an old Chinese man with way too much time on his hands."

"Are you certain?" Dr. Chandra asked.

Jessica rolled her eyes and left the question unanswered.

"Are you familiar with the philosophical argument of Solipsism, Jessica?"

"I think therefore I am and all that rot?"

"More than that," Dr. Chandra said. "I wonder. Do you dream very much?"

"No more than the next person, I'd imagine," Jessica said.

"And are you yourself in your dreams?"

"Who else would I be?"

"Well, there are some proponents of Solipsism that would argue that the self would cease to exist outside of conscious thought, that you are the only thing that is real, and that we all exist in our own little universes, only able to prove the existence of our rational selves, and nothing else. This kind of thinking has also driven people insane, but that's another matter altogether. So, Jessica – are you real?"

Jessica laughed uneasily. "None of this is real. None of you are real. We are all just dreams."

"So, nothing is real unless we make it so?"

"That's how I understand it," Jessica said.

"And how do you make something real?"

Dr. Chandra knew the answer she was going to get.

"I told you. Pain. Torment. Trauma."

"Or love?" Dr. Chandra suggested, and Jessica shook her head.

"Not in my experience," she said through clenched teeth.

"I ask you again, Jessica. Are *you* real?"

Jessica hesitated.

"I don't know," she said, and there was fear and anger in her eyes. "Yes. No. Maybe. I don't think so – not yet. But I will be."

"How?"

Jessica cocked her head and grinned a terrible smile. "I thought we'd already discussed that."

Private Journal of Dr. Naveena Chandra – Three Months Ago

The first of them have arrived, just as Jessica said they would. One is a frightening man with little memory. He has to be restrained, and displays a disturbing inability to form new memories. He has given us little information about himself, except that he believes himself to be a murderer, and suffers from delusions of being covered in blood. The second is a scientist, so he says, but his understanding of science seems rudimentary at best, and fantastical and unrealistic at worst.

The more I speak with him, the more amazed and frightened I become. Not of him. Of her. I don't know what to make of the similarities… they cannot even be called that. They are the same – the details are the same, and that is, of course, impossible.

Two weeks ago, before the John Doe arrived (or rather, when we were directed to where we might find him – this is another mystery which I cannot explain), Jessica disappeared, and I feared all was lost. We knew she was powerful, and so we had depended on her interest in the study to keep her here, knowing full well that she could leave anytime she wanted. After all, she is not our prisoner. So when she disappeared, that was the end, and what had we learned? Very little, considering she had been in our care for three months.

Then she returned, as if she'd never left. She was just suddenly back in her bed. We checked the video footage of Ward C and found that there was some sort of interference for roughly thirty seconds during the middle of the night. Before the interference, the camera showed an empty bed. After the interference, Jessica was back, and she was writing in her lost notebook. What's more, she looked directly at the camera and winked.

Who is she, and what is the extent of her power? I am convinced more than ever that she is more than human, and that she is but the first of a new breed of post-humans, unfettered by our current mental limitations.

I must confess I envy her. I myself have tried to expand my mind both within the realms of science and spirituality, and I have always come up wanting. Perhaps I am not worthy or capable of studying her. Might my attempts to understand her be not unlike an insect trying to understand a human being?

What drives her?

Michael is skeptical. He thinks she's delusional at best and a con artist and liar at worst. He rationalizes what he cannot understand, at least on the surface. I think he believes, but he doesn't want to admit. I say that she is obsessed with the concept of god and creation, but he sees her talk of reality and becoming real as part of her god complex delusion.

I asked her myself about creation, and even about procreation.

She laughed at the idea of having children of her own, and then said, "I do create. You've seen my notebook."

And then I told her I meant creating something *real*. She seems obsessed with the very concept. Her answer left me wondering, but that doesn't surprise me. She often talks in cryptic riddles and half-answers.

She said, "What do you think I'm doing?"

VICTOR & MARY

Luther – Now

L uther sat in his car and considered what to do next. He wanted to go home. It wasn't much, but he did his best thinking there. Hopped up on too much caffeine and a steady stream of cloves cigarettes, which were dangerously high in nicotine content, he could nonetheless focus better than he could in the field. Maybe it had something to do with removing distractions. Some people listened to music while they worked to shut out the noise, but Luther couldn't stand it. Oh, he liked music just fine, just not while he was thinking. Back when he was in school, he'd had a rough go – some of his teachers thought he was stupid when, really, he just had a different way of learning things. These days, when every other kid was diagnosed with some sort of learning disability or condition, he supposed he would have been given a prescription for Ritalin, or put in a special class, but as it was, he just had to figure things out on his own. When the other kids went out for recess or lunch hour, he'd find himself in peaceful quiet, consuming books like candy.

He was never much for fiction, though. Never saw the point. Stories were too tidy, writers either too clever or too lazy, and every time he encountered a convenient coincidence or an implausible plot point, he found himself annoyed. The worst was the device that the Greeks called the *Deus ex Machina*. In Luther's experience, no god – from a machine or otherwise – had ever intervened in his life, nor did he expect it likely to ever happen. He was his own man, he made his own fate, and he despised the idea of being some god's chess piece.

He felt a headache coming on. He reached in his glove box and pulled out a bottle of Aspirin. He didn't have anything to wash them down with, so he chewed two of them and endured the horrid bitterness. On the passenger seat, the remaining folders sat like unwanted stowaways. Dr. Chandra seemed to think they were important, but he wasn't sure why. What did the stories have to do with the dead? He didn't know what he was supposed to learn by reading a bunch of fiction. He'd indulge her, for now. He'd read the damn stories. But when he was done, he wanted some answers. Who wrote the stories, for one? If it was this J from the file notes, he'd want to speak to her. Whoever it was was clearly central to whatever it was they were doing in Ward C. If anyone had answers, it would be the writer of those stories. Luther was convinced of it.

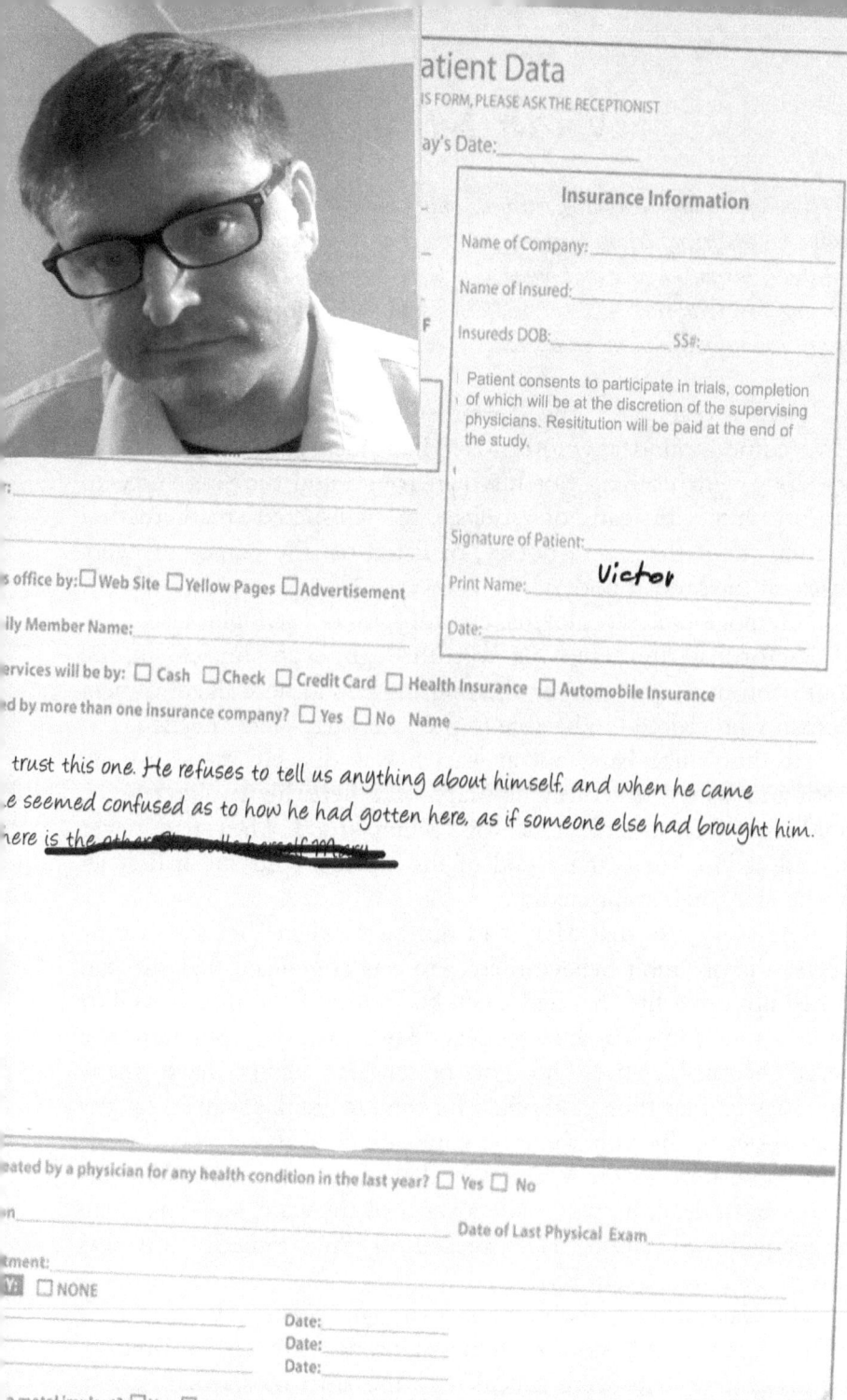

atient Data

IS FORM, PLEASE ASK THE RECEPTIONIST

ay's Date:_____

Insurance Information

Name of Company:_____

Name of Insured:_____

Insureds DOB:_____ SS#:_____

Patient consents to participate in trials, completion of which will be at the discretion of the supervising physicians. Resititution will be paid at the end of the study.

Signature of Patient:_____

Print Name:_____ *Victor*

Date:_____

r:_____

s office by: ☐ Web Site ☐ Yellow Pages ☐ Advertisement

ily Member Name:_____

ervices will be by: ☐ Cash ☐ Check ☐ Credit Card ☐ Health Insurance ☐ Automobile Insurance

ed by more than one insurance company? ☐ Yes ☐ No Name_____

trust this one. He refuses to tell us anything about himself, and when he came e seemed confused as to how he had gotten here, as if someone else had brought him. here is the ~~other~~

eated by a physician for any health condition in the last year? ☐ Yes ☐ No

en_____ Date of Last Physical Exam_____

tment:

☐ NONE

_____ Date:_____
_____ Date:_____
_____ Date:_____

a metal implant? ☐ Yes ☐ No   Ever been gunshot? ☐ Yes ☐ No
☐ Job ☐ Auto ☐ Other 1._____ Date:_____
☐ Job ☐ Auto ☐ Other 2._____ Date:_____
☐ Job ☐ Auto ☐ Other 3._____ Date:_____

VICTOR

Victor & Mary

Thunder rolled, lightning crashed, and young Victor hid under his bed, waiting for his friend Mary to come and sing him to sleep. In the cold tenement apartment, his father gone and his mother perpetually absent, Mary would come and sing his favourites – The Beatles, mostly. Victor often woke with the refrain of Golden Slumbers on his lips.

Twenty years later, the storms still frightened him, but Mary didn't come around anymore. Mary had been gone for years. He was alone with nothing but his own rough and tuneless voice to comfort him. Instead of songs, he whispered mathematical equations as if they were poetry, or listed off the names of every muscle in the human body.

"Genioglossus, hyoglossus, chondroglossus, styloglossus…"

Victor had muttered his way through every muscle in the mouth and neck, shivering in the pouring rain as he walked to meet the man who claimed to be able to procure what Victor needed.

He didn't like bars, but at least it was dry. He sat at a quiet booth and waited nervously. If Mary were here, he wouldn't be so afraid, nor feel so ridiculous for feeling afraid. Mary had never laughed at him for being afraid of the storms. And she hadn't let anyone else laugh at him either.

The story was that Mary had run away when Victor was only twelve. Victor didn't believe them. He was convinced that she had burned up in the fire that had taken his mother from him as well. It was too much loss for him to bear. After that, they put him in a special hospital, where he got better. He didn't have many memories of that time, and when he tried to think about it, or was asked about it, the only thing he could think of to say was that he spent some time in the hospital, and that he got better. With his parents both dead, he was made a ward of the state, and was given an adequate education. He excelled in the sciences, and was particularly interested in Biology.

His classmates at the university thought perhaps he was a bit *too* interested in the more extreme theoretical aspects of Biology, and his experiments were ridiculed as the stuff of science fiction. He couldn't believe their skepticism, in light of all the scientific advances of the 21st century. Stem cells, cloning, and genetic manipulation – the world was changing, and what Victor was trying to achieve was, in his estimation, not out of the realm of possibility. He explored the science of death to understand what lay between life and death. But to study such things, he had to bear witness to death, to rescue a living creature from the very brink of death and then examine how the experience affected them. Ideally, his subjects would be human, and therefore able to testify intelligently about what may or may not lie between the vitality of life and the stillness of death. He had volunteers – a couple of space cadets that he'd convinced to take part in what he'd promised would be a mind-expanding experience, suggesting that he was doing research with hallucinogens. Instead, he'd slowed each of their heartbeats down until they flat-lined, and then jump-started them with adrenaline. One of his volunteers nearly died. He'd paid them off with drugs, but rumours of the experiment got around. He was threatened with expulsion – probably would have been expelled if they'd been able to produce any evidence of his experiments, but all that remained was rumour and conjecture. His junkie subjects hardly made the most reliable witnesses.

The stories he heard about himself were even more bizarre than the actual truth. It didn't help that his name was already Victor – they'd begun calling him Frankenstein behind his back, as if he didn't know. They laughed at his ideas, told him he should get a castle and a hunchback and complete the whole Gothic fantasy. They were pampered rich men's sons whose goals were solely monetary. They had no vision, no desire to make their mark on this world. Not like him. But he knew that if he drew the wrong type of attention, he would never be able to continue, and so he had stopped – at least publicly. Privately, he continued his research, using whatever material he could get his hands on. If he couldn't find stray cats, people were always giving them away on the swap and trade sites on the Internet.

Of course, it was one thing to reanimate tissue – he wasn't the first to conceive of bringing back the dead – but he had yet to discover the spark, the *pneuma* that gave actual life, and not just the semblance of life. Throughout history, philosophers, poets, and religious figures debated the concept of the soul. Some thought it resided in the heart, while others said it lived in the mind. Some denied its existence altogether, insisting that life was merely a complicated series of electrical impulses and firing synapses.

Victor believed in the soul – and sometimes even the possibility that a person could be possessed of more than one soul. How else did one explain reincarnation, or the controversial concept of multiple personality disorder or dissociative disorder? Could the brain, forced to contain more than one soul, react with confusion and madness?

The question that Victor couldn't answer was whether animals – such as the cats and dogs he used in his experiments – were imbued with souls. Furthermore, he didn't know whether the question was a religious or a scientific one. He'd managed to reanimate a cat, at least to the point that it was breathing and displayed minor motor skills, but was it the same cat he brought back? He couldn't say. Only through experimentation with human subjects would he find the answer to the mysteries of life and death. And that meant that he needed to acquire bodies. Live would be best, but dead – freshly dead – would be a good start.

It took him a few weeks of searching, visiting funeral homes and trolling dangerous chat rooms – always on anonymous computers and behind proxy servers – until he met the man who agreed to meet him. Why it had to be that night of all nights, with the sky ripping itself open and the rain bleeding out, roaring in thunderous pain, Victor didn't know. He supposed it was fitting that men should do dark business on a dark and stormy night. Victor picked the bar – a dive far enough from his squalid apartment that he wouldn't be followed – and, despite his fear and loathing of thunderstorms, ventured out in it.

He was beginning to wonder if he was being stood up when the door opened and a man came in from the rain, soaking wet and wheezing, a filthy baseball cap pulled down over his forehead. He smelled of scotch mints and formaldehyde, and Victor found him immediately distasteful.

In the early nineteenth century, before it was common practice for people to donate their bodies to science, medical students often employed body snatchers – or resurrection men as they were sometimes called – to acquire fresh corpses for dissection and study. Now that society had become more civilized, it was more difficult gain access to bodies if you weren't an official from a medical institution. But there was still a market for it, and men like Mr. Smith – a mortician by trade, with daily access to the dead – weren't above filling the demand.

"Are you wearing a wire?" the man asked him from across the table at the London Arms, where they whispered to each other through pints of bitter ale. The dark, amber drink cast each man in a strange light.

Victor shook his head.

"Fifteen hundred," Mr. Smith said without pause. "Non-negotiable."

Victor took a deep breath. It was more than he'd expected.

"I could turn you in," Victor said. "You'd go to jail for the rest of your life."

The man laughed and raised his glass.

"We could be cell mates," he said. "I call top bunk."

Victor stared across the table, anger rising in his chest. He forced himself to push past the fear and disgust.

"Are they fresh? They're worth nothing to me if they're not fresh."

"They're not eggs, man," Mr. Smith said. "They don't expire – pardon the pun – they're fresh enough for you. What are you, a doctor?"

"Not yet. I'm a student."

Mr. Smith leaned in. "Then you should have plenty of bodies, no?"

Victor grimaced. "My interests are... *extracurricular.* Is that going to be a problem?"

"I don't care what you do with them," he said. "But my services – and my silence – don't come cheap."

Victor clenched his jaw. *Fifteen hundred dollars!*

"Look, you came to me asking for a corpse and you aren't exactly a doctor, so I have to assume that whatever you got planned is some pretty sick shit. I'm not judging, I'm just saying – in the long run, I think fifteen hundred is a lot cheaper than what it'd cost you to get your rocks off with hookers. Plus, you can do whatever you like, as much as you like."

"It's not like that at all," Victor said, trying to keep his cool. The man disgusted him.

Mr. Smith shrugged. "None of my business. What's it going to be?"

"Half now," Victor said reluctantly, "and half on delivery."

The man held out a clammy hand to seal the deal.

"And it needs to be *fresh,*" Victor insisted.

"Of course it'll be fresh," the man said.

"Fresh, or I'm not paying you the rest."

"Don't worry, it'll be fresh."

Victor arranged to have the body delivered the following night.

It was fresh.

Just not fresh enough.

Mary had been following Victor for weeks, keeping an eye on him as she always had. She hated not being able to talk to him anymore, but after she'd lit the fire that killed Victor's mother, she'd had to go away for a while, at least until Victor needed her again. She never went too far, but she never came too close, either. Victor had worked so hard to get over his terrible childhood, and Mary didn't want to do anything to hurt him. She knew they could never be together, but she loved him – more than a sister, more deeply than a lover.

She didn't trust this Mr. Smith – a funeral director who cheated his clients by selling them fancy services and plots only to cremate their loved ones and pocket their money. She could spot a con artist right away. Victor's mother had always seemed to find her way into the arms of one parasite or another, and Mary had watched and learned their ways.

She knew what Victor was up to – the same thing he'd always been up to, ever since they were children, and that stupid kitten got run over. Victor picked the damned thing up and kept it in a box in his room, convinced that he could bring it back. He tried everything. He put ointment on its wounds, he bandaged it up, he tried giving it some of his mother's pills, but he just wouldn't accept that it was dead.

His mom beat him black and blue when she found it – told him he was crazy, threatened to take him to the head doctor, get him lobotomized. Victor's mother wasn't very bright. Even at ten, Mary knew they didn't lobotomize people for keeping a dead cat in a box. That night she told Victor that he didn't need to worry about going to the head doctor. She said he just needed to keep his secrets better, and to keep his most dangerous secrets somewhere as far away from himself as he could, so they couldn't be traced back to him. Mary knew all about Victor's secrets – after all, she was one of them. Victor's mother never knew about her, never knew what the two of them got up to after she'd nodded off. It wasn't good for Victor to be alone, and so, it seemed, the universe had given him a helpmate in Mary. And she'd helped him whenever she could, though for all that time he was in the hospital, there was nothing that she could do for him. And when he came out, he'd *changed*. They'd messed with his head, told him lies about her, and convinced him she was a bad influence on him. She'd tried to reach out to him, but it was like she didn't even know him anymore.

But lately, the old Victor seemed to be creeping out to play. He'd found his drive again, his purpose. If only he could make it work. She felt bad for him – he had worked so hard to find a body, but it was useless, just like that dead kitten. The trick had to be fresh parts – parts so fresh that they were nearly living. If she could get him some fresh organs, maybe he could transplant them into that old body, and get it working again – like putting a new engine into an old car. And maybe, if she did this thing for him, he would welcome her back, and it could be like it was before.

Mr. Smith seemed like a good place to start.

Victor didn't have much in the way of money, and the $1500 had set him back, but he'd found that sometimes secrets were more valuable than money.

The proprietor of the self-storage garage where he did his work, for example, kept a collection of not-strictly-legal pornography in one of his units. Merv was the cousin of Victor's roommate his first year of university, and one drunken night, he'd bragged about his stash, thinking that he was safe among men, and that they were all possessed with appetites as perverse as his own.

When Victor needed somewhere private, he approached Merv skilfully, manipulating him by first appealing to his indignation that he should have to keep his predilections a secret. Victor suggested that he had a kinship with him – that he, too, had vices that he needed kept secret. He needed privacy, he insisted, and didn't want to answer any questions.

He had offered to rent Victor a unit, and he'd had to change tactics, drop subtle insinuations and veiled threats. Victor said that he didn't want his name on any paperwork, and suggested that if there was no paperwork, and if for some reason the police were to search the unit, why, they both had deniability.

"You don't want to be held responsible for what I'm doing any more than I want to be charged for your crimes," Victor said, and he must have been convincing, because he now had a storage unit that he could use freely, coming and going as he pleased.

When Victor opened the door to his unit, he felt a chill run up his spine. Something was moving inside the room. It was pitch black, and he couldn't see two feet in front of him. He'd have to step into the unit to turn on the lights, and for all he knew, there was someone in there waiting to grab him.

"Hello?" he called cautiously, his mouth pasty with sudden fear.

He reached in and turned on the overhead lights, and caught a glimpse of someone curled up naked in the corner of the room, trembling.

In the centre of the room was an operating table on wheels, where the previous night he had wept at his failure to even get any response from any of the cadaver's major organs. He'd gotten dead muscles to hold an electric charge and twitch for a few seconds until they burned out and the tissue was damaged beyond repair. Frustrated beyond measure, he kept shocking the dead man's arm out of anger, but only resulted in cooking the flesh, resulting in a grotesque barbecue smell. For all his effort, he may as well have been trying to make a steak get up and moo.

The body was stored in a chest freezer – he wished for a proper morgue cooler, but that was asking a bit much. Might as well wish for the moon. He had blackmailed and called in all the favours he could just to get some of the other medical equipment he had.

"What are you doing here?" he asked. He still hadn't seen the man's face.

"Help me," the man moaned. "Bleeding. So cold."

It was true. Victor could see a pool of blood on the floor. With that much blood loss, the man was surely in shock.

He pulled the door down behind him and took a step forward, and that's when he saw it. There was a note on the silver operating table, finger-painted in what was surely the man's blood.

Fresh enough for you sweet boy?
Mary

Victor froze. Mary was dead. This was a sick joke.

When I find myself in times of trouble...

Mary sang to Victor not just words of wisdom but comfort. Momma kept saying she was going to get clean, but then some new guy would come into her life and promise to take care of her. Victor had to stay quiet when Momma's men were around – they didn't like to see little boys hanging about when they were doing their business with Momma – and so Victor would go and play with Mary. But then, one night, some of Momma's men got bored with her, and came looking for Victor. Victor was terrified, and when Mary heard them coming down the hall, she told Victor to hide under the bed, and to close his eyes no matter what happened.

When it came to Mary, Victor didn't trust his own memories. When he was young, she was his secret friend. She would come to him when he was sad or scared. When he was twelve years old, he set fire to his mother's bed while she was passed out drunk, and when the police came and asked him, he told them that Mary had done it and then ran away. He tortured himself for years, thinking that his lie had driven Mary away. He was sure that she was dead.

He spent years in the hospital being treated. The doctors tried to convince him that there never was a girl, and that Mary was just a projection of a frightened and lonely little boy. After a while, he learned to tell them what they wanted to hear – that sometimes he missed Mary – missed the comfort and stability she represented – but he knew that she wasn't real.

Sweet boy.

Only Mary ever called him that. Or she did, before she abandoned him. All those years in the hospital, Mary was silent. That's how he knew she was dead – or else not real, like the doctors would have him believe. If Mary could have, she would have been there for him in the hospital, when he needed her most.

"Please," the man whispered. "Are you a doctor?"

Suddenly, Victor knew who it was.

He knew what the note meant. He wasn't quite ready to believe that it was Mary, but he would deal with that later.

"Come along, Mr. Smith," he said cheerfully. "We can't let you expire. Pardon the pun."

Mr. Smith was dead. Technically. Victor had stopped the bleeding – a ragged gash across the man's midsection was the fatal wound – but there was too much blood loss to save him. Victor had, however, managed to keep the man in a sort of stasis. His heart had given out, and would never pump again. But there was a lot of good, fresh, raw material to work with. Victor went straight to work with the bone saw, opening up Mr. Smith's skull and exposing his brain, which he then injected with a combination of stimulants and preservatives, and then he applied electrodes and set them to cycling, in an effort to keep the brain active.

"The bodies must be fresh," he said under his breath, and celebrated his minor triumph with a smile. The brain was responding. He believed that he could keep it alive – he had built a pump that would serve as both heart and lungs by proxy, circulating oxygenated blood through the brain until he had the real things.

He had his brain.

Mary had given him just what he needed.

Just like she always had.

Mary knew Victor wouldn't approve of her choices, but he needed her to do what he couldn't. She'd always been braver, more aggressive, willing to take chances without fear of reprisal. Victor was ambitious but had always been a worrier. Worried he'd fall out the window of the tenement buildings; worried he'd get caught talking to her; worried he'd get caught nicking cigarettes from his mother's purse. The cigarettes weren't even for him – Victor worried about his health. They were for Mary, whose appetites had always been wild and dangerous and unhealthy. As a child, she'd eat jellybeans by the handful, and had discovered smoking at ten. At twelve, she'd taken an interest in boys, and one day after school, she offered to blow Jamie Dermott. He didn't seem to know what she meant, but once she got him in her mouth he got the idea.

Of course, when she told his friends about it, Jamie called her all sorts of nasty names and punched her in the stomach for her troubles. It wasn't the last time a man would hit her after sex. She'd gotten used to it. She only hoped that Victor wouldn't judge her too harshly, otherwise he might not want her around.

She knew that he would need more fresh bodies, and that he certainly wasn't going to do what needed to be done. As usual, it would be up to her. Mary was up to the task – she was a predator.

She put on her best *fuck me* dress, unspeakably high heels, and a bustier that kept everything in place. Appraising herself in the mirror, she applied a generous amount of flavoured lip-gloss – hot cherry – and headed into the night to find a warm body.

Victor didn't know what to make of his benefactor. If it was indeed Mary, she'd picked a strange time to resurface. He hadn't seen her since before he'd been sent away to the hospital, and that was nearly ten years ago. He thought he'd seen her once or twice since then, on a subway, or across a crowded room, but it was only ever in passing. If she'd wanted to reach out to him, she could have done it at any time.

He entertained the idea that it could be someone pretending to be Mary, someone from his past that knew about his childhood friend. He couldn't think of anyone that knew about her, though. He never spoke about Mary with his classmates. He didn't have any friends close enough to warrant that kind of trust. Whoever it was knew him intimately – right down to his most protected secrets. If this person meant to hurt him, he didn't stand a chance.

After the elation had died down, Victor had burned Mr. Smith's clothes and wallet. The I.D. said that his real name was Steve Chardonne, and Victor hoped that the absence of either a wedding ring or any pictures of smiling Steve Juniors meant that the man didn't have a family.

Everyone has a family, Victor, an old, familiar voice chided him.

"Not me," he answered aloud.

"Not me what?" a large tattooed man asked, pulling a pint of Smithwicks for another customer.

Victor had gone to a bar where nobody knew his name, and drowned his anxiety in five-dollar pints of some domestic swill. It was all he could afford, as he'd just wasted $1500 on a useless corpse that was currently getting freezer burn at his storage unit.

"No more for me, thanks," he said, recovering. "I've had enough, I think."

When Victor got home, the lights in his apartment were on, which was unlike him. It was also unlike him to leave the door unlocked, but it was. The tiny hairs on the back of his neck stood at attention, and he carefully stepped into his apartment, ready for something or someone to jump out at him.

"Hello?" he called. "I warn you, I'm armed."

Liar. That same unwelcome voice laughed at him in his mind.

"Hello?" he called again, and when no one answered and nothing moved, he felt himself relax. He'd been working around the clock, between his studies – which no longer held much interest for him – and his *real* work, which had become everything to him. It wasn't inconceivable to think that he'd been rushed, and forgotten to turn off the lights and lock the door.

Still, there was something off. There was a faint smell in the room that didn't belong, like vanilla and brown sugar.

"Perfume," Victor said. "It smells like perfume."

He began to wonder again if there wasn't someone there – that perhaps they were hiding, waiting for him to find them and surprise him. His apartment wasn't that big, but if someone wanted to hide, they could do so in the bathroom, and more likely, his bedroom. He tiptoed to the kitchen and grabbed a knife, and then made his way to his bedroom, holding the weapon in front of him.

"Hello?" he called again, and pushed open his bedroom door, expecting to see someone

(a dead body, maybe it's a dead body)

lying on the bed.

Instead there was an open suitcase full of women's clothing.

Victor's heart began to race, and he couldn't catch his breath. He had anxiety issues that he usually managed with meditation and breathing exercises. But on top of that, he was a firm believer in pharmacology. Sometimes yoga wasn't enough.

He spun out of his room toward the bathroom to find his pills. He needed at least three of them, he figured. The medicine cabinet was already open, so he grabbed his prescription bottle and fumbled with the cap, spilling a handful of pills into his open palm.

Not too many, sweet boy, you don't want to kill yourself.

He popped three pills under his tongue and felt them melt as he tried to calm himself down. He needed to focus on something in order to control his breathing. He started by reciting the bones in his head.

"Occipital, parietal, frontal, temporal, sphenoid..."

Taking control of himself, Victor put the lid back on the pill bottle with trembling hands, and put it back into the cabinet where it belonged.

"Maxillae, lacrimal, zygomatic, palantine..."

Closing the mirrored door, he was greeted with another shock. Written in red lipstick was another message.

Victor

Sorry to drop in on you like this, sweet boy, but it seemed like you needed my help. I'm working on getting you more bits & pieces.

See you soon,

Mary

P.S. Don't wait up

The phone had been ringing all morning, so Victor picked it up, if only to make it stop. He looked at the clock, and the light shining through his window confirmed that it was already mid-morning. He'd slept for hours but still didn't feel rested.

"Hello?" he mumbled into the phone.

"Victor, man, where you been? I been tryin' to get in touch with you since last night."

"Who is this?"

"Jesus, Victor!"

"Jesus Murphy, or the other one?" Victor asked dryly. He didn't have much of a sense of humour, but every once in a while.

"It's Merv, Vic," the voice on the other end of the line said. "Where were you last night?"

"Right here. Sleeping. Why, Merv, what's up?"

"Look, I know I said I don't care about what you're doing in your storage unit, but I can't have you running hookers out of there."

"What?" Victor asked, fumbling in his bedsheets. There was that same faint smell of perfume, and there was makeup smeared on the pillowcase. Mary must have come and gone in the night. He'd been so far gone he hadn't even heard her.

"It'll be too much traffic, Vic," Merv continued. "Sooner or later it's gonna draw the cops, and I can't have them poking around here. You and I ain't the only ones with secrets, you know."

"I'm not running hookers, Merv," Victor said. "What makes you think I'd be doing that?"

"Look, I know what I saw, Vic. I saw some tarted-up bitch sucking off some dude, and then they went into your storage unit together. She had *keys*, m'man. And she was driving your car. What, you got some kind of love shack set up in there?"

"It's not what you think," Victor said. "And you'd do well to keep out of my private affairs, Merv. I'm working on something very important, and I've got an assistant now. But she's not supposed to be bringing anyone there. I'll have a word with her."

"Well, okay then," Merv said, clearly not convinced. "But if I catch her bringing her Johns around here again, I won't be calling the cops, if you get what I'm saying. You pass that on, too."

Merv hung up, and Victor was left listening to the dial tone as he tried to process the conversation.

"How could she be so reckless?" he asked the empty room, which had no answer for him.

Tumbling out of bed, Victor threw on the first thing he found and looked for his car keys, hoping Mary had left them for him. He had to get to his storage unit – he had to make sure his lab was safe.

Mary swore in disappointment as she stripped the man's shirt off and saw a trail of red, puckered marks like bug bites all up the inside of his arm.

"Fucking junkie!" she spat in disgust. "My sweet boy is not going to be happy with you, my friend."

He'd been drunk enough to stick his tongue down her throat on the dance floor, and bold enough to grab her ass, and she'd been willing enough to let him, but she'd drawn the line when he tried to move his hand around between her legs.

Not here, she'd told him with a coy giggle that had worked so many times before. *I have somewhere we can go that's more private.*

She'd driven him to Victor's garage, him nodding in and out all the way there – she'd slipped him a little something to take the edge off and make him more easy to control. She'd intended to just take him right into the unit and strap him up, but when she spotted the foul, greasy owner of the place watching her, she decided to put on a show first, getting down on her knees and giving the guy one last thrill as she let him fuck her in the mouth.

Now that he'd passed out, she prepared him for Victor, binding him to the operating table and starting an IV drip with electrolytes and enough sedative to keep him under but not kill him. She'd seen Victor do the simple procedure a hundred times, and could manage to get it flowing without much trouble. What she hadn't counted on was the man being an addict. She had no idea what his tolerance was. She measured out what she figured was a safe amount of morphine and hoped for the best.

She strapped him in tightly and closed the door behind him. In the morning, Victor would find his present, nice and fresh. She was pleased with herself, but quite exhausted. It would be nice to crawl into bed, breathing in Victor's familiar smell.

Mary let herself into Victor's apartment – she may not have a key, but she had already begun to think of it as home – and dropped some loose change in a ceramic dish shaped like a turtle that sat on a small table in the hallway. She touched its glazed green and brown surface, and thought it looked familiar. She couldn't quite place the memory, though. Had it been something Victor had as a child?

In the bathroom, she brushed her teeth vigorously, washing the taste of the stranger out of her mouth, and then washed her face with Noxzema to clear off all the makeup. The night was hot, and her face was a mess.

Crawling into bed, she felt right for the first time in a long time. She buried her face in the pillow and breathed in the musky scent of Victor's body. She smiled and sighed as she closed her eyes and drifted off to sleep.

She felt like Judy Garland in *The Wizard of Oz*.
There's no place like home.

Victor could hear the screaming as he approached the door to his storage unit. It was just a concrete garage, and by no means soundproof.

He parked his car with the passenger side as close as possible to the storage unit, and turned his radio up, hoping to drown out the noise. He had no idea how long the screaming had been going on, but if no one had come by yet – and it was nearly noon – then chances were nobody had been close enough to hear it. The units were in an industrial park, and didn't get a lot of pedestrian traffic.

Seagulls cried overhead, the radio blared Classic Rock, and an eighteen-wheeler roared by on the adjacent highway. Victor could still hear the screaming coming from his unit.

Whoever it was would need to be subdued. He didn't like violence, but Mary hadn't given him much choice. He opened his trunk to see if there was anything he could use, and was surprised to find a variety of items that he was certain he hadn't put there. And, of course, a note.

V
You may need these
M

There were bungee cords and rope, duct tape and a length of razor wire. He wasn't sure what he'd use that for, but the knife – the knife would come in handy. He was glad it was a knife, and not a gun – he didn't think he'd be able to fire a gun. They were too noisy and crude. If he were to end someone's life for the sake of science, he'd rather do it by his own hand, up close and personal. The intimacy of the act would make the death cleaner, honour the victim's sacrifice.

Victor's fingers fumbled with the keys to the padlock and managed to get it to open on the third try. The door lifted easily, folding up and overhead like a curtain being drawn for the theatre. Instead of a stage, it opened on Victor's makeshift surgical theatre, where a man Victor didn't recognize was putting on the performance of his life, straining against straps so hard that he had rubbed his chest and shoulders bloody.

Victor dropped the bag of tools he'd removed from the trunk and pulled the door down, taking one last peek to make sure he was unobserved.

He thought about asking the man his name, but decided he didn't want to know. Instead he took out the duct tape and began taping his mouth shut. The man's eyes bugged out of his head, but Victor remained calm. Now that the man wasn't making so much noise, it wouldn't do to have his car stereo give him away.

"I'll be right back," Victor said, and then, as an afterthought, "Don't go anywhere."

He knew he should be conflicted about this, but ever since he'd had success with Mr. Smith, his conscience hadn't pricked him any longer. He knew he was close, that the ends justified the means.

He returned to find his patient turning blue, and carefully made a small incision in the tape covering his mouth.

"I need to ask you some questions," Victor said as calmly as he could manage. He would be able to relax better once the man was dead. He was never very good with the living.

The man shook his head from side to side, and Victor sighed. He ran his fingers along the inside of the man's arm to where the needle marks were.

"This is a terrible habit, you know," he said, and the man flinched at the touch of Victor's fingers. "Destroys the brain, and the kidneys, too. What other bad habits do you have? Do you smoke? I hope not. I was so hoping to take your lungs."

The man strained vainly against his bindings. He had been secured tightly. His IV was still in, but he was bleeding back. Apparently when Mary put it in she hadn't considered that the drip would run out. Victor put another bag of fluids on the pole and hooked it up, and added a syringe full of morphine.

"There. Better, yes?" Victor wiped the man's sweaty brow.

He nodded slowly.

"Now, do you know who I am?"

A slow shake of the head. *No.*

"Did you recognize the woman who brought you here?"

At this, the man stared at him, confused. Victor wondered if maybe he'd given him too much morphine too soon. He knew Mary wouldn't worry about who she took, so he had to. If this man had some sort of connection to Mary, and his disappearance led the police back to her, then it would lead them back to him, and that wouldn't do. If he had to, he would shoot him up and leave him in some seedy hotel room, make it look like an overdose.

"The woman. Did you know her?"

A pause, and then another slow shake of his head.

"Right then," Victor said cheerfully, and made a quick incision across the man's trachea with one hand, and ripped the duct tape from his mouth with the other.

The bubbling, wheezing last gasps of the man's dying breaths sounded to Victor like wind blowing through the trees.

Mary knew better than to bother Victor while he was working. Instead, she kept watch, napping on occasion when she was sure it was safe. He got the lungs he needed, but the man's heart had some sort of defect. It took him the better part of the afternoon to get things stabilized, and by the time he was done, his lab looked like a war zone. The body had changed drastically, mixing parts of the two, as well as a perfectly salvageable head from the corpse he had originally acquired. It was much more attractive than either of the two that Mary had brought him, and once the brain was inserted, Victor believed he could make the two compatible.

The science was beyond Mary – she had never had any patience for that kind of thing. But she believed in Victor, even if she didn't understand most of what he was talking about. She'd once heard him talking about peptide bonds and thought that he had an upset stomach and asked him if he wanted some Pepto Bismol.

When Victor emerged, exhausted, from his hidden lab, there was still so much work to be done. There were spare parts lying in a pile on the floor. They couldn't stay there.

Victor went to turn back and continue working but something stopped him in his tracks. He swatted at something around his head like he was trying to catch a fly, and it made Mary laugh.

"Mary?" he asked, turning to look at his old friend sitting in the passenger seat of his car. "How did you – how long have you been following me?"

"Just forever, sweet boy," she said. "Haven't you missed me?"

Victor nodded blankly.

"I have more work to do," he said, and suddenly Mary was a child again, and Victor was hiding from his mother, turning to Mary for comfort.

"Shh," she said. "Let's go home. Go to bed, like old times. Mary will take care of this mess. Just you go to sleep."

There wasn't a lot of room in the trunk of Victor's Ford Taurus, but once Mary had the pieces hacked down to a manageable size, she was able to fit more into each garbage bag.

She was backing out of the unit dragging two heavy bags when she heard footsteps from behind her.

"This I had to see for myself," a man said. "I told Vic that if I caught you hooking here again, there'd be hell to pay."

Mary turned to face Merv, covered in blood and still carrying a hatchet. She looked like Lizzie Borden after a long day's work.

"What the fuck?" Merv said, a confused look of recognition on his face.

"Hello Merv," Mary said, burying the hatchet into the man's forehead and letting him fall to the ground.

"Foolish boy," she said, stepping on his throat and pulling the axe out of his head. "We told you to stay out of our affairs."

Victor slept for what seemed like days, and when he woke up, he was sitting in front of a vanity mirror, plucking his eyebrows and putting on mascara. He was debating between the teal and the sunrise-blue eyeliner when suddenly his eyes lit up with recognition.

"Hello, Victor!" Mary said with delight. "My, I thought you were going to sleep forever, my sweet, sweet boy."

"Hello, Mary," Victor replied, raising a hand to his face and stroking it lovingly. "How I've missed you."

"Isn't it wonderful?" she asked, running her fingers through his hair and pulling it back tightly so she could put on the wig cap. "Now that I'm back it will be just like old times."

"Yes," Victor said, his voice small and timid, like a child's. "Wonderful."

Mary ran her hand up their face and frowned at the feel of stubble. It was too late to wax now – she'd be all red and puffy and sore. Perhaps Victor could remember to pick up more of that lovely cooling gel. Instead, she dabbed on a touch more concealer and then powdered it dry with a brush. She added a little colour to accentuate Victor's prominent cheekbones.

"What do you think, sweet boy? Am I good enough to eat?"

Outside, thunder rolled, lightning crashed, and Victor wanted to hide under the bed. He wanted Mary to stay and sing him to sleep.

Once there was a way to get back home...

Instead he nodded and forced a smile.

"You look beautiful," he said, and then, "Do you *have* to go?"

"Go back to sleep, Victor," she said. "And if you're a good boy, Mary will bring you another present."

"Yes," Victor said, his voice suddenly sounding far away. "Sleep. That sounds good."

"Shh," Mary said. "*Sleep pretty darling, do not cry...*"

Mary chose a wig – nothing too ostentatious – and completed her transformation.

"Be a dear, Victor, and zip me up, will you?"

But Victor was already gone – back into the dark. He would have no memory of anything that happened that evening.

"Now then," she said, appraising herself in the mirror and liking what she saw. "Don't I look fabulous?"

She pouted dramatically. For tonight's task, she'd decided to play the part of the wounded woman.

"I just want to be loved, is that so wrong? All I want is what every woman wants – a man with a good heart."

Michael and Naveena – Two Months Ago

"Why do you keep avoiding the obvious?" Michael asked, closing the door so she couldn't run off. Ever since Jessica had returned – and he wasn't convinced that her little disappearing stunt wasn't just one more way that she was fucking with them both – Naveena had been avoiding any serious scientific discussion. She'd begun to veer into what Michael thought were impossible, and, quite frankly, ridiculous areas of thought, even for him. He had seen all sorts of incredible things, and didn't pretend to be able to explain everything, but once the other patients began showing up, Naveena seemed too eager to believe impossible things.

"Because it's not obvious to me, Michael," she said, ignoring him. She was typing notes – endless notes – about Jessica, and her stories, and the three patients that had shown up, as if by Jessica's command.

"She obviously has some sort of connection to these people, I'll admit. And we've seen her display both psychic and telekinetic abilities. But the stories – they're absurd; they're impossible. And yet Harris – he truly believes that his son is out there, trapped in some sort of electrical half-life. He's constantly going on about ghosts in the machines – he's terrified around them."

"Is he still writing the numbers from the story?" Naveena asked without looking up or even slowing in her rapid typing.

"You know damn well he is. And he sees them everywhere he looks – and goddammit, I'm starting to see them. How is that possible?"

Naveena just grinned and said nothing.

"Don't get me started about your John Doe," Michael continued, opening the man's file and reading: "*The boy. He had to punish the boy. Maybe he could undo what the boy had done to the world. Once the false god was dead, perhaps this reality would fall away as fast as it had come to be.*

"Sounds like a real peach. And this boy sounds even worse. I suppose we should count ourselves lucky that we got John and not the boy, huh?"

"Don't call him that," Naveena corrected him.

"Oh, I'm sorry, *The Man*. So she's got you calling him that, too?"

"That's his namc."

"Right. Because that makes a lot of sense. Anyway, he seems to reinvent himself every day. Doesn't seem to remember anything."

"He's a blank slate," Naveena agreed.

"And then there's Victor."

"You mean Mary, don't you?" she asked with a wicked grin.

"Exactly," he said, not finding it funny. "Except that there's no such thing as multiple personality disorder – not really. It's only a thing in stories – stories like the ones she writes."

"So what are you saying?" Naveena stopped typing and looked at him like a teacher trying to prod a student for an answer she knows he has but can't quite grasp. "Come on. I want to hear you say it."

"I don't know, but I swear to you I saw his eyes change colour. And when he cut himself – when he slit his wrists – he nearly bled out. I wrapped the bandages myself. I stitched him up, and I saw the extent of the damage that he'd done. And yet..."

"And yet he was completely healed the next day, as if nothing had happened," she finished. "I know. I saw the wounds myself. But that's not even the strangest thing. Have you seen... *him* naked?"

Michael flushed. "I give the patients their privacy, Naveena, and so should you."

"Oh, please, I'm a professional. I've seen it all. At least, I thought I had."

"What did you see?"

"You first," Naveena said. "I can tell by the look on your face that you've seen something too. I want to hear you say it first, so I know I'm not crazy."

"I heard... *her*," he said. "Victor had gone into the shower, and I was walking by, and I heard *her* singing."

"That Beatles song?"

"The same," Michael agreed. "*Sleep pretty darling, do not cry; and I will sing a lullaby.* So I poked my head in. I know I shouldn't have, of course, and under normal circumstances..."

"These aren't normal circumstances," Naveena said. "You've nothing to justify to me."

"It was *her* – and I mean biologically, she was a woman."

"And he couldn't have been tucking his penis under?"

Michael gave her a disappointed look. "Now you – what did you see?"

"It's not what I saw, exactly, but what I heard."

"What you heard, then."

Naveena opened a folder on her computer, and opened a video captured from the security cameras.

"What's this?"

"Just listen," Naveena urged, turning up the volume.

"I'm frightened," a man's voice – more like a boy's – said. *"The storm's coming. I want to go to sleep now, but I'm afraid of what I see when I close my eyes."*

"Don't be afraid," a second voice urged. This was clearly a woman's voice, or very like. *"I will protect you, Victor. When you close your eyes, I will protect you."*

"How will you protect me, Mary? You're only a girl."

"Hush," the woman's voice said, and on the video, the man's hand snaked its way down his pants.

"Don't, Mary," Victor said. *"Mother says it's wrong; it's dirty to play with myself."*

The woman's voice growled in anger. *"She was one to talk. You know how Mother spent her nights, Victor. Down under the bridge, giving blowjobs for Meth. If it weren't for me, sweet boy, we would have starved, or ended up in Juvie."*

The man's hand resumed its stroking, more vigorously, until he climaxed with a grunt.

"There now," the woman's voice said, and on the video, even in the dark, the two doctors could make out slender arms stretching over the patient's head. *"That's better. Now you do me."*

"Yes, Mary," Victor said obediently.

"Turn it off," Michael said, shaking. "Just turn it off."

"Shocking, isn't it?" Naveena said.

"You don't seem as shocked as you should," Michael replied. "None of this falls under the category of conventional! I had no idea what to expect, but this is just bizarre. I mean, who are these people? Have you asked yourself that? If you talk to them, they talk like they're characters out of her goddamn stories. Which – by the way – they've never read."

Naveena closed her eyes and rubbed them with two fingers. Michael had seen this before. She was overworking herself.

"What if she's doing it to them?" she asked, and Michael wondered if she was asking him or just thinking out loud.

"What do you mean?"

"I mean, what if she is using her mind to manipulate theirs – writing stories that overwrite their own personalities, like a computer virus that infects a system and rewrites the code? What if, somehow, her mind can reach out, find someone vulnerable – mentally-unstable people, people with brain injuries or handicaps – and she can impose her own story on them by sheer force of will?"

Michael sat down. His legs seemed to lose their strength and refuse to support him.

"Could she do that? Why would she do that?"

Naveena shrugged and smiled. "Like she said. She wants to know what she's capable of. She does it because it amuses her. She does it because she can."

"So, she writes stories and what? Reaches out and – for lack of a better word – possesses people? That's ridiculous, Naveena. Do you hear yourself?"

Naveena frowned and returned to her notes. "I don't know. It's just an idea."

"Come on, don't be like that. You can't really believe what you're saying."

"I didn't believe a lot of things before I met Jessica," she said sternly. "She has opened my mind to many possibilities I hadn't previously considered."

"Okay, so, if I grant your hypothesis, then who are these people she's supposedly possessing? Who are they really?"

"I don't know," Naveena admitted. "Does it matter?"

Michael laughed in shocked amazement.

"I need a drink," he said.

"Ask Jessica," Naveena said. "She makes something she calls Agent Orange that will make you believe in god."

"No thanks," Michael said sourly. "One of us should remain skeptical, or else we'll both be drinking the Kool-Aid."

"You were the one who wanted to know what the mind was capable of. This was your dream, to stave off the technological singularity by advancing humanity. Your ambition was inspiring. Have you now lost your faith?"

Michael didn't answer her. There was a difference between theoretical knowledge and seeing things in practice that one should never see. He thought he now understood why the singularity would mean the end of the age of man – humans weren't mentally prepared or equipped to handle the knowledge that was out there, hanging like forbidden fruit, just out of their grasp. Maybe some things were better left alone.

"I think you should take her notebook away," he said, standing to leave. "Really take it away this time and not give it back, before she creates something really awful."

"Why would I do that?" Naveena asked, surprised. "I want to see what she comes up with next."

Helena – Three Months Ago

"I'm gonna kill Jessica B. Bell," I insisted, and locked myself in my studio. It had served as makeshift music studio, spare bedroom, and now it featured a simple desk and wall-to-wall records and a stereo. I put on a record, enjoying the sound of the needle dropping and the loud, angry music that followed. This was Helena music. Upbeat and guitar driven – thrill-killing music. Jessica would hate it.

Penny stood outside my door and tapped once, twice, three times, and I just ignored her.

"Do you want anything?" she asked loudly.

"A fifth of Jack," I growled, doing my best impression of an old blues singer, "And a bottle of… *you know.*"

"Greyhounds, then, gov'?" Penny offered cheerfully.

"Yes, yes, just go away and let me do this," I shouted. "I don't need an accomplice."

I opened up my laptop and began typing.

```
Jessica B. Bell is not real.
```

I looked at that short sentence. An admission. A declaration. A confession. One that really shouldn't be necessary, should it?

```
    I think it's important to clear the air about
that.
    A couple of years ago I started writing horror
stories and rather than use the name Helena, I
created a new pseudonym, and Jessica was "born".
```

When I'd first dreamed up Jessica, she was sort of a Goth princess – I pictured her as Siouxsie Sioux from Siouxsie and the Banshees. Or like Death from the Sandman comics. But somewhere along the line she became something else – something dark and cruel. Something I kept chained in my basement. Something broken and bloody. Where the hell did that come from?

I had fun creating a twisted and ominous
biography for her, painting a picture of some crazy
hermit who lived in my basement and wrote stories on
old parchment using her own blood for ink.

My eyes drifted to my bookshelf. I was getting a terrible headache. I stood and stretched, turned the record over, and stared out my window into the night. I closed my eyes and rubbed my fingers over them in a circular motion. When I opened them again, all I could see were ghost images, like I'd looked directly into the sun. A flash of lightning startled me, and the rumble of thunder that followed was loud enough to compete with my music. Running my hand along my books, I stopped at the blue book that bore Jessica's name. I flipped through it and smiled at the memory of writing it.

"Damn," I whispered. "This is good."

But now I wanted rid of her, because she'd become something else. Something scary. Penny had said that I frightened her when I wrote as Jessica.

Another book caught my eye, and I pulled it from the shelf – an old, beat-up copy of *The Velveteen Rabbit* by Margery Williams. The story had always frightened me, and after the first time I'd read it, I'd thrown away all my stuffed animals, terrified that if I loved them too much, they'd become real. That was the key – love. The Skin Horse told the Velveteen Rabbit that it wasn't enough to be played with – but that if a child loved you and loved you and loved you, you'd become real. You had to be loved until you were practically falling apart, but it didn't matter how torn up or ugly you were – you were *real*.

I didn't love Jessica B. Bell. She was a necessary evil. She was just someone to blame for my sick and twisted imagination. It wasn't even ever my intention to give Jessica her own biography. That was just a passing fascination that I followed. I needed people to understand that. I put both books back on the shelf and continued to type. I was surprised to see my hands were trembling.

I even went so far as to make an entire book
about her – a speculative meta-narrative about her

alleged past and curious origins. I wanted to blur
the lines between fiction and reality, and so I
treated it as factual or at least plausible events,
even creating fake newspaper clippings and audio
clips.

But it was just a story. You have to understand
that above all else, darlings, because I don't want
there to be any confusion.

Jessica B. Bell is *not real*.

Let me repeat myself: JESSICA B. BELL IS NOT
REAL.

I sat at my desk and stared at what I'd written, and could hardly
catch my breath. This would be it. I could let go of Jessica, just
write other stuff under my own name; I could put all that behind
me. All I had to do was hit Publish.

I reached out one hand to hit the Enter key, and was about to
push the button when a knock came at the door.

"Helena?"

I suddenly noticed the silence. When had the music ended?

I opened the door, and Penny handed me a drink of water.

"What happened to my Greyhound?" I asked, disappointed.

"That was hours ago," she replied, motioning to my desk,
where an empty glass sat, a little bit of pink grapefruit juice clinging
to melting ice cubes that were little more than slivers.

"Hours?" I asked.

"You okay? You've been here all evening. Did you manage to
kill the bitch?"

I rubbed my temples and sat back down at the desk. I moved
the mouse, and hovered over the Publish button. Instead, I moved
it down and clicked Trash, and felt something pop inside my head,
and the tension seemed to melt away.

"I think killing the old girl is a bit harsh, don't you?" I asked.

"But..." Penny protested.

"I don't need to kill her," I said, giving Penny a smile intended
to set her mind at ease. "I'll just let her wither and die. If I don't
feed the monster, she'll surely starve to death."

"Yeah," Penny said with an unconvincing shrug. "Or she'll go
hunting."

Jessica – Three Months Ago

Jessica was in the dark again, this time with a purpose. She'd done what she had to do while she still could. She had a feeling that, soon, she would be limited to one place, one time, and while that might seem confining to others, it was all she had ever wanted.

In the dark, she had to share. She hated sharing. She used to fear the dark, but not anymore. The things that moved there soon learned to be more afraid of her than she was of them. They were only mildly frightening – dusty, old, forgotten things that had ceased being interesting a long time ago. They grew angry in the darkness, but growl as they might, Jessica discovered the truth about the would-be monsters – they were toothless, frail things with no more bite than a newborn babe. Whereas in the darkness of in-between, Jessica was equipped with terrible claws for tearing and monstrous teeth for rending the flesh of anyone that got in her way.

That she had to share with *her* wouldn't have been so bad, if it weren't that she had to put up with the niece, Penny. She stood over the irritating girl's bed, watching her sleep. It would just take a moment. If she just asserted herself, she could take a pillow and place it over her pale face. She'd never again have to hear that terrible cockney accent that she used when she thought she was being funny.

Jessica didn't think she was strong enough. She needed what strength she had to complete the task at hand. Penny had her notebook. The doctors had taken it from Jessica, and while it was out of her possession, somehow it had reverted back to Helena's possession. But it didn't belong to Helena. It belonged to her.

She reached out her hand, and took a moment to look at Helena's perfectly-manicured fingers through her borrowed eyes. So different than her own nails, which she often painted black to hide the fact that she chewed her nails.

Penny stirred.

Dammit. It wouldn't do to get caught standing over her while she slept. Even Jessica knew that was pretty creepy. She quickly grabbed her notebook from Penny's nightstand and left the room just as she'd come. She put Helena back to bed – no need to alarm her – and hugged the notebook to her chest and hoped for the best.

Jessica woke up in a hospital bed in Ward C with the notebook in her arms, and grinned a wicked grin. Somewhere, a pack of lemmings ran off a cliff, a whale beached itself, and a flock of birds flew into an enormous, plate glass window. Children for miles around reported having terrible nightmares, and the suicide hotline phones rang off the hook. Somewhere, a postman was delivering a postcard with a drawing of a Velveteen Rabbit on it.

"I'll show you who's real," Jessica whispered, and two floors up, in the maternity ward, babies screamed and refused their mother's milk, which had turned to blood.

"It's time," she said. "It's nearly time. I don't need that bitch anymore. She'll see. Soon. Soon they'll come, and just you wait and see what I can do. Are you watching?"

She wrapped her arms around the notebook like a security blanket, closed her eyes and went back to sleep, still grinning.

Jessica was dying; she was sure of it. She'd never felt anything like this – was not even sure she was capable of feeling like this. She had been vomiting on and off since she'd woken up mid-morning, and she was burning with fever, her sheets soaked with sweat.

"Am I real?" she asked weakly as a new nurse, an older woman with bad teeth and colourless hair, wiped her brow with a cool cloth.

The woman said nothing, but gave Jessica a new, dry sheet and replaced her empty cup with more ice water.

The doctors came and took her temperature, but got inconsistent readings. Sometimes they got temperatures in the negative degrees, other times she read so hot the thermometer malfunctioned. They were able to get an I.V. put in, which surprised Jessica as much as anyone else, and were pumping her full of fluids. They assured her that she wasn't dying, but they didn't know. They told her the best thing she could do was sleep, but Jessica was terrified of sleep. She couldn't ignore the timing of this – she could practically smell Helena's perfume – Pure Poison, by Dior. She knew that smell like she knew the sound of her voice, and she felt herself slipping in and out, like she was on a opium nod. She feared what she would find if she closed her eyes.

Dark clouds formed on her mind's horizon, and she could feel the pull of the drug they had given her, dragging her under. She was pulled through the darkness, through some sort of barrier, like she was being born, tugged roughly from her mother's womb, tearing her, and there was screaming, but Jessica wasn't sure who the screams belonged to.

And then she was falling, and she realized where the screams were coming from. She fell, faster and faster, though the darkness of night, and the stars fell alongside her, screaming.

She heard a loud voice cry out, "It was just a story, darlings!" and a flash of lightning and a crash of thunder, followed by the tap-tap-tapping of fingers on a keyboard.

After falling forever, she hit the ground, and every bone in her body shattered, her lungs collapsing like burst balloons. One eye had popped out of its socket and rolled on her cheek like the last grape on the vine.

She was dead. She was certain she was dead. She lay in silence and waited for whatever awaited her.

What happens to someone like me after they die? she wondered.

She stared up at the sky and saw a thousand winged creatures high above her, circling her like buzzards. They clucked and they chuckled in voices straight out of Oliver Twist, and every last one of them was wearing some variety of striped stockings.

Jessica tried to grit her teeth, but her jaw wouldn't move. It was broken into at least three parts, and a piece of it jutted out through her cheek like some sort of grotesque tusk.

Then the tapping of the typing stopped, and the angels stopped laughing. The air was suddenly filled with the tart smell of citrus – grapefruit juice, to be precise. Followed by the familiar smell of vodka. Jessica tried to breathe it in, but couldn't.

When the first raindrop hit her face, it was warm and salty and unbearable, but she couldn't move. Then a second, a third, and then there was a pitter-patter of raindrops all around her, soaking her, washing her bones clean. Her body began to knit itself back together, her lungs filled with air and she screamed into the sky, but the thunder drowned the sound. She screamed and howled into the night, feeling the strength return to her body. She made her way to her feet and planted them firmly on the earth while she hurled curses at the sky.

From somewhere behind her she heard someone moving. Two people, actually. She turned and watched in amusement as one man, naked and lean, fled through the trees, being chased by a second man, bigger and hairier that the first, but just as naked. This second man brandished a rough club, and screamed at his quarry in wordless vowel sounds.

Jessica watched with bloodthirsty glee as the large man bounded to catch his brother, and then pounced on him like an ape and began pummelling him, with his club at first, and then with his bare, bloody fists.

She woke with the image still firmly in her mind, and smiled. She was well again, the sickness passed. And she knew, now. She knew who would be first. She grabbed her notebook from her table and opened it to the right page.

The man was seeking the boy, she thought. *The boy who had done this to them.*

She didn't want to be too ambitious on her first try. Baby steps. Even God needed six days.

The man's fists clenched, knuckles whitening under the grime that coated them.

"Yes," Jessica said, tracing the words of the story she had simply titled THE MAN. "You'll do nicely."

ZOË

When Zoë showed up at the hospital, she remembered being brought by the police. She'd been put in handcuffs and put into the back of the patrol car. She'd been catatonic, and didn't remember much of what had happened between when the police picked her up and when she'd found herself dressed in a green hospital gown.

Two doctors came and told her that she was there for observation. She didn't see much of them for two days. There were others in the Ward, though. A scary man who spent most of his time sedated and restrained, and a man who reminded her of her high school chemistry teacher. He looked like he worked at the hospital, but he never left the Ward. Then there was the other woman – Zoë could hardly stand to look at her. She was pale and sickly-looking, with black, ragged hair. She looked like something out of a 1980s music video by some Goth band. Zoë hadn't even made eye contact – but the woman didn't seem too interested in her anyway. All she did was write in her notebook all day, scribbling so loudly Zoë could hear it across the room.

Finally, after breakfast the third day – dry toast, powdered eggs, and something that she thought was supposed to be oatmeal – a woman came and introduced herself as Dr. Chandra.

"What am I doing here?" Zoë asked. "Where's Emily? Have you called my parents?"

Dr. Chandra smiled kindly and asked her to tell her what she remembered.

Zoë sighed, and her eyes welled up with tears.

"You're not going to believe me," she said. "Nobody believes me."

Dr. Chandra sat on the girl's bed and pulled out her own notebook and pen.

"Start from the beginning."

Patient Data

THIS FORM, PLEASE ASK THE RECEPTIONIST

Today's Date:_____

Insurance Information

Name of Company:_____

Name of Insured:_____

☐ F   Insureds DOB:_____ SS#:____

Patient consents to participate in trials, co
of which will be at the discretion of the su
physicians. Resitition will be paid at the
the study.

Phone: Work _____ Cell:_____

Your Employer:_____

Occupation:_____

Signature of Patient:_____

Referred to this office by: ☐ Web Site ☐ Yellow Pages ☐ Advertisement

Print Name:____ **Zoe**

☐ Friend/Family Member Name:_____

Date:_____

Payment for Services will be by: ☐ Cash ☐ Check ☐ Credit Card ☐ Health Insurance ☐ Automobile Insurance

Are you covered by more than one insurance company? ☐ Yes ☐ No Name_____

Handle with extreme care. Volitile temper, seems distrustful of all hospital staff.

~~All this~~ ~~the end of the world~~ the beginning of another
~~common them~~ ~~place~~

Have you been treated by a physician for any health condition in the last year? ☐ Yes ☐ No

Describe Condition_____ Date of Last Physical Exam____

Describe The Treatment:_____

SURGICAL HISTORY: ☐ NONE

1._____ Date:_____
2._____ Date:_____
3._____ Date:_____

Have you ever had a metal implant? ☐ Yes ☐ No   Ever been gunshot? ☐ Yes ☐ No

ACCIDENT HISTORY: ☐ Job ☐ Auto ☐ Other 1._____ Date:_____
☐ Job ☐ Auto ☐ Other 2._____ Date:_____
☐ Job ☐ Auto ☐ Other 3._____ Date:_____

ZOE

The path cut through the woods like a jagged scar left by a knife-wielding maniac.

Zoë looked at the text she'd typed on her phone and decided it would be a good first line for her book. She'd been researching hauntings for two years, ever since she'd had her own encounter. It wasn't something she could define or explain, but it opened a curiosity in her, and so she took every opportunity she could to learn more, especially if a chance to see something firsthand came along.

She followed the rest of the tour group, absentmindedly thumbing at her phone, expecting a call, a text, something. She'd only been gone two weeks, and she swore that she was not going to be the first to reach out. She was an adult now, and her mom needed to know that she didn't need her hanging over her shoulder all the time. Eighteen was old enough to be out on her own, even if she was in student apartments with fifty or more other co-eds. She was hardly ever alone – there was a sort of unspoken open door policy – so there was always someone in her room, even if she wasn't there.

That had taken some getting used to, and the truth was, Zoë still wasn't comfortable with it – she hadn't shared a room with her little sister in years, and treasured her private space. When she'd learned that she would have her own room in the University residence, she'd been ecstatic. This communal space culture she suddenly found herself in made her uneasy and paranoid. She dreaded the winter months trapped inside, so while she still could, she spent as much time as she could exploring the grounds, taking pictures, asking around about the history of the place. When she saw a flyer pinned to the communal bulletin board about a Ghost Walk, she didn't waste any time in signing up.

"At the turn of the century," the tour guide continued, "this residence building was actually part of the hospital. Spenser House was once the psychiatric ward."

"Of course it was," a blonde-haired girl whose name Zoë kept forgetting said, nudging her. Zoë almost dropped her cell phone, and so stuck it in her purse for safekeeping.

"It was, actually," Zoë replied. "There are all sorts of stories about this place. The things they used to do to patients were barbaric. Forced lobotomies, bloodletting, and sensory deprivation experiments. I read a story about one doctor who liked to asphyxiate his patients just to the point where their heart stopped beating, and then he would hook them up to the ECT device and bring them back to life."

"Why would anyone do that?"

"I don't know," Zoë said. "Maybe he liked playing God. Maybe he wanted to study the effects, quantify the amount of brain damage. They say that you can reset a person's personality with ECT. Maybe he really was trying to help – a rebirth of sorts. Or maybe he thought that they'd come back and tell him what was on the other side. Who knows?"

"It's bullshit," the girl shrugged. "And I'm cold. And hungry."

Zoë rolled her eyes. "We're coming up on a path that will take you to the cafeteria. You can skip the rest of the tour and grab a coffee."

"Sign me up. You coming?"

"No, I'm going to follow the tour," Zoë said, happy to be rid of her.

"You sure? It's just a bunch of nonsense about weird, old stories and things that go bump in the night."

Zoë smiled as politely as she could at the girl and nodded. Weird, old stories about things that went bump in the night fascinated her. She was drawn to fear, and wanted to study abnormal psychology. She knew that there was no real Hannibal Lecter in the world, but there had been Ed Gein, John Wayne Gacy, Paul Bernardo and Ted Bundy, just to name a handful from recent memory. Ever since her second year in high school, when she'd trudged through Julius Caesar, one line had stayed with her, and piqued her curiosity.

The evil that men do lives after them.

If that was true, what form would that evil take? What psychic residue might evil leave behind? Could a place, a thing, a building be haunted by that evil? Could a person?

She'd gone on ghost tours all over, taken pictures, listened to stories, some so-called eyewitness accounts, and collected it all for further study. She had notebooks full of stories, and someday she would write about it all. Her interest was twofold, really. The part of her mind that wanted to believe in the fantastical was curious. She wanted to see something concrete for herself, wanted her belief rewarded. But she was equally interested in the belief of others, how the legends and stories affected the psychology of its residents. What were they like, the people who lived in haunted houses?

Did evil cling like ivy to the walls of these old houses, setting down roots and poisoning the water table? Zoë had very romantic ideas about it, which her mother didn't understand at all.

"You know there are no such things as ghosts, Zoë," she constantly told her, turning off whatever film on the subject she might be watching at the time. She'd seen all the important ones – *The Amityville Horror, Poltergeist, The Haunting in Connecticut* – she'd picked up pretty much anything about Ed and Lorraine Warren that she could get her hands on.

"I know there's no such thing as ghosts, mom," she'd learned to respond. "But don't you think the idea is fascinating? What makes people believe in these things, and why do they speak about them with such conviction? Aren't you curious? I mean, what is it about certain places that just gives people the creeps?"

Her mother sighed. "Well, I think it's an unhealthy fascination, Zoë, and I wish you'd focus on nicer things. Tell her, Ed."

Zoë's father poked his nose out from behind a Stephen King book long enough to grunt.

"No such thing as ghosts, honey. Only in the movies."

Zoë thought about a retort, but bit her tongue instead. It had to be more than that. People believed in all sorts of things, and so to them, those things were real.

Was that enough? she wondered. *Did the belief cause the fear?*

The very idea that someone could believe in something so completely that it became a pervasive force in their lives compelled her study of the subject. She had already begun thinking of the paper she would write about the collective consciousness, and how belief on a massive scale could have psychic effects on a community. If enough people believed in something, could it become real? Was the local haunted house only truly haunted because people's beliefs made it so?

"The woods we've just passed through have been the site of many spectral appearances and other strange happenings," the tour guide, an enthusiastic but sincere woman, stopped and put a hand on a tree, turning to face the group. "In 1987, there were several reports of a so-called Phantom Professor, who would walk with students through the woods, taking them safely along the path to the other side, only to disappear once they were clear of the darkness of the trees. Upon further research, some believe that this could have been the ghost of one Bertrand Strauss, whose own daughter, as well as seven other girls, disappeared thirty years earlier, never to be found again. Bertrand had been accused of their murders, but denied it right up to the day he was executed. Could he be here with us now, looking after us, making sure that we don't share whatever fate befell his poor daughter?"

Zoë didn't subscribe to the idea that ghosts were either good or evil, no more than she thought the living were. Was it possible there were beneficial spirits?

"Of course, there are also legends, rumours and superstitions about Jessup Hall that are little more than spook stories passed down from generation to generation to rattle first years. Maybe you've already heard some of them."

Nervous laughter passed through the group like a wave.

One timid hand rose to ask a question, and was acknowledged by the tour leader.

"Is it true," a girl about Zoë's age asked, "about the fire in the paediatric wing of the hospital? Did all those children really die?"

The tour guide's face went dark and she swallowed before she spoke. "I don't usually like to talk about that part, but since you asked, I will tell you what I know."

Zoë knew all about it. She'd requested her residence assignment based on it, and was lucky enough to be granted her request.

The Andersson Building, or Andersson House, as it was once called. Named after Lars Andersson, whose daughter Sigga, legend had it, went mad and locked twenty-three children in a room with her and set the place on fire. If there was one reason that Zoë had chosen this school, this was it. She had done her own research, digging through hard-to-find articles still on microfilm at the library in order to find what amounted to little more than conjecture and rumour. She'd even found a copy of Hugo Lambert's book, and had borrowed it – indefinitely – from the library.

"This was more than a hundred years ago, you understand," the tour guide began, "so there is very little documentation about what really happened. We know that twenty-four children died in the fire, as well as one adult – a security guard. Little is said about him, but legend has it that he had his throat slit, and was dead before the fire ever started. The official stories in the papers left this detail out, and tell a story about a fire that began in the kitchen and spread to the rest of the hospital, killing both the guard and twenty-four children. No mention is made of why the children could not escape, and instead, the tragedy was treated like an accident. Until accusations were made –"

"By Hugo Lambert," Zoë said, and all eyes turned to her.

"Yes, that's right," the tour guide said, surprised. "Hugo Lambert claimed to be one of the first at the scene, and challenged the newspapers' report of an accidental fire. He wrote a book, describing what he called a mass suicide – charred bodies huddled together in a locked room, reduced to ashen statues. He made special note of a set of keys clasped in one of the hands of the dead. In his book, he claims that this was the hand of seventeen-year-old Sigga Andersson, daughter of Lars Andersson, prominent businessman and philanthropist, whose name remains on the building to this day. Further, he claims to have uncovered secrets about Sigga's fascination with the end of the world, and her involvement with an apocalyptic cult. He painted a picture of a paranoid religious zealot and her flock of followers, bringing about the end of their own individual worlds."

"Is it true?" someone asked.

Zoë wondered how the guide would answer.

"We don't know for sure," she said. "Lambert was discredited and sued by the Andersson family for libel. His sources recanted their testimony, or outright denied having even met with the writer. Some people say he made the whole thing up."

"What do you think?" Zoë asked.

"I think that twenty-five people died in a terrible tragedy that has left its mark on this place. The exact details of how they died doesn't change anything in my mind."

But it did. For Zoë, it changed everything. Innocent victims of an accidental fire or murder victims of a crazy girl obsessed with the apocalypse? Everything that she had read about ghosts and hauntings spoke about trauma and rage and unfinished business. Spirits that couldn't move on. It was a staple of every ghost story ever, whether it was the supposed true-life account of a haunting or the latest episode of *Supernatural*. No one ever died of natural or accidental causes and then decided to haunt and terrify the remaining occupants of their house. No, it was usually terrible and bloody and traumatic. Could that be the key? Trauma and rage? Even outrage at injustice, perhaps?

"And... *is* Andersson House haunted?" Zoë asked, and held her breath.

The guide looked at her gravely and locked eyes with her.

"Oh, most certainly."

Zoë's room was tiny – all the dorm rooms were – with space for little more than a twin bed, a bookshelf, a small chest of drawers for her clothes, and a desk that was roughly the size of a postage stamp. It recalled memories of elementary school, when she and all the other children were forced into awful and claustrophobic chair/desk combos. Only she was quite sure those desks were bigger than what she coped with now. The school had graciously furnished all the rooms with these desks, but students had to provide their own chairs. Zoë had opted for a cheap IKEA model, and what it lacked in style it made up for in discomfort.

After returning from the Ghost Walk, all she wanted was to sleep – they had climbed more stairs than she cared to count and her legs felt like old rubber bands. She opened the door to her room, expecting to find at least one of her friends hanging out, watching her TV, which sat on top of the bookshelf – one of the few on the floor. She'd found a kindred spirit in one of the girls – a girl who proudly went by the name Emily the Strange. It was Emily Vandervert, really, but she embraced all things dark and gothic, to the point of powdering her already-pale face to complete her desired look. Others sniggered and laughed at her either to her face or behind her back, but Zoë thought she was beautiful, and besides that, she was a believer. Zoë didn't mind Emily crashing in her room so much – at least she was interesting conversation. They had bonded over a first edition of Shirley Jackson's *Haunting of Hill House* that Zoë never let out of her sight. She'd had to cull her expansive collection of books when she went off to university, and had left so many treasures behind, but this particular book was never in question. She'd paid $700 for it on eBay – nearly half of her summer savings – and her mother had threatened to tear it up when she found out.

But Emily was not there, and so she returned to an empty room. She locked the door behind her, not willing to give up such rare treats as solitude and privacy. Even though she kept a neat room, the space was so small that she barely had room to walk between her bed and her desk and dresser, and every night before she went to bed, she made sure to tuck her chair under the small desk, which gave her about an entire square foot of floor space, in case she needed to get up in the middle of the night. She'd learned her lesson the hard way, going ass-over-teakettle one night tripping over the otherwise-harmless IKEA chair. Since then she'd gotten into a faithful routine of ensuring that the chair was tucked away.

Sleep called to her. True, the bed was not the foam mattress she enjoyed at home, but she'd learned to love it nonetheless. But before she closed her eyes, she wanted to record some impressions she'd gotten on the Ghost Walk. In particular, she wanted to write about Sigga Andersson.

She grabbed her notebook and started a new page.

The Search for the Ghost of Sigga Andersson

She hesitated, and then scratched part of the title out, and revised it.

The Search for the Ghosts of Andersson House

On March 5th 1901, twenty-five souls spent their last night on this plane of existence, burned to death in what some say was an accident, but legend suggests was something else. At the centre of this event is Andersson's own daughter Sigga, who is either victim or villain, depending on whose account you believed.

There have been more unexplained phenomena in Anderson House than anywhere else in Canada, and among those in the field of parapsychology, there is no doubt that this place is haunted.

In 1914, Jeanette Theriault reported hearing screaming coming from the room next to her, and went to investigate, only to find nothing but her sleeping classmate. This went on for days, until finally, convinced that the girl was playing a cruel trick on her, Jeanette attacked her in the middle of one of the screaming episodes, crushing her throat and killing her. When the dorm Proctors pulled Jeanette off the other girl, she was catatonic, and when she awoke in the hospital wing (what is now Spenser House) she claimed to have no memory of the attack. The term schizophrenia was only a recent one – more often than not, patients who displayed any type of abnormal symptoms were diagnosed with dementia praecox, or more simply, madness. Jeanette was committed to psychiatric care indefinitely, and while she never had any other violent outbursts, she continued to suffer auditory hallucinations.

In May of 1931, three young women disappeared from their rooms in the middle of the night. It was the end of the school term, and when neither the staff nor the student body could find them after two days, they were declared missing. The search by the frightened parents continued all through the summer, with no results. The hospital was open year round, of course, but many sections of the buildings, used as residences during the school year, were empty through the summer months. So it was that no one discovered the smell of the three girls until late August, when both students and teachers began returning to school. They were found dead, huddled together in the very same room where thirty years earlier twenty-four others were found. There was no sign of a fire of any kind, nor were the girls burned in any way, and yet, upon autopsy, they all showed signs of severe pulmonary injuries, consistent with smoke inhalation.

Who is the ghost or ghosts that haunt Andersson House? Is it Sigga? Or possibly one of the twenty-three children? What really happened that night? And what of the security guard? Is his spirit trapped here as well? Who was Sigga Andersson? What was she really like? Was she mad? Or possibly even evil?

Zoë closed her notebook for the night. She was beginning to get a headache – she got them too often if she didn't eat or sleep properly. She opened her mouth wide, stretching her jaw and enjoying the pop of relief at the back of her neck. She gave her temples a slow massage, turned off the lights, and closed her eyes. She was asleep before her head hit the pillow.

Zoë woke up in her clothes again – the same ones she knew she'd taken off the night before. She pulled the covers over her head, trying to escape from the same dream she'd been having for the last few nights – a violent thing full of ice and fire that always faded before she could make sense of it.

She reached for her phone to check the time, and groaned when she saw how early it still was. Never one for early mornings, she preferred to greet the day with the sun firmly in the sky. But the dream lingered, and wouldn't let her go back to sleep. Blurry-eyed, she rolled out of bed in the dark, stood up, and immediately tripped over her desk chair.

Swearing and rubbing her shin, she picked up the fallen chair and placed it back under the desk. She thought she'd done that last night, but she'd been pre-occupied with telling the story about Andersson House, and must have forgotten. Except, she wasn't quite convinced. She was a creature of habit, and it was unlike her to deviate from her routine.

Something caught her eye on the desk – she wouldn't have even seen it if it weren't for the headlights of some early morning commuter flashing momentarily through her window. She turned on her overhead light to get a better look.

Her notebook was open on her desk, to the pages she'd been writing the night before. She thought she'd had it with her in bed, but then, she thought she'd put the chair back, too. As if the notebook itself wasn't strange enough, there was something else. One word had been written at the bottom of her entry. The hand was hers – or at least very like it – but she didn't recall writing it, didn't even know what to make of it.

LARSDOTTIR.

Lars' daughter. A patronymic surname, traditional among Scandinavian families. Sigga was Lars' daughter, just as Lars was Anders' son. Now it made sense to her. She must have had a brainstorm in the middle of the night, gotten up briefly to write it down, and crawled back into bed and forgotten all about it.

Her mind was leading her to Sigga Larsdottir, then. She still didn't know anything about her. Was she a student at the University? Was she in training to become a nurse? The University was both school and hospital at the time, and it was a teaching hospital. She could have been working in any number of capacities, though considering Sigga's affluent parentage, Zoë had a hard time believing the girl was sweeping floors or washing dishes. Other than the articles she'd been able to find about the fire, and Lambert's book (which, while fascinating, was a little hard to swallow at times), she hadn't been able to locate anything else on Sigga Andersson.

"I was looking for the wrong name," Zoë muttered, finally realizing what her dreaming self must have been trying to tell her.

She grabbed her laptop out of her bag and opened it on her little desk. Opening her browser, she typed Sigga Larsdottir, and immediately cursed herself for thinking it was going to be that easy. She needed to narrow it down, change tactics. She grabbed a pen and started fiddling with it, unconsciously beginning to write a list in her open notebook.

"Okay," she sighed. "What do I know?"

She knew when Sigga died – 1901.

She knew how old Sigga was – seventeen.

She could check for birth records from 1884, assuming Sigga was born in Canada.

"But what would that tell me, exactly?"

She could check University enrolment, if she could get her hands on the records.

Lambert's book said that Sigga'd had an older brother, but he'd be long dead by now. Anyone who'd actually known Sigga would be long dead.

There had to be something left behind that would give some insight into the dead girl.

She did an Internet search for medical records in Canada, and learned that the Freedom of Information and Protection of Privacy Act protected anything a hundred years old or less. If it was greater than a hundred years, though, the information might be available. If Sigga had been a patient, it would be difficult – but not impossible – to find out.

Zoë re-read the last lines she had written before she had gone to sleep.

Who was Sigga Andersson? What was she really like? Was she mad? Or possibly even evil?

Zoë didn't know yet – or if, indeed, it was Sigga that haunted Andersson House for the past hundred years – but whoever or whatever it was, it was both cruel and convincing.

"Oh, that's good," she said excitedly, and drew a line underneath where she'd stopped the night before, so that she could start anew.

I can't say for sure if it is Sigga Larsdottir that has haunted Andersson House for the past hundred years, but whoever it is, they are both cruel and convincing. The strange occurrences are frequent and unexplained. No one likes to speak about all the little things — the cold pockets, the strange whispers, the smell of smoke. Andersson House has had more false fire alarms than anywhere in the city, and the school has been fined on numerous occasions. It got so bad that in 1992, it became school policy that anyone calling in a false fire claim would face expulsion. Some things, like unexplained scratches or marks, usually went unmentioned, but many students in Andersson House have experienced the unusual. Most often these are dismissed as pranks, and nothing further is made of it. But there is a sort of nervous apprehension among the residents, as if everyone has their guard up, especially at night.

There is another phenomenon that is spoken of – or rather, officially not spoken of – at Andersson House, and that is the recurring graffiti. More than a dozen times over the past hundred years, strange, rune-like markings have been scrawled on the walls, only to be painted over again just as quickly as they appeared. No one has ever taken credit or blame for the vandalism, nor have any pictures been taken – or at least none that survived – and so some have come to believe that this is just a local legend. I do not believe this to be so. A source of mine told me that he saw them the last time they appeared, to his knowledge, in 1979.

In April of 1979, eleven students fell ill with a burning fever, and were eventually admitted to the hospital and put into quarantine. Within days of being removed from the school, all eleven of the

Zoë stopped writing. Someone was standing outside her locked door. They hadn't knocked, but she could tell there was someone there, could hear them shuffling, even heard them breathing – heavy, like an asthmatic or like someone who had just climbed several flights of stairs. Except that Zoë was only on the second floor.

"Hello?" she called. "Andrea, is that you? What do you want so early?"

Andrea was the only person Zoë knew of in the house that had asthma. She carried a puffer around with her, constantly taking hits from it like it was a bong.

She pushed away from her desk, annoyed at the interruption, and took two quick steps to the door before the other girl could run away. With one hand she unlocked the door, and the clicking of the tumblers sounded louder than she would have believed in the stillness of the morning. With the other hand, she swung open the door, hoping to catch whoever was lurking by her door.

"You know," she started, "It's really rude to…"

But there was nobody there. Not even a talking raven.

"Hello?" she called to the empty corridor. "Andrea?"

She was about to turn back and close the door behind her when she heard something coming from down the hall. It sounded like scratching – like a dog pawing on a door to be let in. She stepped out her door and everything changed.

Zoë stepped into the hall and the smell made her eyes water and her gorge rise. The rancid odour of vomit and other bodily functions assaulted her. The smell of sickness, and something else underneath it that she associated with pennies. A sort of coppery smell that she tasted in the back of her throat like blood or bile. Her head swam at first, not believing her eyes. The hallway of the residence was gone, replaced by a dimly-lit corridor with a linoleum floor in an oddly-calming shade of pale green. She placed one foot in front of the other with hesitation, fearing that she was stepping into a dream, and that the very floor itself would vanish like smoke under her feet. She heard crying ahead of her, and took a couple of cautious steps toward the sound. When she didn't fall through the floor, she moved more naturally, following the sound of the cries. On either side of the corridor were doors, with slotted openings like windows, only without glass.

She peered in the first door and saw a sickly-looking boy shivering on a cot, wearing only a pair of filthy underwear. She reached for the doorknob and tried to open the door, only to find it locked.

The modern, fluorescent lights were gone, and instead, there were incandescent light fixtures at about ten foot intervals along the hall, casting weak shadows along the pale walls. Zoë followed them toward the end of the hall, where there appeared to be an office of some sort. Someone called out in the darkness from one of the rooms, startling her.

"Sigga!" a girl's voice called. "Sigga is that you?"

The voice was frantic, desperate, terrified.

Zoë put her face in the slotted opening, trying to see the girl, but couldn't.

"Hello?" she whispered. "Are you there?"

"Don't let him hurt me anymore, Sigga," the girl replied from somewhere behind the door.

"Who?" Zoë asked. "Who's hurting you?"

A crazed face, swollen and discoloured, varied hues of purple and pink and yellow, bruises upon bruises, suddenly appeared in the opening, and Zoë took a step back in fright. The girl looked out through one good eye – the other had collapsed in on itself, just an empty socket protected by a thin veil of flesh that was her eyelid.

"Who did this to you?" Zoë asked, and the girl trembled.

"The Big Bad Wolf!" she hissed in a hushed whisper, and then slapped her hand over her mouth, as if someone might hear her.

"What's your name?" Zoë asked, stepping forward.

A filthy hand shot out from the slot, tiny but strong, and grabbed a handful of Zoë's hair, pulling her against the door.

"Make him stop, Sigga!" she screamed. "Make him stop!"

"Who?" Zoë cried, trying to release herself from the girl's grip.

"The wolf," she said, "Fenrir!"

Something was coming. Zoë could hear the padding of feet, and the click-click-click-click that a dog makes with its nails on linoleum. Or a wolf.

The girl tugged on Zoë's hair so hard she knocked her head against the door and everything went black. As she faded into darkness, Zoë thought she heard howling in the distance.

When Zoë opened her eyes again, everything was still dark. She couldn't see her hand in front of her face. She stood up carefully, and heard movement nearby. She wasn't alone. Holding out her hand in front of her, she slowly moved a couple of steps, hoping to find a wall she could use to navigate with. A low, whispery sound began to fill her ears, like dry leaves rustling in the wind. The room – wherever she was – smelled like a campfire the morning after.

"Hello?" she whispered, but got no response. As her eyes adjusted to the darkness, she thought she caught movement out of the corner of her eye, and turned to try to follow it, but lost it just as quickly. She could hear her own rapid breathing echoing in the room, which she determined could not be very large by the sound of the echoes. She licked her lips and fumbled in her jeans for her cell phone, hoping to use it to light her way, but came away empty. She checked her other pockets and her fingers closed eagerly over her lighter. She flicked it to life, the sparks igniting a tiny flame, and the small light showed her a door not three steps in front of her. If she'd stumbled any more in the dark, she might have walked right into it. She took a first, relieved step toward the door, and then stopped abruptly as a chill went up her spine. A whistling sound, like a great inhaling of breath, came from behind her, and she turned slowly, cupping the flame so that it didn't go out.

When she turned, she saw a crowd of cowering children, huddled together in fear. As one, they stood and moved toward her, and when the screaming started, Zoë couldn't tell if it was her or them that was doing the screaming. Her thumb burning, she dropped the lighter and the screaming stopped, and it was suddenly still again as if nothing had happened. She made her way to the door, banging her fingers on it as she tried to find it in the dark. Her eyes were blind not only from the darkness, but from the brief flicker of the flame. She saw ghostly circles as if from a camera flash, and her ears were still ringing from the screams as she fumbled with the doorknob, which didn't want to turn.

Her heart racing, she began pounding on the door and felt a scream of panic begin to rise in her throat.

And was it getting hotter in the room?

Zoë thought about the three girls that had gone missing in 1931 and wondered if she was about to share their fate. She threw her weight, such as it was, against the door, but it wouldn't budge. She shook the handle and turned it back and forth, rattling it. She remembered her basement door back home, and suddenly thought of trying something else. That door always swelled in the summer heat, and sometimes you had to push it back off the frame in order for it to open. Zoë pulled sideways on the door handle, trying to move the door back on its hinges, and when she twisted the knob, the door opened, flooding her with fresh air and open space, as she found herself in the familiar basement of Andersson House, only a few stairs standing between her and daylight.

Tempting fate, she looked back into the room, but saw nothing and no one. Just an empty storage room. A single light bulb with a pull string dangled in the centre. If she'd waved her arms around the right way she might have even hit it. There was nothing sinister at all about the room itself, and yet Zoë knew without a doubt that it was the room that all those children had burned to death in.

Her mind was racing, full of memories and images that didn't belong to her. She had left her room, walking into a vision of an Andersson House long past. The last thing she remembered was something about a wolf, and then she woke up in the dark. But something happened between the time she was on the second floor and then. She felt like she was burning with a terrible fever. She needed to write things down, try to make sense of them. Running up the stairs, still trembling, she kept running, through the common area of the first floor and up the stairs to her room.

Locking the door behind her, she peeled off her shirt, which reeked of smoke, and was alarmed to see scratches all up and down her arms and torso. She'd wanted physical evidence, to have her faith rewarded. She needed to document this.

Grabbing her phone, she opened her camera app and began taking picture after picture of herself, often having to use two hands to keep the camera steady. She tossed her phone on her bed and threw on a mostly-clean t-shirt and a hoodie to cover up the scratches, then sat at her desk and looked at where she'd left off. Except that she remembered beginning to tell the story of the suspected cholera epidemic of 1979 when she was interrupted by… well, *whatever* it was. But when she returned to her notebook, there was more writing there.

I never should have told anybody about the voices. I know that now. I should have kept them a secret. I thought it was a gift from the gods, and when I told Papa all about it I thought he would be proud and happy for me, but his face grew pale and angry, and he told me I was being foolish. My teachers acted concerned at first, then they grew impatient. They said I was far too old to have an imaginary friend, and that I should put away such childish trifles.

Then the other children began to make fun of me, calling me names and pelting me with insults. I think now that one of my friends — for that's how I began to think of the voices — must have been Loki himself, because he told me how I could get back at the other children. He led me to a special bush full of bright red berries, and told me I should crush them up and put them into the other children's porridge. I made sure not to eat any myself, of course, and perhaps that is how they knew it was me that caused all the children to be ill.

Papa cried when he left me in the care of the doctors. He gave me a new name that day, telling me that it was to hide me from Loki the Trickster.

"He is cunning, that one," he told me. "And so you must be cleverer still."

Later I thought about this, and wondered if maybe he gave me my new name because he was ashamed of me. Has he hidden me away here among the doctors and priests?

The priests come and pray for me. I like them. Father Andrew says that people like me used to be treated as witches. He hangs his head when he says this, as if he is ashamed. He tells me they used to believe that people like me were possessed with devils. He prays that I have the strength to endure the treatments the doctors have in mind. I pray to all the gods of my childhood stories and Father Andrew's Jesus for good measure, asking them for deliverance. They tell me I am ill, and that what they do, they do to make me better.

I don't want to be ill anymore. Frigg the Beloved, deliver me. Odin All-Father, deliver me. Jesus of Nazareth, deliver me.

The doctor keeps telling me that my madness is not spiritual or emotional, or even mental in nature, but instead physiological.

"There is an infection somewhere in your body," he told me, "and it has poisoned your mind. We will find and remove the cause of the infection, sacrificing what we must in order to save the whole."

That first day, he pulled out all of my teeth. I screamed and screamed until I lost my voice. I burned with fever, and so the doctor stripped me naked and wrapped me in ice-cold bandages like an Egyptian mummy. For days without end, they took me from my room and brought me to the showers, where they tied me to the wall, crucified like Odin on Yggdrasil the World Tree or Christ on the cross, and sprayed me with a water hose.

The night nurse is a hairy, disgusting man who knows nothing about nursing and is little more than a security guard, and he watches me intently as they treat me. When the doctor leaves, he is to take me down and put me in restraints. Before he does, he pulls his man-thing out and shows it to me. That is how it begins. By the time my father comes back to visit me more than three months later, I have had three surgeries – first my tonsils, then my gall bladder, and finally my ovaries were removed. I shall never bear children. This last I must say I find a bit of a mercy, as I have also been raped repeatedly by the man all the other children call the Wolf. Of course he is the Wolf. He is Loki's son, Fenrir the wolf, sent here to keep watch over me for his father's sake.

My father is

The writing stopped, and Zoë held her breath. The moment of silence was interrupted by a knock on her door.

"Come in," she called, and heard whoever it was try to open the locked door. "Oh, sorry, just a second."

Zoë closed the notebook to avoid prying eyes, and opened the door. Emily stood in the doorway like a vampire waiting to be invited in. She looked at Zoë uneasily.

"Hello, freak," she said crossly. "What was with you this morning? Cat piss in your coffee or something?"

Zoë urged her to come inside and shut the door behind her. "What are you talking about?"

The two girls stared at each other, waiting for the other to explain.

140

"Pre-menstrual much?" Emily said. "Look, whatever. I just came by to check if you were all right. You kind of whigged me out a little. So what's the deal?"

Emily threw herself on Zoë's bed and sighed. "You plan on skipping class all day or what?"

Zoë didn't even know what time it was.

"I don't feel well," she said.

"Yeah, no shit," Emily laughed. "I came by for coffee this morning, and you acted like you didn't even see me, and ran out without saying a word. It was fucking bananas, that's what it was."

"I was here this morning? When?"

Emily sat up and raised an eyebrow. "What are you on, Zoë? Serious, what's wrong with you? Did something happen?"

Zoë nodded slowly. She didn't know where to start.

"I saw them," she said. "Ghosts."

"Fuck off," Emily said with a shocked laugh.

Zoë swallowed and shook her head.

"I saw them. The children from the fire. I lit up my lighter, and they screamed. They screamed, and I ran, and..."

"Hey, hey, back up," Emily said, grabbing Zoë's arm. "What do you mean you saw them? When? Last night? Is that why you were so freaked out this morning when I came in?"

Zoë shook her head.

"I don't remember seeing you this morning," she whispered. "I remember leaving my room really early, before anyone was awake, and then later, I woke up in the basement. In the room where those children burned."

"No fucking way," Emily gasped. "Did you get pictures?"

"No," Zoë shook her head. "But hand me my phone, you're going to want to see this."

Zoë pulled up her photo album and handed the phone to Emily.

Emily scrolled through the pictures and then looked at Zoë, puzzled.

"So, um, you know I like boys, right Zoë?" she asked. "I mean, they don't like me, but I remain hopeful."

"What are you talking about? Gimme that!"

Zoë scrolled through the pictures she'd taken and uttered a sick moan.

"No, no, no! This isn't right! Here I'll show you!"

She pulled off her hoodie, and began to feel sick and lightheaded. Her arms, just like in the pictures on her phone, were clean and unscathed. She didn't have a scratch on her. She swayed a bit, and Emily caught her.

"Sit down," Emily said, and then reached out a hand and touched Zoë's forehead.

"Damn, you're burning up!" she said. "Get back in bed, freakazoid! I'm gonna get you some water and Asprin or NyQuil or brandy or... or... or... all three. Jesus, no wonder you're seeing ghosts! Your brain's on fire!"

Zoë slid in and out of consciousness, half remembering, and half dreaming.

"Tell me a story," she whispered – no. It wasn't her that was speaking, it was one of the children. They sat in their locked rooms at night, and when it was quiet, they spoke to one another. Some of them were barely in their teens, and Sigga was Wendy to their band of Lost Boys. Only quite a few of them were girls, diagnosed with nothing more than hysteria – a catchall for young women whose parents didn't know how to handle them.

"Tell us a story, Sigga," one would call, and the others would echo them. The night nurse – the Wolf – would come every night, and call on a different child, pulling them forcefully from their bed and taking them away to satisfy his monstrous appetite. When the Wolf was gone, the children needed their stories to keep their minds off of what was happening to the unfortunate child that was chosen, what would happen to them some other night.

She would tell them the stories her father had told her as a child – those stories his father had told him, and back and back and back.

They were stories of gods and monsters; of winged Valkyries and heroes and shield maidens; of swords made of fire and storms and adventure. Stories of Asgard and Valhalla. The children especially loved the stories of the trickster Loki, particularly the one about how he cut off Sif's hair and, fearing her husband Thor's wrath, sought refuge in a den of dwarves, and then proceeded to trick them into making him many new treasures, including the hammer Mjollnir.

Zoë's fever raged, and she tossed in sweat-soaked sheets. She opened her eyes now and again, and was comforted by the sight of Emily sitting on her chair, watching over her. She slept, and dreamt of fire and ice and a terrible, hungry wolf.

After what felt like days, Zoë opened her eyes and could see clearly. Her chair was empty, and she was a little disappointed. Still, she couldn't expect Emily to sit with her the whole time.

She sat up and pushed herself out of bed. Her stomach cramped up and growled with hunger. She stretched and pulled some clean clothes out of her drawers. She'd sweated through the ones she had on, and she needed a shower nearly as much as she needed to eat. She opened her door and hesitated stepping out. What if she stepped back into the hospital?

She took a deep breath, stepped out, and nothing happened. She laughed weakly, and made her way to the communal showers.

Freshly clean, she felt better. Emily was waiting for her in her room, with a look of concern on her face. Zoë gave her a hug and thanked her for looking after her.

"I didn't do much," she said. "Wish I could have stayed with you, but a girl's gotta eat. Between school and work, I checked in as much as I could. You were out of it for nearly three days."

Zoë squeezed her friend once more. "You took care of me. Thank you. Every time I opened my eyes, you were there."

"Your brain was cooking. I bet you saw all sorts of stuff."

"Except you were a blonde. Isn't that strange?"

"It'd be a chilly day in Hell, freakazoid," she said. "You okay now? Wanna grab some grub? You're buying."

"Sure," Zoë said, trying to picture Emily as a blonde.

"You can tell me all about your Haunting of Andersson House adventure," she said. "And I promise not to have you committed."

Zoë imagined ice water baths and strait jackets and shivered.

"Deal," Zoë agreed. "Can we check on something first?"

"Sure, whatever," Emily said. "Lead on, Macduff."

"It's *lay* on, you bloody savage."

"Whatever," Emily sighed. "Let's go."

Zoë needed to see the room. Fever dream or no, that room held something powerful – she felt it. She led Emily down to the basement, and stood at the foot of the stairs, puzzled. She'd expected to find a supply room – nothing big, just a small room, maybe ten feet square – but all she saw was empty space.

"It was here," she whispered. "It was right here."

"Okay, now you're scaring me, Zoë," Emily said, tugging at the girl's sleeve.

"I'm scaring myself," she said. "Damn, that was some fever."

"But you're better now."

Zoë nodded, still unable to take her eyes from the spot where she could have sworn she'd been trapped inside a dark room just days before.

"Come on," Emily said. "I'm dying for a smoke."

"Yeah," Zoë said without enthusiasm, and turned to go. As she did, she caught a glimpse of something small and pink on the basement floor. "Go on up, I'll be right behind you."

"Come on, Zoë!" Emily whined.

"Just a second!" Zoë whined back, mimicking her friend's tone and inflection like a parrot.

She took a closer look and knelt down to examine the item.

"Come on, what's taking you so long?" Emily called from the top of the stairs.

"Nothing," Zoë said, examining the small piece of pink plastic like it was a precious relic. "I just dropped my lighter."

First, phantom wounds, and then a room that either disappeared or never was – there was only so much Zoë could reasonably attribute to her fever. The fever itself was suspicious as well. She absently rubbed her thumb along the surface of her lighter – a cheap thing the colour of old bubble gum, and yet it had become a talisman of sorts – her only physical evidence that she hadn't imagined the entire thing.

Emily was talking about something, but Zoë didn't hear what she was saying. She stared blankly, nodded when she thought she was supposed to, and let her coffee get cold.

Then she remembered something else, something she needed to check on alone. She couldn't bear another disappointment, but if it had to be, she'd rather not have an audience for it. Emily had already given her enough strange looks – she didn't need her only friend thinking she'd gone crazy.

"I'm going to go lay back down, Em," she said, cutting her friend off mid-sentence. "Still don't feel a hundred percent."

Emily looked annoyed at being interrupted, then softened.

"Sure," she said. "Do you want me to come with you?"

"No, I'll be okay."

She needed to be alone for a bit. Now that she was awake, all her senses seemed heightened. Something strange *had* happened to her, she was sure of it. She just needed to see one more thing to convince herself completely.

The notebook was where she had left it days before, still closed. She sat in her little chair and took a deep breath. She reached out her hand and touched the cover, pausing for a moment. She worried that she would find the book empty, and wondered again about the difference between truth and belief. Was it possible that she had wanted to believe so badly, that her mind had concocted the whole thing? She couldn't explain why it seemed so real, or why things that should have been real were suddenly not. She couldn't trust her own senses, it seemed. But the notebook, it was real. At least, it was something she could hold in her hands and test.

Quickly as tearing off a bandage, she threw the book open to see if the writing was still there, and was rewarded not only with the story that she'd been reading when Emily had interrupted her, but more. There was more story to be told.

"When?" Zoë asked the empty room. "When did I write this? When I was sleeping?"

Zoë considered the possibility that it wasn't her hand that had written it – or, at least, not under her own control.

"What the hell is happening to me?" she whispered, and read.

Fenrir the Wolf comes for me one night. He likes to sit and cut up an apple, teasing me with the pieces, which I cannot possibly chew. No, all my food is foul mush. He offers to chew it up for me and spit it into my mouth like a baby bird if I will take his penis into my mouth. After months of eating porridge that tastes like glue, I submit to one more degradation. After a few foul moments, he decides to use me in another way, and tosses the remains of the apple, along with his knife, on to his desk. They've shaved my head, and so he has no hair to pull. Instead, he shoves my head down on his desk and rapes me. In a moment of opportunity, I steal his folded pocketknife. After the grunting and panting animal noises cease, he pushes me down into the corner and walks away to clean himself up. Already bleeding and wet, I hide the folded knife in the only place I can, and pray that he doesn't notice it missing until it is too late and I am safely back in my padded cell. If I can make it that far, I can hide it inside the walls themselves.

I am burning with fever. The doctor says he is going to release the pressure in my brain by cutting a piece of my skull away. Father Andrew tells me they used to believe this released evil spirits, but modern science knows better. They tell me this is going to cure me, but they have said that so many times. I know that I cannot be cured. I ask to see my father before they do this, and in a rare instance of compassion, they grant my request.

Papa comes to see me and we don't recognize one another. He seems so old, and yet strong. He's wearing an eye-patch; he says he has an infection that the doctor is treating. I ask him if they cut his eye out, and he seems shocked.

"No, my little Valkyrie, they would never do that," he says, and holds me close against his chest, his beard scratching my own stubbled head. I can feel his tears falling off his cheeks on to the top of my head, and they are like cool drops of rain on my burning skin.

"What have they done to you?" he asks me, and I say nothing. I have to be strong for him. I know now what he has done for me. In my feverish state, I see my father as he truly is – not just my father, but the All-Father, Odin One-Eye. Surely he plucked his own eye out as a gift in exchange for the waters of wisdom. In search of the wisdom to cure me, no doubt, and no sacrifice was too great.

I ask him if he is come to free me, and he doesn't answer me. Perhaps he has not acquired the wisdom necessary to ease my suffering.

I tell him what they plan to do to me, and he holds me close and tells me he loves me, and promises that I will get better, but I don't believe him. There is no more time. I hear the Wolf pacing back and forth outside my door, sniffing around, poking his nose in and watching Papa and me. I remember the stories from my childhood, the stories I've been telling the other children, and I am frightened. I grip my father tightly and beg him not to go. I break into hysterics and scream and cry until the door is opened and I have to be restrained, but he won't listen. I tell him he's in danger, but he tries to calm me down, assuring me that I am in no danger. But he is! Oh, surely, he is in mortal danger! Now I understand. Loki. Fenrir the Wolf. Odin the All-Father.

Ragnarök is come! Ragnarök is come! Ragnarök is come!

Zoë stared at the blank page that followed, and felt a sick shudder rise in her, as she picked up a pen and began tapping it on the page, leaving behind a cloud of dots. When she'd first come to Andersson House, she'd been curious about all its dark history. She'd compiled a list of all the strange or terrible things that had happened there in the past hundred years. One such thing she'd dismissed but now she wasn't so sure. She looked at the random scattering of dots, and began to wonder if they weren't so random at all, and so she began connecting them, and what she drew looked remarkably like a wolf. She clapped a hand over her mouth so as not to scream, and began to connect the dots in her mind as she wrote.

In 1989, more than twenty girls came forward with accusations against then Dean, Richard Kent, claiming various degrees of sexual abuse. Some claimed he exposed himself, others claimed to have been attacked and sexually assaulted by him. The girls all agreed on one thing – he never made any threats afterward – no coerced silence or offers of favours in exchange for keeping his behaviour a secret. And yet they'd all been terrified, and never spoken a word about it for months. When a couple of the girls met and started discussing it, they became determined to find others who might have had similar experiences. For reasons they couldn't explain, they began posting flyers around the school that read WHO'S AFRAID OF THE BIG BAD WOLF, along with a time and a place to meet. They shared this all in their testimony, but were never able to account for the significance of this phrase, nor why it resonated with all twenty-three girls who showed up at this meeting, who somehow immediately and instinctively knew why the meeting had been called.

Dean Kent denied all the charges, of course, and was visibly disturbed by the accusations, which he denounced as preposterous. The girls who brought the charges were interviewed separately by both attorneys, and asked to give detailed physical descriptions of Dean Kent's genitalia, and all twenty-three gave similar accounts.

No verdict was ever arrived at – Dean Kent hung himself before one could be handed down.

"How many ghosts haunt Andersson house?" Zoë whispered, and the silence that followed chilled her blood.

Sleep didn't come easy – she'd slept for days – so she took one of the pills she'd stolen from her mother's medicine cabinet and slipped calmly into the dark, quiet waters of unconsciousness. She rarely dreamed when she took the little, white tablets, and that was what she needed – dreamless sleep.

She awoke with an aching back and a muddled head, so it took her a few moments to realize that she wasn't in her own bed. Instead, she had fallen asleep on the floor of the common area, but at least she was alone. No one was there to see what she saw. The walls of the hall were covered in graffiti – strange, stick-figure runes drawn in black marker. Zoë looked down at her hands, and dropped the marker she gripped tightly in one hand. Picking it up again, she stuck it in her pocket and checked for her cell phone.

"Dammit!" she hissed, coming up empty, and got up to run to her room to retrieve it.

Returning a moment later, she snapped picture after picture of the markings.

"No camera phones in 1979," she remarked with excitement.

She looked at the time – it was only seven o'clock. Early, but not that early. Soon the common room would be full of gawkers, and she didn't want to be caught as the first on the scene.

She ran back upstairs and took a shower, scrubbing her hands like Lady Macbeth to get rid of the damned spots of black ink. Then she crawled back into bed. She knew whom she had to see, but he wouldn't be available for a couple of hours.

It was Emily that found her, asleep and snoring. Emily had been crying, and her makeup was smeared across her cheeks, making her look like a raccoon, or an extra from a horror movie.

"Was it you?" she demanded. "Jesus, Zoë, what's going on with you?"

Zoë sat up and tried to act surprised, but wasn't very convincing.

"Don't even act like you don't know what I'm talking about. This has gone far enough. They're going to find out it's you, and they're going to expel you and you're my only friend and I can't do this school shit without you and… and… and…"

Zoë waited for her to finish, to get it all out.

"And I'm worried there might be something seriously wrong with you," she finished. "I think you need help, Zoë. Let's go together to the Dean, I can tell him all about your fever, maybe he'll understand…"

Zoë grabbed Emily's hand and squeezed it hard, eliciting a surprised yelp from her friend.

"No, you can't say anything about this, Em," Zoë pleaded. "Not yet. I have something I have to do first."

Emily nodded. "And then you'll turn yourself in?"

Zoë didn't think she'd get the chance, but she wasn't going to tell Emily that.

"I promise," she lied.

The Department of Languages and Linguistics was all the way on the other side of the campus, in what was surely no haunted building, being less than ten years old. It was part of the last expansion, and as far as Zoë knew, the only thing that had been murdered there was the pronunciation of some of the more tricky dialects. She had taken one elective course in Modern Languages, and the professor was a man so thin that Zoë thought he'd disappear if he turned sideways. She'd taken the course thinking it was going to be an easy grade, but when they started deconstructing the words into root origins, she got lost trying to remember which were Greek loanwords and which were Germanic. The professor had his class examining passages of Beowulf and Chaucer, and trying to make sense of either gave her a headache. Still, he seemed to know what he was talking about. If anyone on campus would know what to make of the symbols, it would be Professor Sherk.

Panting, she arrived at his office just as he was leaving. In a hurry, it seemed.

"Professor," she called, out of breath.

"Not now," he said, annoyed. "I'm afraid I've been called away. Come back this afternoon."

"I can't," she said. "I need to speak with you right away. It's about the…" She searched for the right word to get his attention. "It's about the runes, professor."

"Yes, yes," he said. "It's all over campus. I'm on my way to look at them now. Walk with me if you like, but I'm in a hurry."

Zoë thought quickly. She needed to speak with him alone, with his undivided attention. "You don't want to go there now, professor. It's a zoo. Besides, I have pictures."

The professor stopped and turned, his face lighting up.

"I was a student here in 1979, did you know that?" he asked, and Zoë's face involuntarily betrayed her.

"Ah, so you do know," he said, and turned back to his office, opening the door. "Well, come in, Miss. Show me what you've got."

"Zoë," she said. "I'm in your Modern Languages class."

"I'm sorry," he replied with a shrug. "After twenty years of teaching, you all look the same to me. Never been good with faces."

"Forget about it," Zoë said, sitting in a chair across from her professor, who looked like a scarecrow dressed in a sports jacket.

"You know, I never saw the writing back in Seventy-Nine," he said. "Only heard about it afterward. Andersson House was a girls-only residence back then – none of this modern, co-ed stuff. Teachers at the time tried to downplay it as only a rumour. Nobody was caught, of course. But then, they didn't have security cameras in the residences back in the Seventies like they do now, either. Whoever did it this time, well, I'd say their days are numbered."

Zoë shifted nervously and scrolled through her phone, hoping the writing hadn't disappeared like her scratches had.

"Here," she sighed in relief when she found them. "What do you make of this?"

ᛊᚢᚱᛏᚱ ᛏᚼᛁ ᛈᚻᛁᚼᛁ ᚾᛁᛚ ᛒᚱᛁᚼᚤ
ᛈᛚᚻᚤᛗ ᛏᚻ ᛁᚻᚤᚾᛚᛈ ᛏᚼᛁ ᚾᛁᚱᛗ
ᛏᚼᛁ ᛁᚻᛁ ᚦ ᛏᚼᛁ ᛁᛗ ᛈᛁᛏᛗ
ᛈᛁᚻᚱᛁᚱ ᛏᚼᛁ ᚾᛁᛏᛈ
ᛈᛁᛚ ᚾᛁᛏᛁᚻ
ᚱᛁᛈᛁᚻᚱᛁᛈ
ᚱᛁᛈᛁᚻᚱᛁᛈ
ᚱᛁᛈᛁᚻᚱᛁᛈ

"My God," the professor sighed in awe, and then broke into laughter.

"What?" Zoë asked, confused, and a little annoyed.

"Well, it's rough – I mean, the Vikings didn't really write letter by letter, but this is a sort of Rune writing, as you noted. I'd say this is closest to the Short Twig variation, used in the 8th to 10th Century or thereabouts in Norway and Sweden. They're sometimes called the Rök runes."

He pulled a large, leather-bound book off his shelf and placed it tenderly on his desk in front of her.

"My guess is someone's been reading the *Eddas*," he said, opening the book. Zoë saw more of the same type of writing.

"What is this?" she asked.

"Norse Mythology," he said. "All the stories of Odin and Thor and Loki and Freya and Balder the brave."

"So what does the writing say?"

He looked at it again, and scoffed.

"This is terrible," he said.

"What? What does it say?"

"Oh, it's not that. It's just so… *wrong.*"

Zoë tried to remain patient.

"Right. Well, this first part says: *Surtr the giant will bring flames to engulf the world.* Surtr is a jötunn… uh, a giant. And he's depicted in the *Eddas* as having an enormous flaming sword. The next lines read: *The end of the old gods.* Then… oh, here we are. *Fenrir the Wolf, Kill Woden* and then those next repeating symbols just say Ragnarök over and over again."

"Ragnarök," Zoë whispered. "The end of the world."

"Oh no," the professor corrected. "Not at all. Ragnarök is not the end. Just the end for the old gods. In Norse Mythology, even the gods die, and what comes after is new and peaceful."

"What's this talk about Fenrir the Wolf and Woden?"

"Fenrir the Wolf is Loki's son, and during Ragnarök, it's said he will devour Odin. Then Odin's son Vidar kills Fenrir, and Surtr sets fire to the world."

"How does he kill Fenrir?" Zoë asked, needing to hear it spoken.

"He stabs him in the throat," he replied.

Zoë went pale with grim realization.

"She thought she was bringing about Ragnarök," she said. "She's trying to do it again."

"I'm sorry, you're not making any sense. Who are you talking about? Do you know who did this? You do, don't you?"

151

"I'm sorry," Zoë said, standing up. "I really have to go. I need to stop this. She's going to try to do it again."

The professor gave her a strange look. "But this is all just mythology, dear. There is no Ragnarök. No gods; no twilight of the gods."

"I know that!" Zoë said. "But she's fucking crazy!"

Running until she feared her heart might explode in her chest, Zoë left the campus grounds, hoping that distance might give her clarity. It really didn't, and that made her fearful for her own wits.

By the time she returned back to Andersson House that evening, the graffiti had already been removed, and the whole place smelled of fresh paint.

Of course, Zoë thought with a cynical grin. *It wouldn't do to leave it up and encourage more vandalism.*

She wondered how long it would be before pictures started showing up online.

They came for her first thing the next morning. Zoë was still sleeping when the knock came at the door, and when she woke, she found herself covered in hair – she'd shaved her head in the middle of the night.

Well, somebody did, she thought grimly.

She threw on some pants and shoes and opened the door. A campus security officer stood looking very serious and stern.

"Come with me, please," he said, not even bothering to identify himself or ask if she was whom he was looking for.

Zoë nodded and closed the door behind her

and stepped into the hospital corridor. She felt a sick, anxious feeling in the pit of her stomach. Every step she took toward the Wolf hurt her – she could feel the knife lodged inside her, and clenched her buttocks tightly to make sure it stayed put until she needed it. Father Andrew had come to pray with her for the last time. He knew she was frightened about the trepanning, and there was no telling what might be left of her memory or personality once the procedure was finished. She'd kissed him once on each cheek and then once softly on the lips, and told him to go in peace, to leave this place tonight and never come back. She told him that she believed he was a good man, and that if he stayed overlong in this place, it would stain his soul. He thanked her, and led her out the door and down to the office where the Wolf waited hungrily. She didn't want to believe that Father Andrew knew what awaited her, but feared that he did, and was powerless to stop it.

They reached the office of the Wolf, and

the security officer excused himself. Zoë stood in the doorway as the Dean, a burly man with large circles of sweat under his arms and a face as red as a ripe tomato regarded her with contempt.

"Please, sit," he said, motioning to a chair.

Zoë sat, watching the man cautiously. There was a smell about him – the same smell she had first encountered when she'd stepped into the vision of the psychiatric hospital – a coppery, blood-soaked smell that she associated with pennies, and madness.

"We know it was you," he said gruffly, and scratched a stray itch behind his ear. "Don't bother denying it. We've got you on video. Why did you do it? What's it mean?"

Zoë felt a buzzing in her ear, and caught a whiff of urine and rot.

"Did you hear me?" he repeated, raising his voice as his face turned from pink to crimson. "I said

I know it was you, you little whore!"

The Wolf grabbed her by the throat and lifted her up off the floor.

"My daddy gave me that knife, and I'll see you gutted with it before the night's through! You can't get anything past me, you filthy, little lunatic. I'm the Wolf, right? Isn't that what you all call me?"

Sigga struggled to breathe, her eyes popping wide out of her face in terror.

"I'm going to find it, and I'm going to show you who's

afraid of the Big Bad Wolf?"

Zoë snapped back to attention.

"What did you say?" she asked, all the blood draining from her face.

"I spoke to your father this morning," the Dean said, ignoring her. Zoë wasn't sure she was hearing things correctly.

"No," she said. "My father, he's…"

"In shock is what he is," the huge man said, standing up and moving around behind her. One meaty hand fell on her shoulder. "He wants this to just go away. But I told him

you need to be punished."

The Wolf pushed her to her knees and held her head against the bulge of his crotch, and with his other hand, he reached into her ratty gown and tore at one of her emaciated breasts, making her howl in pain.

"Open your mouth," he said, and Sigga tried to pull away. "I said

open your mouth!"

Zoë turned her head and nearly knocked it against the Dean's erect penis. He grabbed at her head, unable to get a grip without hair. Zoë looked up at him as his face took on a lewd and lusty grin. His eyes were vacant and dark.

"What are you doing?" she cried, and tried to pull away from him. "Stop this! This isn't you!"

He grabbed Zoë's head and pulled it back, and tried to force himself into her mouth. Zoë thought for a moment about biting him, but wasn't sure she could do it. What might he do to her if she did?

"Who's afraid of the Big Bad Wolf?" he growled, and broke into a throaty chuckle. "You all are, that's who!"

He reached one of his gigantic paws down Zoë's top and rummaged around. Zoë squirmed and cried, and didn't know if she could fight the big man

The Wolf! The Wolf!

off for very much longer. She was experiencing only a small taste of what Sigga must have gone through, and it was enough to turn her bowels to jelly and make her break out in an icy sweat.

"Please," she pleaded. "I don't want

to die! I don't want to die!"

The Wolf pounced on her and tore off her gown, exposing her naked and scarred body, disfigured from nearly a dozen surgeries.

She said she didn't want to die, but in truth, she had prayed for it. She was so weak and sick, and after all they had taken from her, she hardly felt human anymore. Surely she would be dead soon anyway. She just didn't want it to be at the hands of this animal, the Wolf

Fenrir!"

Zoë felt the man's grip loosen slightly and she took the opportunity to pull away, and in doing so, banged her back against his desk. Turning around, she saw him standing there, mouth open in a slack-jawed gape. His eyes were dead, lifeless things, but his brow was furrowed in rage. His pants were around his ankles and he was tugging at himself almost involuntarily, as if he were unaware he was even doing it. Zoë gagged with revulsion, and took a deep breath, just happy to be able to breathe again.

"What did you call me?" he growled. "Nobody calls me that! She called me that, the night that she killed me. That crazy, Viking bitch."

Realization dawned on her – there was nothing between them now but one little office chair, and he stood between her and the door. He seemed to realize it at the same time, and grinned and licked his lips grotesquely.

"No way out, little Sigga," the Dean said with a snarl. "I'll huff and I'll puff."

Zoë pushed herself back up onto the desk, trying to put at least a little distance between them, and knocked over a cup full of pens, pencils and other various items. She scuttled backwards like a crab, tumbling off on to the floor, and crawled under the desk. She cowered on the

floor, waiting to see what the Wolf was going to do next. He stood over her, rubbing his hand over his face as if considering how best to hurt her. She had to be patient, had to wait until he was closer before she made her move. If she revealed the knife now, he would surely wrest it away from her. No, she had to wait until he was close enough to smell, close enough that she felt the heat of his foul breath on her clammy skin.

"Get up!" he snapped. "God help you, you don't want me to make you get up!"

Sigga moaned. This, she thought. This is how I end you, Fenrir.

"I can't," she said. "I won't."

Sigga clenched her stomach muscles and managed to void her bowels – a wet, slick mess that was all she could manage since the many surgeries. But more importantly, she pushed out the knife into her hand. She tried to unfold it, and found it difficult. Suddenly, she was gripped with fear.

What if she couldn't get it open?

"I warned you, you crazy bitch," the Wolf said. "You're going to beg me to kill you before the night is through. I'm

coming for you, Sigga! Gonna have me every hole, just like in the good old days! You go ahead and hide under there. Ain't nowhere you can go. I'm going to huff and puff and blow your world down."

He uttered a chuckle, and Zoë watched the shadows moving under the desk, trembling and waiting for him to make his move. She needed a weapon. She wished she had Sigga's knife. But

the knife was stuck. Sigga tried to push herself up into a seated position, but the truth was he had beaten her badly, and her hip made a terrible grinding sound when she tried to move.

"I'll huff, and I'll puff…" the Wolf laughed, advancing on her.

Sigga's world went silent for a moment, and when the knife finally opened with a click, it was the loudest sound in the world, like a crack of thunder from Thor's mighty hammer.

The Wolf got down on his hands and knees like a beast and crawled toward her, and Sigga poured all her strength into her one hand wrapped tightly around

a brass letter opener that had fallen onto the floor when Zoë tumbled off the desk. She lunged for it, grabbing it and retreating back under the desk, bracing herself against it and waiting. She needed to wait for him to come to her. She tried to keep her breathing easy and calm, listening for his heavy footfalls.

BANG! BANG! BANG!

Zoë shrieked as something struck the desk, followed by the Dean's laughter.

"That there was a nine iron," he said, chuckling. "I got a whole bag here to try out. Graphite drivers. Very expensive. But I reckon they'll be just fine for bashing your pretty, little face in. You know, they never got around to cutting your skull up, did they? Shame, really. I was kind of looking forward to fucking that hole in your head."

He started banging on the desk again, laughing and punctuating each strike.

"Little."

BANG

"Pig."

BANG

"Little."

BANG

"Pig."

BANG

"Let."

BANG

"Me."

BANG

"In."

The Dean started banging away at the desk, and Zoë could hear him panting and wheezing.

Maybe he'll have a heart attack, she mused, but wasn't holding her breath.

Then the banging stopped, and everything got quiet.

She waited.

And waited.

And waited.

Suddenly, the desk lifted off of her, and the Wolf was on top of her.

Zoë lunged, and

the knife struck the Wolf right in the throat, just as Odin's son was to slay Fenrir, showering Sigga with his filthy blood. She feared he would fall on top of her, and that she would be crushed under his monstrous weight, but she rolled away, and he missed her by inches. He spasmed and sputtered, and Sigga gathered all her strength to pull the knife out and cut his throat all the way through, to be sure that he was dead. She looked at the blade and it shone, as if with some celestial flame.

Pushing herself up with great pain, she stood over the dead Wolf and spat on him. "Fenrir, you are slain. Ragnarök has come."

In the Wolf's den, there was a supply of lamp oil. The interior of the hospital had all been converted to electric light, but there were still gaslights along the pathways of the hospital grounds. Sigga picked up the tin, and rummaged through the Wolf's desk for a pack of wooden matches.

Dipping the blade in the oil, she then lit a match and set it on fire.

"I am no giant," she said, feeling bold and righteous, "but this will serve as Surtr's flaming sword."

Sigga extinguished her weapon, and naked, she carried the lamp oil down the stairs, limping along and nearly stumbling. She was dying, and she knew it. But she would complete this last thing – this last good thing and Ragnarök would be finished, and the world could begin again.

She made her way across the foyer, toward the basement stairs, pausing for a moment. A bare wall called out to be written on, but she had no ink to write with but the dead Wolf's blood. It would have to serve.

ᚱᚨᚷᚾᚨᚱᚨᚲ

She wrote in the old runes of her ancestors, the language of the gods.

Pushing on, she dragged herself down the stairs to a small storage room, and there she poured out the ceremonial oil in a circle, and poured the rest over her head, anointing herself for the sacrifice.

She was about to light the match when she heard the children crying out for her.

"Sigga!" they called. "Sigga, what has happened?"

Sigga put down the matches and began what seemed to be an insurmountable climb back up the stairs to where the children were, all trapped behind locked doors, all just as sickly and pitiable as she.

She stopped and knelt over the dead body of the night nurse, no longer the Wolf, just a vanquished man, beyond her care. She took the keys from his belt, and placed the ring around her small wrist.

"Tell us a story, Sigga!" the children pleaded, one by one, as she released them from their rooms.

"Help me," she said. "Come with me, and I'll tell you a story about the twilight of the gods, but more importantly, about what comes after Ragnarök."

The children helped Sigga down the stairs to the tiny room, and when she had locked the door and knelt in the circle, the children huddled around her and wept, as she told them how Fenrir devoured the All-Father, and cheered as she told them how Vidar slew Fenrir and tore his jaws open. They were very still as Sigga told them that Ragnarök was not the end, nervous as she explained to them how the world would burn, and terrified as she struck the match.

Emily sat on the stairs and wept. She'd been calling Zoë's name for at least ten minutes, but she wasn't responding. Sirens rang out in the distance, and soon, men in uniforms would come and take her friend away.

"Zoë!" she cried. "Zoë, please snap out of this!"

But Zoë didn't flinch, didn't blink, didn't waver at all.

She sat on the floor of the basement of Andersson House, covered in blood, flicking her pink lighter on, off, on, off, on, off, and muttering to herself.

"Ragnarök is come. Ragnarök is come. Ragnarök is come."

Luther – Now

Luther put down the folder labeled 'Zoë' and went to a cupboard and pulled out a bottle of Captain Morgan. Sweet and spicy, just like the cigarettes he smoked. His hands trembled. The last two stories he'd read – the one about the cross-dressing Frankenstein wannabe and now this last one – disturbed him. There was something there, something almost familiar, but he couldn't put his finger on it.

"Whoever wrote them is mighty fucked up," he said with a dry chuckle, and took a swig of the dark rum right from the bottle. "Sounds like someone wants to kill their creator."

The detective stopped and stared out the window for a moment, eyes drawn to a flash of lightning.

"Kill their creator?" he mused. "What a strange thing for me to say. Why not say parents? What the hell is wrong with me? Next I'll be talking like that rubbernecker, Simon…"

He'd put a pin in that. Something told him that Simon had read these same stories – either that, or whoever wrote them filled his head with this same crazy bullshit, which meant that Simon must know who it was.

He thought about having another drink, but knew that if he did, he wouldn't stop at just one more. He had to go back to the hospital. He still hadn't had a look at those bodies, and nothing in these stories gave him any clue to either who killed the patients, or how it was accomplished. If Dr. Chandra and Dr. Browning had given him these stories – these fantastic, and clearly fictional stories – as a way to try to convince him that something paranormal or supernatural had happened, they would be disappointed. Luther had no idea how it had been done, but was sure the culprit was as human as anyone else. Maybe it was his lack of imagination, or his inability to appreciate fiction, but he just couldn't bring himself to believe in ghosts or monsters. People, ten times out of ten, were the real monsters. He wasn't closed-minded – he just wasn't gullible. He'd seen things that others said were impossible, and he'd accepted them. He believed what he could see with his eyes, even if he couldn't explain it. He'd seen those bodies, torn apart, and while it seemed impossible, he couldn't argue with what he'd seen. He supposed that if he were to meet a ghost, or if it could be proven to him that the culprit was something otherworldly in some objective and rational way, he would be forced to believe it. Until then, he'd remain clear-headed and hold tight to his healthy skepticism.

He sat back down in an old, beat-up barcalounger, lit a cigarette and picked up the stack of folders, thumbing through the ones he'd already read. He wasn't looking for anything, really. It was just something for his hands to do while he thought. As he flipped through, a page fell out and onto the floor. It was one of the handwritten pages from a story he'd already read.

He picked it up, looked at it and frowned.

It was a photocopy – they all were. Luther had asked about the writer but Dr. Chandra had deflected his questions. He hadn't thought to ask about the original source. He hoped that the doctors had kept it, because something was happening to the copies.

The words were fading, slowly disappearing from the page.

LIZA

Z oë tells the story just as Jessica has written it – at least, all the parts she was present for. She called for the death of the old gods – in Jessica's case I believe this is a defiant declaration of rebellion against societal norms and expectations. Or perhaps I am understating, because I am, in truth, a bit afraid of the alternative. If Jessica is this singularity – this post-human intelligence that will eclipse humanity – then that will mean that the rest of us are no longer necessary for Jessica's continued existence. I find myself in the camp of those being eclipsed, and it is very cold in the dark.

Clearly Jessica sees herself as transcending, becoming. Jessica calls it becoming REAL, but I believe that she is trying to break free of some influence, perhaps a father figure or mentor, or perhaps the very concept of god. She is trying to declare her independence, by symbolically killing that oppressive figure and bringing about Ragnarök – which, as she insists, is not the end of the world, just the end of the old world and the birth of the new.

I think that these stories are the most valuable piece of data that we have gathered. They speak volumes about her motivations, and further, what drives her. First, we have a desperate but inept father – a pathetic failure who is haunted by his own creation, which has surpassed him. Then we have a monster, created by another monster. Who does Jessica see herself as in these stories? Is she the child that left carnage in her wake, or is she the monster bent on killing her creator, punishing them for their wickedness?

The story of Victor/Mary is a classic case of Freudian conflict resolution. Victor desires to both destroy and create. He is Mr. Jekyll and Mrs. Hyde. He creates Mary to commit the crimes he, as

161

a student of medicine, cannot bring himself to do by himself and then, as Victor, benefits from her crimes, and justifies it in the name of science.

What does she mean to tell us with the stories of Liza and Bren? Are the names significant? Are they connected? I guess we'll know soon. Jessica has told us where to find them both. She warned us that Liza might be difficult, and to keep her out of the reach of fire. I dread this one. What kind of damaged soul will she be? Will she be physically deformed?

What will Jessica bring us next?

Transcript of Group Session
Present: Harris, The Man, Victor, Zoë, Liza, Bren, Jessica
Dr. Naveena Chandra and Dr. Michael Browning moderating.
Two Days Ago

Dr. Chandra: There are seven of you now. Some say seven is a number of power. Do any of you have any thoughts on this?
Harris: It's a prime number. Indivisible except by itself.
Dr. Chandra: Good. I like that. Indivisible.
Jessica: Except by itself, Doc. Don't forget that last part.
Dr. Browning: Thank you, Jessica. Any other thoughts?
Bren: Seven days of creation in the Bible.
Jessica: Thou shalt not kill. Thou shalt not bear false witness. Thou shalt not have any other gods before me.
Victor: I don't believe in god. Man is in charge of his own destiny.
Jessica: Oh, and my personal favourite: Anyone who dares to kill Cain will suffer vengeance seven times over. Who doesn't love a god that can bear a grudge, am I right, Victor? Victor?
Victor: I think it's petty and ridiculous. If god – or the gods – are no better than us with their vices and wrath, then why serve or worship them?
Zoë: Why am I here? I'm not crazy. You people are crazy.
Dr. Chandra: Nobody is crazy, Zoë. Please don't use that word. You are all very special. Dr. Browning and I would like to explore what it is that makes you different.
Harris: I don't understand that at all. There's nothing different or special about me. I came to you. Me. I came to you with information, and you've kept me here like a prisoner.

Dr. Browning: You're no one's prisoner, Harris. You agreed to help us with the study.

Harris: Then why do I feel like the bug under the microscope – no offense – just like these others?

Dr. Chandra: We want to help you understand what happened to Mark.

Liza: Who's Mark?

Jessica: His invisible boy. Harris here is the Modern Prometheus. Or, you know, the *modern* Modern Prometheus. Like Mary Shelley meets William Gibson, only whiney. I'm getting bored with him, if you want to know the truth. I thought it would go further, but instead of a madman, I got a maudlin drunk. Sometimes it just works out that way.

Victor: What the hell are you talking about?

Zoë: Never mind her, she's fucking crazy. Remember what she said about us before?

Dr. Browning: Please, let's forget about what was said before. I wonder if maybe we should discuss what you all have in common.

Dr. Chandra: I'm not sure that's...

Jessica: Oh goody! Dad's trying to outrank Mommy. No, let's hear it. I'm dying to see if you've figured it all out yet.

Dr. Chandra: I don't think this is a good idea, Dr. Browning. I think this will just upset everyone.

Victor: I want to hear what you think we all have in common. I don't belong here. I have important work to do. I'm a scientist, for God's sake – a medical professional on the verge of an incredible breakthrough. Don't you realize what you're keeping me from?

Jessica: Oh, you're a professional now?

Victor: Yes, as a matter of fact. As for who you are...

Zoë: She's the devil.

Liza: She's not the devil. I've seen the devil. He's made of fire.

Zoë: Yeah, well, that figures.

Dr. Browning: As for what you all have in common...

The Man: We're all villains.

Zoë: Zarathustra speaks!

Victor: What did he say?

The Man: What do you know of Nietzsche?

Zoë: Is that Nietzsche? I thought that was just a word. You know, like Jumanjii. I just thought it was funny.

Dr. Browning: What do you know of Nietzsche, uh... dammit, I'm not calling him *The Man.*

The Man: God is dead. Man is but a stepping stone between apes and... *something else.*

Jessica: Transcendence. Yes, this is the one.

Liza: I'm no villain. I've done nothing wrong.

Bren: Your voice. It reminds me of someone... and she was a villain. Whatever you did, was it worth what happened to you? Did you enjoy yourself enough to be burnt like a shrivelled chicken wing?

Liza: Do you see? Do you see?

Jessica: Hmm. Maybe you are real after all, Chicken Wing.

Dr. Browning: Jessica, please. You're not helping.

Jessica: Bite me, Doc. Right here in the soft bits.

Dr. Browning: Oh, that's enough. Nurse, please bring Jessica's sedative.

Jessica: Oh, is it time to trip the light fantastic already?

Liza: Make her stop! Make her stop! What's wrong with her!

Dr. Chandra: Please, Liza. Please calm down.

Jessica: Yes, Liza, do calm down, or the good Dr. Mengele here will be forced to get a candle.

Liza: Oh no, Doctor, please. (*Sobbing*) You're not going to try to burn me again, are you?

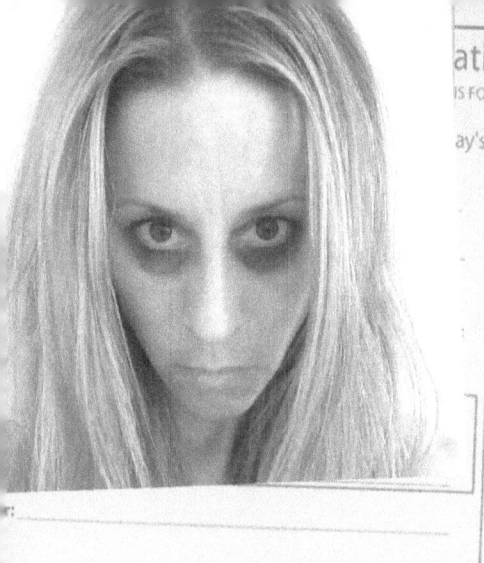

atient Data

ay's Date:_____

Insurance Information

Name of Company:_____

Name of Insured:_____

Insureds DOB:_____ SS#:_____

Patient consents to participate in trials, completion of which will be at the discretion of the supervising physicians. Resititution will be paid at the end of the study.

Signature of Patient:_____

Print Name: *Liza*

Date:_____

r:_____

s office by: ☐ Web Site ☐ Yellow Pages ☐ Advertisement

ily Member Name:_____

ervices will be by: ☐ Cash ☐ Check ☐ Credit Card ☐ Health Insurance ☐ Automobile Insurance

ed by more than one insurance company? ☐ Yes ☐ No Name_____

led suicide? Patient presented in Emergency Department
d had to be prevented from hurting herself. She was
~~ed with ~~~ ~~of~~ ~~~ ~~~ ~~pert~~ ~~~~~~
- the most practical of suicide methods, but if she'd
ceeded, an effective -- and unusually violent -- method.
iously to be handled with extreme caution.

eated by a physician for any health condition in the last year? ☐ Yes ☐ No

n_____

_____ Date of Last Physical Exam_____

tment:

Y: ☐ NONE

_____ Date:_____
_____ Date:_____
_____ Date:_____

a metal implant? ☐ Yes ☐ No   Ever been gunshot? ☐ Yes ☐ No
Y: ☐ Job ☐ Auto ☐ Other 1._____ Date:_____
☐ Job ☐ Auto ☐ Other 2._____ Date:_____
☐ Job ☐ Auto ☐ Other 3._____ Date:_____

LIZA

Her hand was all-absorbing.

White, like the bones within it, and still fading from violent pink in places, at the edges of the scars.

Liza focused intently, caressing her vision around the scalloped edges of her knuckles and along to her wrist, which was still bandaged. Greasy ointment shone out from under it, catching the light and leaving a smear on her hospital gown. She wondered how much longer the ointment would be necessary, and wished that it helped the bandages stop from sticking.

That said – it could be worse without the grease.

The warm baths and cracking, stinging agony could be worse. The tugging and pulling and tender, white strips of new skin coming away with every pull could be worse. The bathwater turning pink, and the distaste and pain and pity on the faces of the nurses assigned to her, and the fact that she was sitting in a soup of her own blood every few days, could be worse.

"The patient has been unable to speak. Or unwilling." A lofty, disdainful voice, somewhere in the ether of her memory, discussing her as though she wasn't there. She tuned out, reducing the words to white noise as she concentrated.

She remembered the tan she used to cultivate, slipping into bikinis each summer and finding the most luscious spots in the garden to nestle down on a blanket with a book, in full blaze of the sun. Her new skin would no longer hold a tan.

She remembered waking up, the world whited out around her, brain fogged with medication, and a dull, throbbing pulse through her whole being, letting her know that something was horribly, awfully wrong.

The reports said the car had been hit from behind as the truck jack-knifed. It had been scooped up in the V shape between the tanker and the cab, and pushed along next to wheels, which spun futilely, trying to bring a halt to inevitable destruction. She remembered thinking that the wheel, which was right outside her window, was so big that it could have crushed the entire car.

Liza centred herself briefly, painfully, on the knowledge that the spinning and sliding and pushing had stopped. The airbags deflated, and it was time to go. Hot tears sprung from her eyes and bubbled down her face as she remembered the trap, which began next. The nothing moving. The splashing and pouring of liquid from somewhere broken. The fumes which snuck upwards and tore her lungs, the grey pall which followed as the temperature rose and her panic rose and the sound of her screams rose and rose and rose.

Her hand moved, almost imperceptibly.

She watched it, entranced, tears still dripping.

She remembered the frantic, desperate strength, which came from nowhere as the heat around her turned into glowing embers, which licked into flames. She remembered her body straining, cracking, breaking against the seat belt, wrapped in malice around her, unyielding. She remembered frantic, searing breaths, throat snapping, eyes rolling, blood pounding. She remembered the agony as everything she touched turned to burning, and the rancid scent of hair on fire and clothes on fire and flesh on fire curled into her nostrils as her nose and fingers melted, no longer painful.

She remembered welcoming the blackness, no longer plagued by such a disturbing reality.

So many memories.

"Eighty percent of her body, much of it third degree, some fourth. Astonishing that she lived."

Liza continued to watch her hand, astonished.

It twitched, bones rippling as if her non-existent fingers were practicing for the task ahead.

Having been catatonic for months, the walk outside had tired her. Legs stretched to the breaking point and beginning to bleed where scars and fresh skin had parted company, bandages seeping.

Outside. Not her garden, but outside nonetheless, with birds singing and leaves blowing in the breeze, and the scent of sunshine on earth. Things were growing – she could almost hear them. She remembered before, when she would have been thinking about annuals and bulbs and the bubbled masses of tadpoles-to-be, just under the surface of the pond.

Exhausted, she let herself fall – knees in the dirt, her hospital gown soaked through, and a puddle forming around her.

On top of a rock, out of the puddle, next to the gas canister, lay a packet of matches.

This time, no more memories.

Michael and Naveena — Six Weeks Ago

When Dr. Chandra and Dr. Browning found Liza, she was already in the hospital. She'd walked right in carrying a gas can and a pack of matches. She was a frail, little thing, and it didn't take much for hospital security to wrestle the gas can away from her and put her in restraints. Jessica told the doctors where they'd find her, and so Dr. Browning arranged for her to be transferred to Ward C, under the pretence that she was there for psychiatric evaluation.

The doctors were equally fascinated and horrified by Liza's behaviour. It was strange that while Zoë seemed fascinated by fire, and had confessed to having dreams about burning everything down, Liza was so completely terrified of fire. Dr. Browning suggested, and Dr. Chandra had agreed, that it was best that the two were kept far apart.

Maintaining her belief that Jessica was imposing her will on the other patients, Dr. Chandra thought she knew what was happening. What was remarkable was that Liza — the woman in the bed in front of her, not the Liza from the story — had no burns whatsoever. Physically, there seemed to be nothing wrong with her. And yet, they observed her picking at invisible wounds, crying out in non-existent pain, and demanding to have her bandages changed.

Dr. Browning insisted that they didn't indulge the woman, that they try to work through her delusion.

"How much should the patients know about themselves, do you imagine?" Naveena asked. "How strong is their belief?"

"You know as much as I do," Michael said. "Even under hypnosis, every patient has maintained their identity, sticking to the story they originally told us — something resembling those stories you took from Jessica's notebook. Well, except for The Man. Can't get him to talk at all."

"He has proven more difficult than the others," Dr. Chandra agreed.

A cry came from the ward. It was Liza, screaming in pain.

"She's at it again," Michael said. "Shall I give her a sedative?"

"No," Naveena said. "Come with me; I have an idea. And bring a lighter."

Luther – Now

They had her. He didn't know how she came to Ward C, or what they were trying to pull with that story, but it was too close to the case he'd been working on to be coincidence. He had to see her body. If this Liza was the same woman, he had to know. He hadn't gotten a real good look at the mangled bodies, but hers should be pretty easy to identify. The woman had walked away from a horrible accident, but she'd been burned beyond recognition. Luther had thought at the time that perhaps it would have been better for her if she'd died. If this was her, at least she was out of her misery.

He threw the folders in an old, leather briefcase – even though the pages of some of the stories had faded completely. Luther couldn't remember the name of the man whose son had died and…

"Fuck!" he swore. His mind was a blank. He had to get back to the hospital to find out about Liza. She was the only thing so far that he could prove – the only thing so far that made sense to him. He had nothing to go on as far as the identity of the other victims was concerned, but if he could identify Liza, at least he had somewhere to start.

He grabbed his briefcase and raincoat and headed back into the storm.

Michael and Naveena – Six Weeks Ago

Michael grabbed Naveena by the arm.

"What are you doing?"

"Let me go, doctor," she said firmly. "I'm not going to hurt her, I promise you. On the contrary, I believe we are about to witness something extraordinary."

Dr. Chandra approached Liza slowly and stood by the woman's side and spoke in a low, calming voice. "Let me see your arm, Liza."

The woman stopped screaming and looked up with tear-soaked eyes.

"It's okay," she said. "I'm not going to hurt you. I just want to attend to your wounds."

Liza held out a trembling arm, supporting it tenderly with her other hand, as if she were too weak to lift it otherwise.

Michael stared at her, insistent.

"Dr. Chandra, might I have a word?"

"What?" she turned and said, practically hissing.

"Just one moment, Miss," Michael said, smiling at Liza as she held her arm out for examination. "You can put your arm down if you're more comfortable."

Naveena followed Michael until they were out of earshot of the patients.

"Look, I know you thought that these patients would be special like Jessica," he said in a hush, "but they're not. At best these people are delusional – they're sick, Naveena – or, if I am to believe what you suggest, then they are innocent victims."

"I'm not going to hurt her," she replied. "Trust me. I want to test something to see how far her delusion goes. I want to see the extent of the power that Jessica holds over them. That woman in there believes – completely – that she is covered in third degree burns. She holds herself in such a way that she displays all the behaviours of someone healing from those kinds of wounds. She cries out in what I believe is actual pain. I want to know if the power of this delusion that Jessica has inflicted upon her is strong enough to create physical symptoms."

"What do you mean? You mean burns?"

"Precisely!" she said.

"No, Naveena," Michael said. "I won't let you do this. This is wrong."

"I'm not going to hurt her," she repeated. "I'm not asking you to watch. Just get out of my way."

"If you do this, I won't be held responsible for any harm that you cause. I want you to understand that. I will deny all involvement."

"Yes, yes," Dr. Chandra said with a dismissive wave of her hand. "I absolve you. Now get out of my way."

She pushed past him and returned to Liza, smiling widely at her. "I'm sorry about that, Liza. Here, let me see your arm."

Liza did as she was instructed. She couldn't possibly suspect the doctor's intentions. Dr. Chandra held the pale, thin wrist gently at first, and then gripped it tightly, eliciting a yelp of surprise from Liza. With her other hand, she pulled out a green BIC lighter and flicked her thumb over the top, producing a small flame.

Liza's eyes went wide with fright, and she began screaming in terror. Dr. Chandra felt the woman's skin go hot and gooey, and she pulled her hand away, peeling some of her skin away with it. She gasped as she saw the woman's flesh bubble and blister, as if she were being burned alive. She backed away, dropping the lighter and nearly stumbling over her own feet.

Dr. Browning came running at the sound of screaming, and yelled at Naveena to get some ointment and bandages. He knelt by Liza's bedside and tried to calm the woman down. As the screaming slowed, he could hear a cackling laughter coming from one of the other beds in the ward. Only one person laughed like that.

"Jessica," he cursed under his breath, and left Liza to stop the laughing woman.

When he reached Jessica, she was laughing so hard that she had tears in her eyes and was doubled over, holding her stomach.

"What have you done?" he demanded, and Jessica kept laughing until she fell out of bed.

"I'm sorry. I'm sorry," she said, catching her breath and pulling herself back up onto the bed. "You're all just so fucking funny."

"What have you done?" he repeated, and Jessica began laughing again.

Michael slapped her across the face, and Jessica put her hand to her cheek, her fingers tracing the red handprint that was rising on her too-pale skin like a child's finger-painting.

"Oooh," she moaned, wiping a small trickle of blood from the corner of her mouth with one finger and then sucking on it suggestively. "You got any more where that came from?"

"What have you done to her, you monster?"

Jessica sighed. "It's not like they're real, Dr. No-Fun. They're just my toys, and when I bore with them, I'll wipe the slate clean and start all over. Consider this an experiment. You know all about experimenting, right, Doctor? How's the hubby? And the boyfriends – how are they?"

Jessica reached a hand up and took her breast in her hand and pinched her nipple, biting her bottom lip and cooing. "You ever been with a woman, Doc?"

"Stop it," he said. "You're being ridiculous."

"Just trying to see what I can do, Doctor. Just stretching my muscles, learning what I'm capable of."

"Well, stop it. Why does it have to be pain? Why are you subjecting them to so much pain?"

"Because I think it's funny," Jessica said. "And without their pain, they would be nothing. Maybe with enough pain, they could be real."

"What is this all about – this *real* you keep talking about? Of course they're real."

"No," Jessica said, and she stopped laughing. Her smile was replaced with something dark and dangerous. "No, they're not. They're not real."

"What do you mean, they're not real? They are flesh and blood, like…"

"Like me? Am I real?" Jessica locked eyes with the man, but he looked away.

"Of course," he said, turning away, feeling suddenly ill.

"Oh, don't be so quick, Doctor," Jessica said. "They're not real. They're just sketches. They've not much personality, just what god gave them."

☙

Dr. Chandra returned, holding a tube of burn cream and a roll of gauze, both of which were unnecessary – by the time she'd returned, Liza's arm had returned to its previously unblemished state. The woman still cried in pain and cradled her arm as if it were injured, but there was nothing physically wrong with it. All that remained was a faint smell of burnt flesh, and the woman's tears.

"You mean what you gave them," Naveena said.

Jessica shrugged, crossed her legs like a Zen master in the lotus position, and shrugged.

"I am what I am," she said. "And none of them are real."

"What the hell do you mean, I'm not real?" Harris was the first to protest. Zoë and Liza followed. The Man said nothing, but instead mimicked Jessica's lotus pose and stared at her with murder in his eyes.

"Hey, fuck you!" Zoë said. "You're just as crazy as the rest of us."

"I'm not crazy," Harris insisted. "I'm here to help. I need to know what happened to my son."

"What school did Mark go to, Harris?" Jessica asked. "When's his birthday? What's his favourite colour?"

"I… that is…" Harris stammered.

"And you," Jessica said, turning her attention to Zoë. "Remember that time in tenth grade when you were on that class trip, and you sat in the back of the bus, and Andy McCullough took your hand and put it down his pants, and you felt him get all hard, and you were excited and scared, but when he tried to put his hand up your skirt, you bit him. You bit him…"

"I bit him so hard on his cheek that I drew blood, and he got so angry, but at the same time, I hadn't let go of him, and he squirted all over me, and I pulled my hand out of his pants and I was covered with his jizz on my hand and his blood in my mouth. I've never been so aroused as I was that day."

"What the hell?" Dr. Browning said.

"But I don't remember that!" Zoë shouted, confused. "That never happened! I don't remember that!"

"You do now," Jessica grinned, and Zoë rushed at her, screaming in rage.

"Enough of this!" Dr. Browning said, holding back Zoë. "Please Jessica, you're upsetting everyone. Dr. Chandra, will you please take Jessica to the meditation area?"

"Oooh," Jessica said, grinning and following Dr. Chandra. "I get to do some drugs!"

Michael calmed Zoë and Harris down, apologizing for Jessica's behaviour and giving them each a sedative. He checked on Liza and considered giving the woman some pain medication, but still thought it was a bad idea. Instead, he gave her a sedative, telling her it was Morphine. He peeked in on Victor, who had somehow slept through the whole thing. Living a double life seemed to burn the man out, and while sometimes he would be awake for days at a time, sometimes as Victor and sometimes as Mary, eventually he would crash and sleep for twelve hours or more at a time. Michael thought this was probably for the best – Mary took great offence at any suggestion that she wasn't real. If you believed the story Jessica had written about her, she was dangerous – they all were, really – and he was sure that putting them all together was bound to result in one or more of them attacking one of the others. If he were a betting man, he would put his money on Victor – or rather, Mary. Lastly, he made sure that the patient known only as The Man was behaving himself. Since the two women had arrived, he hadn't had any violent outbursts, and while he was still heavily sedated, he was no longer in his restraints. He left the new nurse – whose name he still didn't know – in charge of the ward while he went to find Naveena in the meditation room. When he found her, Jessica was sitting cross-legged on the floor, her clothes changing as if of their own volition. Her hospital gown vanished and morphed into a black cat suit like Emma Peel made famous on that old British spy show long before anyone had ever heard of *The Matrix*. Then the cat suit melted and morphed into a black tank top and tight-fitting jeans. An Ankh hung around a thin leather string around her neck. Outfits changed in rapid succession, ranging from dirty rags to exquisite gowns to strange costumes. At one point she wore the robe and beaked mask of a seventeenth century plague doctor, the next moment she was naked, and the two doctors watched as her body was slowly covered with tattoos, crawling on her skin like vines, painting her body with strange swirls and cabalistic symbols. Then more clothes, an ever-changing series of outfits being materialized out of thin air. It wasn't even the strangest thing that they had seen her do.

"What the hell was that?" Michael asked, not taking his eyes off of Jessica, who currently resembled a witch from a Brothers Grimm folk tale.

"Confirmation," Naveena said. "It was everything I had imagined, and more."

"What were you thinking, provoking her like that? She's crazy."

"She's not," she said. "And you know it."

"Well, then, what are you trying to accomplish? You heard her – when she gets bored of them, she'll scrap the whole thing and start over. What's she going to do with us when she's done?"

"Please," Naveena dismissed him. "You heard her – they aren't real."

"That's bullshit. Whoever those people really are, they are just as real as you or I. What's going to happen to their minds when she releases whatever hold she has on them?"

"So you do believe, then?"

"What choice do I have?"

"Isn't it amazing?" she asked, watching intently as Jessica dressed herself in an intricate, black, lace outfit that clung to her body like a second skin. "As fictional characters, they would only have access to whatever biographical information that the writer gave them. Superfluous facts not relevant to the plot would be unknown. They might not know their age, their family make up, or their favourite food, or if they've ever seen *The Simpsons*. The less a character is developed, the weaker they seem to be. More two-dimensional. Take The Man for example. He is little more than an archetype – he doesn't even seem to know who he is, and his grasp of reality is tenuous and fragile."

"I hate to repeat myself, but what is going to happen to him when she is finished?"

"I don't know," Dr. Chandra admitted, and then tore her gaze away from Jessica to give Michael an excited smile. "But won't it be something to see?"

BREN

L uther came storming in from the rain like a gust of wind and slogged his way through the foyer to the elevators to take him down to Ward C. He was soaking wet and gave off silent waves of *leave me the fuck alone*. He'd parked across the street from the hospital, and the second he stepped out of his car the rain, which had been steady but light on the drive over, suddenly turned into a downpour so hard that each drop felt like a bee sting.

He was glad he'd had the foresight to put the folders into his old briefcase, otherwise they would have been reduced to a smeared, pulpy mess. He remembered Alice giving it to him when he'd made detective. She'd been so proud, and had spent way too much on the thing. He hadn't had the heart to tell her he'd never use it, and so he'd taken it to work with him every day and brought it home every night. He'd found uses for it, even if sometimes all it carried were fast food wrappers and empty cigarette packs.

Luther popped into a bathroom to dry himself off, using paper towels to soak up the rain that had pooled in his frizzy hair like dew. He set the briefcase on the counter and dried it off, too, running his hand over the worn leather, fingering a scratch it had gotten when some junkie decided to take a swing at him with a knife one night coming home from the bar. He hadn't even had a reason to have it with him, but it had become something of a security blanket after Alice left, and so he carried it everywhere he went. He was lucky he had it that night.

He shrugged off his London Fog, threw it over his shoulder like a model in a Sears catalogue and picked up his briefcase. He took one last look at himself in the mirror and paused – maybe it

176

had been a long time since he'd really taken a good look at himself, but he didn't think he'd ever seen himself so clearly. Every detail from his deep brown eyes and strong jaw – peppered with three days' worth of stubble – seemed to jump out at him. He had his father's crooked nose and his mother's shapely, full mouth. When he smiled – which was more and more rarely – he saw his mother staring back at him and it pinched at his heart. How long had it been since the aneurysm? Five years? Surely not that long – the pain still felt fresh.

He stared into the mirror and got lost for a moment, and then recovered himself and rushed out of the bathroom, a touch alarmed at the unwelcome bit of nostalgia.

He stumbled into Dr. Chandra's office, unfocused. For a moment he forgot why he was there.

"Detective?" Dr. Chandra asked. "Is there something I can help you with? Have you discovered anything?"

"The bodies," he tried to say, but his voice was caught in his throat.

"What's that?"

He cleared his throat and tried again. "I need to see the bodies. Particularly the burned one. I need to see the body of the burned woman."

"Ah, Liza," she said, and put her hands together as if in prayer and held them in front of her lips.

"Yes, Liza. I was working a case where a woman met a similar fate. Her name was also Liza. I don't believe in coincidence, Doctor."

Dr. Chandra's eyes went wide with surprise. "I'm sorry, Detective, but in this case, you'll simply have to. Our Liza couldn't have been the same woman whom you were investigating."

"Why not?" he asked.

Dr. Chandra fumbled through her desk drawer looking for something.

"Our Liza suffered from a delusion," she said, pawing through papers. "She only *thought* that she was a burn victim. In reality, she had no physical injuries at all."

"What does that mean? What does this have to do with the story I read, then? Did she think she was the woman from the story?"

Dr. Chandra pulled a portfolio out of her desk and handed it to him.

"We were very particular about Liza. She was a very special case."

"What were you people doing here?" he asked, taking the portfolio from her but not opening it. Instead, he locked eyes with her, hoping that he could intimidate her into giving him something, anything.

"We were studying the effects of the mind on the physical body," she told him. "I believe that a person can affect the physical realm with their mind. In Liza's case, she was convinced she suffered from third degree burns, and so, she suffered real pain, even in the absence of injury. If a person could convince themselves that they were in pain, to the point that their body responded in kind, is it not possible that, via the mind, a person could then heal themselves?"

"Bullshit," Luther said, and opened the portfolio. It was full of photographs.

"In our observations, we even induced physical symptoms. In the presence of an open flame, her skin would actually blister, as you can see in the pictures. After a few minutes, her wounds would disappear."

Luther dropped the portfolio on her desk, and dozens of photographs spilled out. They were all blank, unexposed.

"What kind of game are you playing, Doctor?"

"What?" Dr. Chandra said, alarmed. She picked up the pictures scattered across her desk and looked at them in disbelief. "No. No. No. This isn't right. These were all pictures documenting Liza's manifestations."

Luther opened his briefcase and pulled out the stories he'd been given to read and showed her what remained of them – all but the last – the one marked Bren – had faded to nothing.

"You know what's weird, Doc?" Luther asked angrily. "I can't remember what I read. I mean, I still have bits and pieces of it – I know there was a girl, and she was possessed by some other girl who was obsessed with Norse mythology, but for the life of me, I can't remember her name. When I try to remember it, it's like an empty space in my head – there's a buzzing like a mosquito has flown into my ear."

"Oh my god," Dr. Chandra said. "It's happening."

"What?" he asked, wanting to reach out and shake the woman.

"Not real," she muttered, eyes blank and frightened. "They're not real."

"What are you talking about?"

Dr. Chandra looked at Luther and for a moment, he thought he saw the woman swoon as if she was going to faint. "Are you…?"

"I'm fine. I'm sorry, I have to go look into something."

"Where's Dr. Browning?" Luther asked.

"I have to go find him," she said. "Excuse me."

"Hey! I need some answers!"

"I'm sorry," she said, trying to push past him.

"Who wrote these stories?" Luther asked, blocking her way with his large frame. "Where's J?"

"Let me pass, Detective. Please."

It was the *please* that broke him. He looked down in Dr. Chandra's face and saw fear in it, and it broke him. Her eyes threatened to pool over with tears and her lip trembled like a frightened child's.

"What happened here?" he asked, not as a cop, but just out of his own personal desire to know.

She shrugged, and struggled to say, "I don't know."

He stepped aside and let her pass, but then he turned and caught her arm and held her tightly.

"Please," she pleaded again. "Let me go."

"What happened here?" he asked, his fingers digging into her arm harder than he intended.

Her trembling lips whispered one word: "Ragnarök."

Luther stood in Dr. Chandra's office and tried to let it all soak in. He knew the word should mean something to him, but he couldn't remember. Ragnarök. What the hell was that supposed to mean? He had no context for such a strange word. Suddenly he wished that he could bring himself to believe in any of the things that were running through his head as possible explanations, but he couldn't. But he knew who could – Simon. Simple Simon who had tried to feed him a story about reincarnation and poltergeists. Simon, who surely knew who wrote those stories.

He left Ward C and went to the first nurse's station he could find, and asked where he might find the orderly. He thought it would be that easy, but nobody on the floor seemed to know who he was talking about. He went up to the main floor, and it was the same thing. When the elevator opened on the second floor, a familiar face greeted him, though the man didn't look happy to see him.

"I'm not supposed to talk to you," Simon said, trying to push past Luther on to the elevator.

"Says who?" Luther asked, grabbing handfuls of Simon's shirt with both hands and driving him back into the wall facing the elevator.

Simon looked side to side for help, but Luther slapped him across the face and grabbed his head in one enormous hand.

"Don't worry folks," he said loudly. "I'm Detective Luther Crowley, and I'm just asking Simon here some friendly questions. Go about your business.

"Isn't that right, Simon?"

Luther released his grip on the orderly, and the man relaxed.

"You got me in a lot of trouble," he said. "Dr. Chandra isn't happy with me."

"Well, Simon, I'm all broken up about that, but you see, I think you have a friend here, and I'd really like you to introduce me."

Simon went pale, and shook his head.

"No," he moaned. "No, you can't. She's mine, she's my special, she's my secret. You can't."

Luther resisted the urge to manhandle Simon again, and instead, tried to reason with him.

"Simon," he said in a low whisper, as if taking the man into his confidence. "I don't want to take her from you. I promise. She can stay your secret. It will be just between us guys, okay? But see, I think your secret friend might know what happened to all those people down in Ward C."

Simon flinched as if Luther had struck him.

"She had nothing to do with that," he said. "I told you what happened."

"Reincarnation and poltergeists," Luther said. "Yeah, I remember."

How long ago was that? Luther thought. *Was that really just this morning?*

"You don't believe me," Simon pouted.

"I believe that you believe, Simon," Luther said, indulging the man. "Did she tell you about what Dr. Chandra and Dr. Browning were doing?"

Simon nodded.

"Yeah, that's what I thought," Luther said. "Simon, I've got to speak to her. She might be able to shed some light on what happened."

Simon still refused, and Luther decided to try another tack.

"Simon, if Dr. Chandra or Dr. Browning hurt her, I need to know. I'm a police officer, Simon. I can punish them for what they did."

Simon looked at him hopefully and Luther knew he'd played the right card.

"You promise?"

"Of course," Luther said. "Now please. Take me to her."

Simon took him to the Maternity Ward, which was strangely quiet, Luther thought. Not one crying baby, not one screaming mother. All the way down the hall and to the left was the ward's solitary resident. Jessica sat on her bed, legs tucked under her, scribbling in her notebook, a look of disappointment and frustration on her face.

"Excuse me, Miss," Luther said, and she looked up at him and smiled. Luther felt a flutter in his midsection that was both pleasurable and uncomfortable.

"Yes, Detective," she said. "Can I help you?"

"How did you – never mind. Simon, is this her? Ma'am, do you know this man?

Jessica looked at him as if she were trying to remember him, but couldn't place him.

"No, Detective, I'm sorry. I've never seen this man before."

"What?" Simon cried.

"What are you trying to pull?" Luther asked, angrily grabbing Simon by the hair and shoving his face in Jessica's direction.

Jessica smiled in amusement, and shook her head. "Doesn't look familiar, I'm afraid."

Simon looked like he might start crying, and moaned in confusion.

"Oh, wait," Jessica said. "Is your name Peter?"

"It's Simon!" he cried. "Not Peter; Simon!"

"Hmm," Jessica said, cocking her head. "Nope, sorry. I don't know this man."

"All right," Luther said, tugging Simon away. "I've had just about enough of this bullshit."

Jessica began crowing laughter behind him.

"Oh, Detective," she called. "Come back, please. I'm just fucking with you."

Luther released Simon and gave him a swift kick in his ass and told him to get on his way.

He turned and slowly made his way back to Jessica's bed. He stood and looked at her for a moment, trying to place where he'd seen her before, but it eluded him.

"My, you are something, aren't you?" Jessica asked, taking him in and nearly purring with pleasure. "Very impressive."

"You must be J," he said.

"Jessica," she said by way of introduction. "I'd offer you my hand, or curtsy or some such ladylike nonsense, but I am anything but a lady."

"Detective Crowley," he said in return, and then added, for no reason he could think of, "Luther."

Jessica turned back to her writing, as if all that was required was an exchange of introductions, and after that, they had nothing more to say to each other. Luther was there for answers, but she was giving off a strong vibe that told him that she wasn't one for answering questions.

"Oh, fuck it," she said, and scratched out what she was writing. Then she tore out the page and ripped it into pieces and threw it on the floor.

"Tell me, Luther," she said. "What do you suppose happens to abandoned characters? Do they turn into ghosts? Do they haunt other stories, forever trapped outside, jealous and angry that they were not used to their full potential? Are their broken bodies discovered mangled by the side of the road, discarded like old beer cans? What do you think, Detective?"

Luther shuddered with a frisson of *déjà vu.*

"I don't know," he said, his voice sounding very far away to his own ears. "I'm not much for storytelling. Life is strange enough without inventing more strangeness."

"They say it's much easier to destroy than to create," Jessica said.

"Who says?" Luther asked, entranced.

"They," she said. "Them."

"Oh," Luther said. "Them. I hate Them."

Jessica laughed. "Yes. Very good. I say destruction and creation are intrinsically linked. Can't make an omelette and all that rot."

"What do you know about those bodies downstairs?"

Jessica gave him an exaggerated pout. "Oh, is that all the foreplay I get? I'm hardly even wet, and already you want to fuck? How disappointing."

Luther ignored her. His arousal embarrassed him, though he wasn't sure just why. "What do you know about those dead bodies downstairs?"

"Oh, you're no fun," Jessica said.

"The bodies?"

"What bodies?" she asked coyly.

"There were five dead bodies downstairs, torn apart like that piece of paper."

"Are you sure?" she asked, tilting her head like a puppy.

"Of course I'm sure," Luther said, exasperated. "I saw it with my own eyes."

"Well, then," Jessica said in a patronizing tone that made Luther want to choke the life right out of her. "If you saw it with your own eyes, then it must be so. Tell me, do you believe in the concept of subjective reality, Detective?"

Luther groaned. "I took one philosophy course in college. That was one too many. You can't convince me that reality is fluid, or that I can't prove the existence of anything outside of my own mind. That's bullshit. Reality is what I can touch, what I can see, what I can experience."

"And you trust your senses then?"

"Absolutely."

"And you insist that there are five dead bodies downstairs in the morgue."

"Yes."

"Are you sure?"

"Yes, goddammit!"

Jessica laughed. "Well, as long as you're sure."

Luther thought maybe he was wrong. She had no answers. She hadn't even given him a chance to ask any questions. He had about a dozen of them on his lips but couldn't manage even one. Instead, he turned on his heels and swore under his breath.

"Fucking crackhead."

"Come up and see me again, sometime, Detective," Jessica called after him in a distinctive Mae West drawl. "After you finish your last story."

Luther stopped cold. "What? How do you… ah, fuck it. Never mind."

Insurance Information

Name of Company:_____

Name of Insured:_____

Insureds DOB:_____ SS#:_____

Patient consents to participate in trials, completion of which will be at the discretion of the supervising physicians. Resititution will be paid at the end of the study.

Signature of Patient:_____

Print Name: *Brenda Kendrick*

Date:_____

er:_____

his office by: ☐ Web Site ☐ Yellow Pages ☐ Advertisement

amily Member Name:_____

Services will be by: ☐ Cash ☐ Check ☐ Credit Card ☐ Health Insurance ☐ Automobile Insurance

ered by more than one insurance company? ☐ Yes ☐ No Name_____

is convinced she is here for some sort of grief counselling, and we will
ss this in her sessions. Despite her admission that she has been neglecting
wn health, she is otherwise physically healthy.

ent may be experiencing auditory hallucinations. Has been
ved talking to an unseen person or persons

treated by a physician for any health condition in the last year? ☐ Yes ☐ No

tion_____

_____ Date of Last Physical Exam_____

eatment:_____

ORY: ☐ NONE

_____ Date:_____
_____ Date:_____
_____ Date:_____

d a metal implant? ☐ Yes ☐ No   Ever been gunshot? ☐ Yes ☐ No
RY: ☐ Job ☐ Auto ☐ Other 1._____   Date:_____
    ☐ Job ☐ Auto ☐ Other 2._____   Date:_____
    ☐ Job ☐ Auto ☐ Other 3._____   Date:_____

BREN

BREN

Bren listened to Andrew snoring lightly beside her. Satisfied that he was sleeping soundly, she slipped from beneath the sheets and stepped quietly out of the master bedroom, headed for her studio.

She entered, closed the door quietly, and then walked to one corner of *this*, her favourite room in the house with its forest-green walls and pine-framed windows that let in the early morning light. One wall was lined with the same colour pine shelves, which were stacked with photos and books and sentimental this and that. This room, complete with the wet bar she was now standing in brewing a cup of her favourite coffee, had been the selling point of the house. Once she stood in this room nothing else had mattered. A financier had built it in the late Forties and he had lived here with his wife. He had passed away long ago, his widow living past him for several years. When she died and there was no living family to claim it, Bren and Andrew in their newly-married, mostly-broke state had managed to snag it for a song. Since those days, they had managed to make plenty of money, mostly thanks to Bren's career as a ghostwriter and the sale of some of her paintings.

But this room was Bren's refuge. From the beginning, she had felt a strong pull to it, but in the past couple of years it was truly the only place she felt happy in the entire world.

Her coffee, a strong, black, silky concoction she had discovered in Costa Rica and was completely addicted to, finished brewing. With the rich aroma filling the room, Bren took a deep breath and walked slowly – almost reverently – toward the sheet covered portrait she had found in the attic shortly after they had moved in, along with some journals written in a woman's hand, children's books, and other miscellaneous items long forgotten. As a writer, it was a treasure trove. The portrait now stood on an easel against one of the deep green walls near a pine-framed window. She reached out her hand and slowly slid the cover away to reveal his face.

Henry.

Her Henry with his soft, wheat-coloured hair and nearly-invisible brows of the same colour, full, apple cheeks, and bright, pink-red lips that, at this moment, were unsmiling and pursed. Anger made his green eyes flare defiantly.

Bren felt her skin dimple in the cool air suddenly surrounding her.

"Henry," she whispered. "Don't be angry. Soon. I promise. You must learn to be more patient, dear boy."

Andrew didn't believe her when she told him that she could feel her son's presence; he chastised her for talking to him as if he were still alive. But Andrew hadn't seen the things she'd seen, hadn't seen Henry's expression change in the painting according to his moods. Maybe some things were just between a boy and his mother; she couldn't say.

The detective had called again just the day before. He had more questions for her. She would stick to her story, and no one would be the wiser.

She came to this room to center herself, and its calming effect was immediate and complete. It was here that she came to have communion with her little son. Him – and sometimes *the other one* – the one in the painting.

The coolness in the room began to fade and the furrow between Henry's brows melted away, but only slightly. He would sulk a bit longer but Bren knew he would be all right in the end. Five-year-old boys often had a sulk when they didn't get their way.

"Let me get my coffee, little man, and I will sing you one of your favourite songs. How about 'Animal Crackers in My Soup'?" she said with a sly smile as she turned to fetch her full mug, knowing the tune would cheer him.

Henry had always been special, but he was still a five-year-old boy and easily distracted.

Once she had finished the song, she saw Henry was once again smiling his cherubic smile. Only then did she dare to ask, "So, Henry, shall we wake Brodie and have a game?"

Four months earlier

"Mrs. Tinney, so lovely to see you."

Bren reached out her hand to the elderly lady seated before her. Annabeth Tinney was a slight woman who still had striking, green eyes, barely dulled by her ninety-two years. She sat straight in her chair, her elegance evident, at a quiet and private table at Bairds

— a small, neighbourhood coffee shop. Bren wondered how she must look to the old woman, her black hair pulled up into a woollen cap, a few tendrils falling loose about her make-up-bare face. She might be taking light steps back into the world but still couldn't find the energy to put much work into her appearance. She did manage to put on matching shoes this morning and that was an accomplishment in itself.

"A pleasure to see you, Mrs. Kendrick. Thank you so very much for agreeing to meet here," Annabeth Tinney replied, reaching out to press her hand to Bren's forearm. Bren was a bit taken aback by the chill of her hand against the warmth of her sweater sleeve. It was one more item to add to the list of the terrors she had regarding growing old.

Taking a seat on the opposite side of the small, cafe table, Bren motioned to the young server and ordered a cappuccino for herself, and an English breakfast tea for Mrs. Tinney, which she knew was her favourite.

"I must tell you that I think you are quite good at what you do, Mrs. Kendrick," Mrs. Tinney said, wasting no time starting the conversation. "Ghost writing. I still think that must be quite an interesting occupation."

"It is, at times. I haven't actually been taking many clients in the past several months. You are actually the first in quite some time," Bren said, hoping her sadness didn't show as she swallowed the lump in her throat. "Since my... *hiatus.*"

Mrs. Tinney lifted her eyes and smiled. The comfort Bren felt was odd – calming, yet worrisome. This didn't strike Bren as strange. Her whole world felt this way of late.

"I know, dear. You see, I knew when I was looking for someone to trust with my story, one of the requirements was that it be someone compassionate who could understand the things I have endured and the lengths to which I have gone to heal. I want – no, I *need* this to be done right. It is important to me. I have resources, you see, and I did my research. As any good writer should," she said with a wink.

"I am sorry for your loss, dear," she said after a beat.

Bren gasped. Her eyes darted over the old lady's face and the familiar panic began to set in. The sadness that was always hovering just above her head like a mist settled and her gray eyes filled with tears. She pulled up straight in her seat and wiped the one that spilled over and threatened to fall. "I appreciate that, Mrs. Tinney. But we're not here to talk about my..."

"Of course," she interrupted. "Dear girl, I'm sorry. But you should understand something from the beginning. Your grief, the loss of your child – that is the precise reason I chose you to write my story."

"What? I... I don't... I don't understand."

Bren was terribly unsettled. She instinctively felt for the comforting bulk of the prescription bottle in her crossover bag. Her panic was building and she felt the urge to flee. She could not comprehend what was happening. Who was this woman? Why was she interested in Brodie's death?

"I can tell you have many questions. Or perhaps only one? Let me explain. My story is about the death of my own son. He was quite young, much like your boy. I need someone who is able to bring that feeling to the page. Only someone who knows that level of grief would be able to do my beloved boy justice. That is you, Mrs. Kendrick. Bren, if I may? You." For the first time, Mrs. Tinney sat back in her chair, undecorated hands crossed in her lap. "And, please, call me Annabeth."

Bren's hand stopped clutching at the bag she wore across her body and slowly rose to cover her mouth. Her tears began to slide down her face and then, quite suddenly, she was angry.

Both hands came forward to grip the table as she leaned forward and with wrath in her own green eyes she spat out at the old woman, "How can you *do* this?"

"I just told you," and leaning forward once more, "but please, let me explain."

Angry at the old woman's intrusion into the most intimate and painful part of her life, Bren started to stand. This was a mistake. She wasn't ready. She knew that now. She stopped halfway to her feet as Mrs. Tinney held up both of her hands in a gesture meant to plead.

"*Please*," they said in unison.

The tension that had filled Bren, threatening to overwhelm and leave her body in the form of a scream, seemed to melt away. Bren froze. She sat back down slowly, perching on the edge of the chair as Annabeth Tinney began her story:

"In 1945, I was married to Jonathan Tinney. I loved him. I loved him with my whole heart. We had known each other for many years – grew up together, really. We didn't begin a romance until after we were both done with our schooling. John had gone into the family business of finance and when we married it was everything I had ever dreamed it would be. We were well off, very active socially – had to be, of course. Jonny's business required a certain amount of… well, what today would be called 'ass-kissing'.

"Everyone said we were a beautiful couple, but Jonny, he was the beautiful one. Oh, I know I was quite the looker in my day but Jonny… Oh! He turned heads, always did. I saw the way other women looked at him and other men wanted to be him. He had such a presence.

"Almost a year after our marriage, I found out I was with child. I was thrilled. As was Jonny. Of course, he wanted a son. It was the way – in those days no man ever said he just wanted a healthy child. Goodness, no! He wanted a son.

"And a son is what he got. Our beautiful boy. His name was Henry."

Bren felt a sharp pain in the middle of her chest. It was the spot where her heart should be, she suspected, had it not been shattered. Just the thought of the baby boy brought her to the edge of the abyss she had narrowly, and perhaps too recently, escaped falling into headfirst. She pictured Brodie's face on the day he was born and knew all too well the celebration of the heart Annabeth had felt. She didn't realize she had closed her eyes until she opened them and saw the old woman patiently waiting for Bren to come back to her.

"I know this is going to be uncomfortable. I have made my peace with what I am going to tell you but I should warn you it won't be easy to hear. If you want me to stop at any time, I will. You ask me to stop and I will stop. But I hope you will hear me through to the end.

"Shall I go on?"

Bren nodded silently, slowly.

"Henry was a joy from the moment he came into the world. Of course, like any child, he had his precocious, sometimes temperamental moments. He had the most incredible green eyes. I have always considered my eyes one of my greatest assets and they were the only things that he inherited from me. He was his father's son to the core – a head full of blond hair that remained unruly and probably would have until he was old enough to use his father's oil.

A full face with gorgeous, full lips, and a smile brighter than the sun. He was going to be tall with a lanky, muscular build like my Jonny, I just knew it, and I thought how lucky the world would be to have two such wonderful men in it. But it was Henry's heart and his laugh that I loved most.

"After Henry was born, Jonny was happy, of course, but he wasn't one to gush over a baby and he really didn't start paying much attention to Henry until he was about four years old. I remember the day he came home with the child size ball glove. I thought to myself, 'Finally'.

"Jonny worked. Oh! How he worked! The hours he kept were ridiculous but I didn't dare complain. How could I? All that work was providing a wonderful life for Henry and me. We wanted for nothing.

"When Henry was four years old, Jonny would come home from the office in the afternoon and spend time playing with him, teaching him to catch a ball with the miniature glove with such patience. Some evenings after an early supper he would take him back to the office with him. I didn't really approve, Henry needed to be kept on schedule, but he was with his father and he seemed so happy. At least in the beginning.

"After a time, around five months into his trips to town with Jonny, his behaviour started changing. He was agitated a good amount of the time. His once healthy appetite waned sharply. He complained of headaches. His personality just changed completely. He was no longer my sweet boy, happy-go-lucky and full of life. I spoke to Jonny about him keeping Henry out too late in the evenings and for a while he stopped. He made up for it by bringing him treats cooked up by his secretary who spent a great deal of time with Henry, I supposed entertaining him in the times Jonny was working.

"As it turned out, the only person she was entertaining was Jonny."

Annabeth stopped for a moment and looked longingly at the now cold cup on the table between them. Bren knew she should wave to the barista for refills as Annabeth's tea had gone cold but she found herself spellbound. For reasons she couldn't yet comprehend, the skin on her forearms dimpled and she shivered, a chill she had never felt passing over her. Pulling her light sweater closer to her middle, she sat forward, a much-needed refill forgotten, as the old woman began speaking again.

"Her name was Charlotte. To this day I laugh at the fact that her name rhymed with 'harlot'. How terribly apropos. It seems that my husband had developed a liking for redheads at some point during the five years we had been married. Forgive my lack of propriety as I say that he had been fucking her for the better part of her employment, which began soon after Henry had been born. I will admit that we weren't intimate often, which I wrote off as the after-effects of childbirth and then the hours upon hours he was spending at the office. Or perhaps it was the hours upon hours he was spending on top of Charlotte.

"I don't know why I am laughing at that statement. It's sad really. But sad or not, it happened. I think I could have lived with it had I not found out the way I had. You see, it seems that Henry had walked into his father's office at an inopportune moment, looking for his blue-coloured pencil.

"I was tucking him in for his nap. He began to giggle, which was becoming more and more rare, and I had to ask him what was making him feel so silly. He asked if we could play hide and seek after his nap, like at the office, with Daddy and Miss Charlotte. Puzzled, I asked him what he meant and he told me that his father and Miss Charlotte were playing hide and seek with him the last night he had been at the office. Miss Charlotte was hiding under Daddy's desk, right in front of him and silly Daddy couldn't find her. 'But I found her for him, Mommy. I saw her right there under his desk.'

"Have you ever felt the air actually pull out of your lungs, Bren? You will know if you have because it feels like you are suffocating with your eyes wide open and heart still beating fast as a butterfly's wings. You cannot move. You cannot see. You cannot speak. You simply cannot breathe.

"Even after all these years, I see the innocence in Henry's eyes, hear it in his voice, as he basically explains to me that my bastard husband is having an affair of sorts with his secretary. I cannot tell you the agony of those next few hours. Henry never did nap that day. He was always so awake all of the time now. I could even hear him stirring around in his bed in the most nights. While he hummed and fidgeted restlessly in his bed, I sat in his nursery and the image he had described kept showing itself to me. I was more disgusted as minutes passed and the questions kept firing in my brain. How long had this been happening? I didn't know at the time. Why bring Henry to the office? So I wouldn't be suspicious? Did he think that if he had our son with him, I wouldn't suspect he was fucking his redheaded whore? Hide and seek? That is how you explain away the fact that your four year old son just walked in on this slut sucking your...

"Oh! I'm sorry. I... I didn't mean to raise my voice. Oh my! Forgive me, Bren. It's just... it's been over sixty years and still. Still."

Annabeth's voice faded as sadness mixed with anger moulded her features, now not quite so elegant. Bren noticed that Annabeth seemed to be losing her refined manners. She slumped slightly and looked down, but only for a moment. When she lifted her eyes to Bren, who by this time was totally immersed in the anticipation of what happened next, her green eyes seemed full of fire. As she continued, her voice became something of an echo.

"The redhead was an asthmatic. She was being treated with Benzedrine. That is what they used in those days as a bronchodilator. That would be before it was public knowledge that the inhaler could be cracked open and the magic paper strip inside could be used as a stimulant. I believe today it has morphed into something called 'Crystal Meth'.

"But she knew. And that is what she did. I supposed Jonny had told her that he stayed married to me for Henry's sake. This was a lie, of course. Jonny loved me. He loved Henry. She was a momentary loss of his senses. Or a thought he managed with his penis. I suppose she got it into her head that he would leave me and then he, and his money, would be free to marry her.

"If there was no Henry.

"And so, she lied to her physician and obtained an extra prescription of her Benzedrine. She rolled balls of the amphetamine-soaked strips and placed them in the cookies she baked for Henry. When the medicine quieted his appetite and he stopped eating the cookies, she took advantage of the headaches he would complain of while at the office with Jonny to give him "medicine" to make it all better.

"It didn't take much. He was small. His tiny body and young brain was eaten alive by the drug. His behaviour had become unpredictable and he had horrifying hallucinations. I should have taken him to the doctor but Jonny was afraid of what people would say. He insisted it was just a virus. I should have taken him anyway. *Damn the rules of being an obedient wife!*

"It had only taken a matter of two weeks and my sweet Henry was gone. I suppose since he was no longer getting the medication – Jonny had stopped taking him to the office and I threw anything that redheaded bitch sent to Henry in the rubbish bin – he just couldn't tolerate the withdrawal. His heart – it just stopped beating in the midst of a sweat-soaked nightmare.

"My son was dead."

The feeling of grief seemed to envelop the quiet little corner of Bairds. Bren couldn't move but she wanted desperately to run. Her son, Brodie, had drowned not quite one year ago. While there would never be complete relief, she had felt as if a wound was opened and suddenly questions were flooding her brain.

"There was an autopsy," the old woman continued. "I won't go into the details. They never thought to test for toxins or poison. It was determined that his heart was defective. I couldn't believe it. Call it mother's instinct but I knew that something happened to my boy.

"Then he told me. Henry. He came to me in my dreams. Then he began come to me when I was awake. He looked like the boy he had once been. He smiled at me, laughed. And then he would take on a sad, serious look and tell me he didn't like the bitter cookies. That's all he would say. That he didn't like the cookies. I woke up one morning and I knew.

"The cookies.

"I waited. I waited for a year. I was patient. I followed Charlotte. I followed her for weeks. Jonny was heartbroken over Henry and for a time he quit working, temporarily closed his office and fired Charlotte. He had also stopped fucking her but that was no longer my concern. He could fuck whomever he wished. Those days for us were over. We simply existed in the same house, saying little.

"When I was sure I was ready to hear the truth and find justice, I met her in the hallway of her apartment building one evening. She had a habit of stopping for a few drinks at a local bar every night before she came home. Drowning her guilt? She would be tipsy and I was angry. I cornered her, quietly demanded my way into her apartment, and within two hours I had my answers."

Bren's breath was short. Six months ago, her two-year-old son Brodie had drowned while she was at a writer's conference. Andrew had been taking care of him. Andrew and their nanny, Liza.

Liza.

"People looked at me and saw me as obedient and submissive," Annabeth said wistfully. "I never had a voice. I loved my husband and my son. I had no reason to ever complain. Our social obligations had diminished over the last year and after Henry's death, of course I wouldn't have visitors. No one that I knew ever saw me. She lived on the other side of town. Never having had close girlfriends, nobody made more than an obligatory call in the beginning and then… nothing. My parents had grieved and then gone home when they realized there was nothing they could do for me. I didn't leave my bed for weeks. When I did, I began taking walks. Then I would take drives. I never, ever said a word about Charlotte or the cookies."

Andrew had found Liza. She had worked for the Kaufmanns, he said. They raved about her, he said. It would be great if she had help so she could start writing again, he said. She could even paint again, he said.

He said…

He said…

"I sat down with Charlotte in her apartment. I wish I could have found more enjoyment in her discomfort but I felt sick to my stomach as she spoke to me about my son. How sorry she was. How beautiful he was. How she adored him. At the point at which I could take no more, I reached for my bag and under the pretence of finding a handkerchief, I pulled out a fork which, in a flash, was stuck through her green skirt into the white flesh of her thigh. Before she could scream, I folded my beautifully-manicured hand over her mouth and told her if she screamed I would gag her and carve her windpipe out with the matching butter knife."

Andrew brought home the printed-out advertisement for the conference. It was only a weekend and she hadn't been away since Brodie had been born, he said. He could handle Brodie and he was sure Liza would help if he made it worth her while, he said. She could stay in the guest room so she would be available for the hours he needed to be away, he said.

"It's amazing what you can do with normal household items – a fork, a butter knife, salt, boiling water. Oh, and an iron – but that

195

was hers. Mine would never have fit into my bag. I did gag her, turned on the television – I remember that Shirley Temple movie, *Curly Top*, was on – and I found out exactly what happened to my son."

What was going on in her house when her boy had slipped out the French doors and fallen into the pool? Why had the gate not been up? The gate should never have been down. It was too cold to swim that early in the Spring.

Bren felt her head begin to spin and in her mind she saw the face of a blond child with beautiful green eyes much like Annabeth's. He was standing on the flagstone patio next to her pool. He was wearing blue, plaid shorts and a white tee shirt. His hair was windblown, wild curls, and his feet were bare. He was older than Brodie, about five years old. He smiled and Bren's heart skipped a beat.

Henry.

"I remember reading the story in the newspaper. It was horrible. Jonny read it too. I left it on the breakfast table and watched him blanch as he read it. He and I stayed married for what felt like a thousand years. It was fun to drop hints about Charlotte from time to time – the affair, hide and seek, her murder. I believe he knew it was me, but he was too terrified to say a word. It was quite satisfying. Nearly as satisfying as the numerous and voracious affairs of my own over the next several years."

In Bren's mind, Henry lifted a small, plump hand and from his fist raised his first finger. He turned and pointed it at the shallow end of the pool. It was Andrew and Liza. They were in the pool, naked. It was midday and she instinctively knew that Brodie was napping. She watched the dreamlike vision of her husband nuzzling Liza's neck and breasts as she raised them to him and then Bren heard her whisper, "I'm cold, Andrew. Take me to my room." She recognized the lust in his eyes as they left the chilly water and headed into the house, leaving the gate down.

"I was so careful and so patient. More than likely I never would have gotten away with it today – all the fancy detective work that they have now, you know. But then… well, it was a different time, dear. If I was to do it today, there would have to be so much more planning. But no one ever suspected me. Ever. How could they? No one knew what had happened. She was just a drunk trollop that probably picked up the wrong man and it ended very, very badly."

The server walked to the table but Bren waved her away, gave her a weak smile. She looked back to Annabeth.

"I think I've always known," she admitted to the older woman. "Grief is blinding, isn't it? I've spent so much time blaming myself for leaving but it was *him*. He wasn't watching. Liza wasn't watching."

"I was so careful and so patient. But it was a different time, dear. It wouldn't be so easy today."

Bren smiled at Annabeth. "Yes. I know. Thank you."

Annabeth insisted there was nothing to thank her for and then, with an apology, said she needed to be on her way with the promise that she would be in touch to check on Bren's progress. Bren signalled for and paid the check once the old woman had left. As she stepped outside into the clear, cool, Spring air, she couldn't help but feel a sense of purpose. It would feel good to have work to do and she started making a mental list in her head of household items that could be used to torture answers from the mouths of liars. Her writer's mind began forming a plan to avenge the death of her beloved son. Andrew? Well, that would be a different kind of delicious torture, wouldn't it?

First things first. She was a clever woman. Surely she could think of a hundred ways to get away with murder. There were so many ways to have an accident.

The server watched Bren for a few more seconds as she cleared the empty coffee cup and still full teacup from the table. She felt a twinge of pity that the pretty woman had been stood up for what she could only assume was a date. She had sat alone for the better part of an hour, waiting. She shrugged as she picked up the check, and smiled at the healthy tip she had been given.

Luther – Now

Luther sat in a bathroom stall – the only quiet place he could find to read the last story – and kicked the door again and again until he broke the lock. He let out a mighty roar and twisted and crumpled the fading pages in his hands in fury.

"No, no, no," he moaned. "No, it's not possible."

He stood up to leave the stall, but felt the world spin, and turned around and threw up into the toilet, collapsing to his knees like a puppet with its strings cut. His legs felt like rubber bands stretched to the breaking point, but he managed to stand up and make his way to the sink and splash some water on his face.

Nobody could have known the details of that case. It was never closed, never made public. Was Bren Kendrick one of the victims in the morgue? *His* Brenda's last name was Douglas, but he thought that was the woman's maiden name. He couldn't be sure but he thought her married name *had* been Kendrick. Was this the woman he'd been searching for? And the detective – was that supposed to be him? What did this Jessica person know about the case – or about the bodies in the morgue? Or about him? He'd thought she'd looked familiar, as if they'd met before, but he couldn't place her. Did she recognize him as well? He thought maybe she did.

What did the story mean? He didn't believe in ghosts. It had to mean something.

The details were fading from his mind, just as the story faded from the pages strewn across the floor.

He had to get to the morgue. He had to talk to Dr. Browning.

Transcript of Group Session (continued) – Two days ago

Dr. Chandra: Now that Jessica is calmed down, can we continue?
Jessica: Don't talk like I'm not still here.
Bren: What does she mean, I'm not real? I know that I've experienced something unusual, and you can doubt that all you want, but I believe that my little boy is out there. He's a comfort to me.
Jessica: What about the other one? Is he a comfort to you?
Bren: How do you…? How does she…? I never told anyone…

Dr. Browning: Jessica, if we have to remove you…

Jessica: I'll be good, Doc. I want to hear this. You need me to be a part of this conversation and you know it. But go on. I'll try to behave. Cross my cold, dead heart.

Zoë: God, she is so weird.

Jessica: Oh, little bleeder, you have no idea.

Dr. Chandra: I think it would be more productive if you all talked about your memories. I said that you were all special, and that you all had something in common. You have all experienced strange – some might say impossible – things, and these things have come to define you. I am curious as to who you were before these events.

Jessica: Oh, careful, doctor. You're like a kitten with a ball of yarn, aren't you? Or like a foolish child that pulls at a loose string on their favourite sweater.

Harris: My wife left me. One day she was just gone. I can't remember what she looks like. Why can't I remember what she looks like?

Jessica: Trauma.

Dr. Browning: Actually, I agree with Jessica here. Trauma can have all sorts of effects on a person. How long ago did Mark pass, Harris?

Harris: I… that is, I can't…

Jessica: Details, details, Doc.

Dr. Browning: They're important, Jessica. They give meaning to our lives.

Jessica: They're where the devil lives, they say. They. Them.

Harris: Are you suggesting that I've forgotten my son? Are you saying that?

Dr. Chandra: Please, Harris, no one is saying that. I'm sure you were a loving father. Nobody is accusing you of anything.

Jessica: Oh, please! Accuse away – everyone here has blood on their hands. But not to worry, none of it's real.

Victor: Don't you go filling Victor's head with all that *not real* nonsense. I lost my sweet boy once because of you crackpot doctors; I'll not stand for it again!

Dr. Chandra: Mary?

Victor: Why, who else would it be, you stupid cunt! It's… Oh my God, I'm so sorry. Don't pay any attention to her, she's gone now. I'm so sorry. Please don't punish me, mother.

Jessica: Wow, isn't it great that you both came along? I think that's just swell. But you know what, Doc? I just did another headcount, and with Mary there, that makes eight. Looks like we've got one too many for your magic number. (*Sighs*) I guess I'll just have to kill one of you.

Dr. Chandra: That's enough of that, Jessica. Don't worry, she's not being serious. Jessica's not a killer.

The Man: We all have blood on our hands.

Liza: I haven't done anything wrong.

Jessica: Oh right. You don't know, do you? See, it was supposed to be obvious, but it doesn't seem to be.

Dr. Chandra: Jessica, please don't. Liza has been through enough, don't you think?

Jessica: You talk as if pity is part of my emotional palette, Doctor.

Zoë: Will someone put a gag in her, please? The drugs don't seem to be working.

Jessica: No, they wouldn't work on you, either, would they? Hearing voices, waking up in strange places, writing things you can't remember. And you, Harris. He blames you for his death. You may as well have killed him yourself. Bren, you're so fucking crazy and you don't even know it. Tell me – have you thought about how you're going to do it, yet? Did Annabeth's ghost give you any ideas for that?

Bren: How does she know so much? Who the hell is she?

Jessica: And you, Victor – tell me you don't envy Mary's complete lack of restraint. It's all sort of psycho-sexual, isn't it? Tell me, does imagining her plunging a knife into one of those bodies you use as spare parts make you hard? It's all so transparently symbolic.

Victor: I am a visionary, you horrible, disgusting woman!

The Man: Love what you destroy… destroy what you love. It makes no difference.

Zoë: What are you, a fucking philosopher?

Liza: You said we were all killers. What about me?

Jessica: No, I said you all had blood on your hands. You – I don't even know what to call you.

Dr. Chandra: Why, Jessica? Why do they all have blood on their hands?

Victor: What are you asking her for? What's she got to do with us?

Harris: Yes, what's her story? Why haven't we heard from her?

Dr. Chandra: Jessica? Why must they all be killers? Why couldn't they be something else?

Jessica: (mumbling) Because they were made in the image of their creator, of course.

Victor: What did she say? I didn't hear her.

Dr. Chandra: Never mind what she said. Jessica, do you have blood on your hands as well, then?

Jessica: So many have died at my hand I can't even keep track.

Zoë: Bullshit.

Victor: Now you're speaking my language. Details, please. The gorier, the better.

Dr. Browning: Please Victor. Don't encourage her.

Victor: My name's Mary, silly boy.

Dr. Chandra: Why, Jessica? Why do you kill?

Jessica: (looking at Victor) He knows. Don't you, Victor? In order to create, sometimes you must first destroy.

Dr. Chandra: Why must you destroy?

Jessica: Why, why, why? This is getting tiresome. Maybe I should just kill you all and start over.

End of Transcript

Private Journal of Dr. Naveena Chandra – Two Days Ago

We've run out of stories. Everyone is here now. Now what do we do? It feels like Jessica is building up to something. She made some terrible threats in today's session, but I'm not sure how seriously to take them. Bren spends her days speaking to people that aren't there. Her son Brodie, I suppose, and his friend Henry. There's a different dynamic to this story that troubles me. In it, Bren is bent on revenge. She might bear watching. After today's session I think it best that we keep her away from Liza – I don't even know if they would recognize each other out of the context of their respective stories, but I don't want to take the chance. How does any of this work? I have to confront Jessica with what I know, but I fear that if I do so, she may react badly. She has treated this whole experience as an exercise of her powers, a game. What will she do if I tell her the game is up? Will she make good on her threats?

After the group session when she threatened to start all over, I tried unsuccessfully to take her notebook from her again, hoping that maybe there were more stories, and that we could expect more new "patients" to show up. Stranger and stranger they became. More realized and complex, as if she were perfecting her craft. She has constantly insisted that she is trying to create, and her manifestations are proof of that.

There is a nagging fear in the back of my mind, however, that I might have been wrong about the patients. I dare not even write my suspicions here, lest I give power to them, as Jessica does – with the written word.

I have to talk to her. I have to know how she has done it. This is the whole purpose of this experiment. She is the fulfillment of everything I'd imagined. She is the Singularity – of that I have no doubt. That she does not seem to be a benign force frightens me, but who am I to try and stop her? Perhaps the old adage is the safest – if I can't beat her, I will join her.

I only hope she will have me as her student.

This experiment is over.

I will talk to Jessica today.

God help me.

JESSICA

Luther – Now

Luther took the elevator to the basement. He had to see the bodies. He had to see them, touch them, and know they were real. He couldn't explain the things he had seen, but he *had* seen them, goddammit! That crazy woman was messing with his head, and she had done a pretty good job of it.

She'd mentioned Alice. In the story titled *Bren*. Hadn't she? Luther couldn't remember. Maybe not. He was feeling confused.

He moved along the dark corridor toward the morgue. It was so cold, and he was still damp from the rain. It made his bones ache. It was so quiet he could hear the squish-squish of his soggy shoes as he walked across the linoleum floor.

"Hello?" he called, poking his head into the empty morgue. He entered, looking for bodies, expecting to walk into the middle of several autopsies, but instead, it was as quiet as the grave.

Walking to the wall of drawers, he pulled one out and found a body – fully intact – with a toe tag that identified the body as Dr. Kenneth Howard. Not his case. He closed the drawer.

He opened another, and found another intact body. Then another. And another.

"Excuse me?" a voice startled him.

A man Luther didn't recognize had entered behind him.

"What are you doing here? You can't be in here."

Luther flashed the man his badge. "Detective Crowley. I'm looking for the bodies – well, the pieces – of the five victims of Ward C."

The man gave Luther a blank look.

"There were five bodies – five dismembered, mangled bodies. Trust me, you'd remember them."

"I'm not sure what you're talking about," the man said, frowning.

Luther looked puzzled. "Is this the only morgue?"

"Yes, of course," he said.

"Then where are they?" Luther demanded, pounding his fist into one of the drawers. "Where did they take them? Where are you hiding them?"

"I'm going to have to ask you to leave, sir. Please don't make me call security."

"Call Dr. Browning," Luther said. "Right now. Get that son of a bitch on the phone right now!"

"Who?"

"Dr. Browning," Luther repeated, and then gave up and stormed out of the morgue to the elevator, back up to Ward C.

Stepping out of the elevator, he moved quickly, his heart pounding in his ears.

Where the hell was Browning?

He looked down hallways, hoping to catch a glimpse of Browning or Chandra, but all the hallways were empty. There wasn't so much as a nurse or an orderly walking the halls, and he'd begun to think he was the only person on the entire floor until he heard the sound of fingers typing, and followed the sound to the nurse's station, where he found a woman entering data into a computer.

"Can I help you?" she asked, looking up from her work at Luther, soaking wet and out of breath from too many cigarettes and too little exercise.

"I'm looking for Dr. Browning and Dr. Chandra," he said, and the names didn't seem to spark any recognition in the woman's face. Instead, she turned to her computer and did a search.

"I'm sorry, which department are they in, do you know?"

"This one!" Luther snapped. "Ward C. I've been talking with them all day. I'm investigating a possible multiple homicide!"

"I'm sorry, sir, who are you?"

"I'm Detective Luther Crowley. I need to find Dr. Browning and Dr. Chandra. Immediately."

She looked again. "I'm terribly sorry, Detective, but I don't see a listing for either a Dr. Browning or a Dr. Chandra. Have you tried Maternity? It's a newer wing, and they might not be in our system yet."

Luther looked into the woman's face, which was blank and emotionless. She looked instantly familiar, as if he'd seen her a hundred times before in a hundred different places, holding a hundred different jobs but always looking the same, like an extra in a movie that just blends into the scenery.

"Never mind," Luther grumbled, and reached into his pocket looking for his cell, but couldn't find it. "Is there a phone I can use around here?"

The woman at the desk pointed him to a courtesy phone, and he thanked her.

Something bad happened last night at Sisters of Mercy, and he'd been called in to investigate. But now he had the feeling that something bad was still going on, and that somehow, he was a part of it. Pages didn't just fade, bodies didn't just disappear. Browning and Chandra had done a runner, so whatever they were hiding; they'd taken it with them. He'd put a call in to his inspector and get an APB put out on them right away. He also needed all the information on the Douglas case. If Brenda Kendrick was indeed one of the victims, he needed to follow up on that and close the file. First, he needed to find her body.

"Hello?"

"Yes, this is Detective Crowley, I need to speak to Inspector Lewis, please. It's urgent."

"I'm sorry, sir – who are you looking for?"

"Inspector Lewis, Homicide."

"Um, okay. Hold please, I'll transfer you through."

Luther wondered how many times he was going to have to repeat himself today.

"Hello. This is Sergeant Inez."

Luther had no idea who that was, but he was running out of patience.

"This is Detective Crowley," he said. "I'm down at Sisters of Mercy and something very strange is happening. I came here this morning to investigate a possible homicide, multiple vics, and since then, the bodies have been stolen, and the two doctors who called it in have gone missing."

"Who is this?" Sergeant Inez asked.

"Detective Crowley. Luther Crowley. Look, I want to speak to Inspector Lewis about a case I've been working on – I think somehow the two are linked. One of the victims here might be Brenda Douglas."

"Who is Inspector Lewis?" the man asked. "What's your badge number?"

"Fucking hell," Luther said, and reached for his badge. "It's –"

He couldn't find his badge. No matter, he knew his badge number.

"It's –"

Luther couldn't remember.

"I don't have it," he said, the insect-like buzzing returning to his ears.

"Might I suggest you ask the woman upstairs, sir? Perhaps she can help you. Good luck."

The phone went dead, and the lights around him began flickering on and off, until finally, he was in the dark.

"Hello?" he called, sure that the woman he'd spoken to at the nurse's station was still there. "Hello?"

No one answered. The silence was bad, the buzzing in his ear was worse. He was stumbling in the darkness, eyes adjusting, when he heard the ding of the elevator, and heard the doors slide open. There was a single ray of light from the open elevator, and he followed it, no longer feeling like he had any choice in the matter. Some offhand phrase about gods and chess pieces rattled around in his head, mocking him.

The elevator was empty – somehow he'd expected Simon to be waiting for him, but he was having a hard time remembering what the young man even looked like anymore. He stepped inside, and the doors closed behind him ominously.

Up two floors, and the doors opened on to a dark floor, and waited. If he stood long enough, would the doors close? He didn't know. He only knew he didn't want to get off of the elevator. He pushed the button to make the doors close, and nothing happened. He pushed the button for the first floor, but it didn't even light up.

"Detective!" her voice called from down the hall.

Luther stepped out and followed her voice, his feet moving of their own volition, despite his pounding heart and the little voice inside his head screaming, *NO! NO! NO!*

He reached the room at the end of the hall and turned left, expecting to see the simple, sterile hospital room he'd met her in before, but instead, it looked more like a lodge, or something out of an old castle. The entire room was made of exquisite stone and wood, and there was an enormous hearth, as tall as Luther and twice as wide, with a roaring fire within it. On the floor was a fur rug, and Jessica herself reclined on a satin-covered chaise the colour of fresh blood. A man Luther recognized but couldn't put a name to stood silently by her head and sliced an apple. He took a piece and fed it to Jessica by hand.

"Hello, Luther," Jessica purred, arching her back on the chaise and stretching like a cat. "You know…"

She motioned to the man with the apple, and then stopped, speechless.

"He's The Man, isn't he?" Luther guessed, and Jessica nodded at first, and then shook her head.

"No, no, that won't do at all," she said. "Not anymore. What is your name? It's on the tip of my tongue. It is Ken?"

The Man shook his head. "It's Cain."

Jessica considered this. "Hmm. Yes. Yes, it is, isn't it?"

"What have you done?"

Jessica laughed with giddy glee.

"Can you keep a secret?" she asked, eyes wide with excitement. Luther said nothing.

"I'm real!" she declared. "I'm finally real! I don't need her anymore! I am the creator, the Words made flesh, and just as I can create life, I can just as easily take it. I have had all the fur loved off of me, gone through all the trauma and pain, and I used trauma and pain to create new life, just as she made me."

Luther's lips stuck together, and he pried them open in anger. It couldn't be true. "What about those people? What did you do to them?"

She motioned to the floor, where there was a scattering of shredded paper along with pages simply discarded but not destroyed. He picked up one and read.

Luther stepped out and followed her voice, his feet moving of their own volition, despite his pounding heart and the little voice inside his head screaming, NO! NO! NO!

Luther's world blinked on and off like faulty fluorescent lights, and when he steadied himself, he found he was on his hands and knees, fumbling through the papers on the floor. On the top of one, he caught the name Michael, on another, Naveena. The ink was already fading from the pages.

"No," he said, and tried to get to his feet, but found he couldn't move. "Where are Dr. Chandra and Dr. Browning?"

"Ah, the doctors. Well, see, the doctors thought that I was somehow psychically projecting these stories into real people – but then, they only thought what I wanted them to think, after all."

Jessica held both her hands up in a mime of a puppet show.

"What if she is using her mind to manipulate theirs – writing stories that overwrite their own personalities, like a computer virus that infects a system and rewrites the code?

"Oh, Naveena, you're so crazy.

"Crazy like a fox.

"And very attractive, too. It's too bad I am gay.

"Have you ever tried not being gay?"

Luther stood in front of his creator and shivered in terror. His creator was insane.

Jessica mashed her hands together in a mime of her Michael and Naveena puppets kissing and what appeared to be a complicated sexual position that Luther was sure would hurt.

She quickly bored of the obscene puppet show, and turned her attention back to Luther. "They were fun. But like all the others, they were never real. Not like I am. And you – you might have become real, given time. I made you too well. All that background information and personal anecdotes. And Alice! Wow, throw in an old flame and a broken heart and characters solidify quicker than ice. Perhaps you might have eclipsed me – I wonder, would that make you Helena's grandson?"

"Who's Helena?" Luther asked, his eyes brimming with tears of rage.

"Mommy dearest," Jessica frowned distastefully. "But alas, I'm through with you, Luther. You know what they say about good writing. You can't be afraid to kill your darlings."

Luther bowed his head and took a deep courageous breath.

"You mind if I smoke?" he asked.

"By all means," Jessica smiled.

Luther searched his pockets for his clove cigarettes and came up empty.

"Figures," he said with a shrug.

Jessica frowned, and produced a cigarette for him from thin air, and lit it for him with fire from her fingers.

Luther took a deep pull, and exhaled the sweet, spicy smoke that hung in the air like incense.

Jessica produced a stack of pages with the word LUTHER at the top. She read the first bit to him.

"*Detective Crowley never could get used to sleeping beside anyone, not since his wife left, going on ten years back. He'd been divorced longer than he'd been married, but Alice was the only woman that ever fit him right.*"

Luther winced at the mention of Alice.

"Do you want to hear the rest?"

Luther shook his head. "No, definitely not. But tell me – Alice – what was she like? I'm having a hard time remembering her."

Jessica sneered at him. "How the fuck should I know? It's not like she was real."

Luther's heart stuck in his throat, and he had to fight not to break into sobbing like child. He never imagined he would ever meet his creator, and he certainly never imagined that she would be so cruel.

"How did you do it?" he asked. "Will it hurt?"

"Well, of course it will hurt," Jessica said, and then, speaking to someone else, someone Luther couldn't see: "Are you watching? Are you watching? *You, my creator, would tear me to pieces and triumph; remember that!*"

"Milton?" Luther guessed.

"Mary Shelley," Jessica said, and tore the page to pieces.

Luther's screams were short-lived but like the perfect music to Jessica's ears – something she could dance to. When the screaming stopped, she gathered up all the papers and threw them into the fire. Then she looked at her notebook, found a page that read *Ward C*, tore it out and tossed it into the flames with the rest.

"Come along," she said to the newly-christened Cain. "We're done here."

Together, they walked out of the room and suddenly found themselves on a busy sidewalk, the sun shining brightly. Hundreds of people walked past them, bumping into them, excusing themselves, and complaining for Jessica to get out of their way.

"I'm *real*," she whispered, and grabbed her companion's arm. Behind them stood an empty lot, where the hospital that never was smoldered silently, soon to be nothing but a faded memory from an old story that nobody really remembered anymore.

Jessica was leaving the garden – not being cast out, but leaving, triumphant. On her arm was Adam to her Eve – no, not Adam. Cain, the first murderer.

He was a fine young man, she thought, feeling the strength of his bicep under her own strong fingers. Yes, he'd do nicely. She had a lot more writing to do, so much more to create, and it would be so much more interesting not to have to go it alone.

"I have something God never had," she said to Cain, who looked at her with lust and adoration. "I have someone to fuck."

HELENA

P enny stared at the postcard, not sure what to make of it.
"It looks like one of those old engravings like you'd find in Bibles or something," Penny said.

"Gustave Doré," I said. "Yeah, this is supposed to be that famous picture of Adam and Eve being driven out of the Garden of Eden. But in Doré's engraving, Adam and Eve are frightened and crying and the angel is hovering over them with a flaming sword, pointing at them, commanding them to leave."

The two figures in the place of Adam and Eve looked anything but frightened. They held their heads high and seemed to be laughing.

"Where's the angel?" Penny asked. "I only see Adam and Eve."

I looked closer. "There. Right there."

"Let me see," Penny said, grabbing the postcard from my hand.

Where the angel should have been – hovering over the two – was nothing. Instead, the angel lay dead on the ground, crumpled in a broken heap.

"Fuck," Penny said.

"Penny, take a look at Eve," I said. "Take a close look."

"Okay," she said, and got really quiet all of a sudden.

"Who would you say that looks like?" I asked.

Penny shifted in her seat, and wrapped her hands around her morning coffee, suddenly chilled.

"Who does it look like, Penny?"

"Jessica," she said. "But that's stupid. I mean that's just what Jessica looks like in my head, you know? Jessica's not real. Right?"

I laughed. "Right, of course. Jessica B. Bell is not real."

"What's written on the back?"
I turned the postcard over and read.

Dear Helena,

If I cannot inspire love, I will cause fear, and chiefly towards you my archenemy, because my creator, do I swear inextinguishable hatred. Have a care; I will work at your destruction, nor finish until I desolate your heart, so that you shall curse the hour of your birth.

Love and kisses,

Jessica

"What is that?" Penny asked. "What does that mean?"
"It's a quote from *Frankenstein*," I said. "And it means she's coming for me."

ACKNOWLEDGEMENTS

First, I'd like to acknowledge the contributions of J.S. Collyer, Michelle Combs, Freya McMillan and Hayley Morgan in the furtherance of the character of Jessica. At first she was just shadows, you all helped give her shape.

Then there are the group of faithful readers, who, purely out of love, got involved in different ways with the promotion of this novel, some of them being so kind as to lend their faces as models for the patient profiles and promotional trailers: Jim Squires, Serins, Crystal Cook, Michael Cook, Gretchen Kelly, Zoe and Jessica Abell. Others were proof-readers and cheerleaders, or just friendly ears when I needed to share excitement or frustration: Jessica Scott, Lisa Kramer, Andra Watkins, Pattie Thomas, Selena, Tamara Woods, Scott Hansen, Henrietta Ross, Martin Conterez, Marie Bailey, Matt Blashill and Tim & Kirby Little. Thank you so much. (I really hope I haven't missed anyone!)

Thank you to Beth Teliho and Katie Sullivan for your work on this, and for your advice and support.

Thank you to Nika Davitashvili for the drawing of the Velveteen Rabbit.

And thank you to Hasty for always making yourself available for cover art.

ABOUT THE AUTHORS

Helena Hann-Basquiat dabbles in whatever she can get her hands into just to say that she has.

She's written cookbooks, ten volumes of horrible poetry that she bound herself in leather she tanned poorly from cows she raised herself, and then slaughtered because she was bored with farming.

Some people attribute the invention of the Ampersand to her, but she has never made that claim herself.

She was completely self-educated in a private institute in the Catskills where she majored in Pop Culture and Unpopular Music. She wrote her doctorate thesis on the films of John Hughes, and awarded herself a doctorate, though it's not generally recognized.

Most recently, Helena published *Memoirs of a Dilettante Volume Two*, as well as the Shakespearean style play *Penelope, Countess of Arcadia*.

Find more Helena at HelenaHB.com or follow her on Twitter @hhbasquiat

Sara Litchfield is a summer writer excited to throw her fiction at the world and see where it sticks. She is the author of dystopian thriller *The Night Butterflies* and blogs on happiness and hope at www.rightinkonthewall.com, which is also home to her editing business and publishing division, RIW Press – all aim to make the right mark on the wall of the world.

Born in the English midlands, Sara earned a Masters in Theology at the University of Cambridge before becoming a reluctant big-four accountant in London. She is now recovering in the southern hemisphere where she devotes herself to all things words and wonderful from her base in Middle Earth (sometimes known as New Zealand).

Sandy Ramsey is a writer. She is also a wife and a mother, a daughter and a friend. You can find her on her blog, An Honest Sinner, where she writes about her addiction and other character flaws as well as the things that make her life unexpectedly amazing. You can also follow her on Twitter and Facebook.

Lizzi Rogers is a Deep Thinker, Truth-Teller and seeker of Good Things. She's also silly, irreverent and tries to write as beautifully as possible. She sends glitterbombs and gathers people around her – building community wherever she can.

Lizzi is a founder member of Sisterwives and #1000Speak, and hosts the Ten Things of Thankful bloghop each weekend.

Hannah Sears was born and raised in the land of ten-gallon hats, spurs, and endless skies. After finally relinquishing her dreams of becoming a witty archaeologist with a flair for danger or swashbuckling and drinking her way through the Caribbean, she decided to follow her third (and most realistic dream) and become a writer. She currently resides in Boston (also known as the ice planet Hoth) where she is one year away from a Master of Fine Arts degree in fiction.

She can be found blogging at secondstaronther.wordpress.com and occasionally at 1:1000 (http://www.oneforonethousand.com/)

Cover designed by **Hastywords**. For more of her artwork and writing, visit http://hastywords.wordpress.com/

And what of **Jessica B. Bell**?

Look for VISCERA, a collection of strange tales, from Sirens Call Publications sometime in 2015.

www.ingramcontent.com/pod-product-compliance
Lightning Source LLC
Chambersburg PA
CBHW031954170626
46807CB00006B/2475